COPYRIGHT

Something in the Way He Needs
Copyright © 2013 Cardeno C.
Issued by: The Romance Authors, LLC, April, 2016
http://www.theromanceauthors.com

Print ISBN: 978-1-942184-42-3

Editor: Jae Ashley
Interior Book Design: Kelly Shorten
Cover Artist: Jay Aheer

REVIEWS

He Completes Me: This is probably one of the best books I have yet read in the M/M romance genre.

— *Ebook Addict*

In Your Eyes: Every single title in the series thus far has been pure pleasure to read.

— *Smoocher's Voice*

Jumping In: It was delicious, beautiful, hot and sexy and lots and lots of other words that just wouldn't do it justice.

— *Archaeolibrarian*

Just What the Truth Is: An incredible story that is charming, loving, witty, humorous, touching and moving.

— *MM Good Book Reviews*

McFarland's Farm: A touching love story with the amazing character depth that Cardeno C. always brings to the table.

— *Kindle Romance Reviews*

More Than Everything: If you love Cardeno C, if you have never read any of CC's books I highly recommend this book. This book is a must read.

— *Gay List Book Reviews*

Perfect Imperfections: Witty, Smart, and hard to put down

— *Naughty Vixen Mafia*

DEDICATION

To readers: Thank you for supporting my writing and giving me the opportunity to do something I truly love.

CHAPTER 1

"You better not call me an asshole or tell me I'm selfish or any other bullshit for the rest of our motherfuckin' lives," Asher Penaz growled at his friend.

Of course, it was entirely possible that Oliver couldn't hear him or wasn't listening. There was no way for Asher to know because there was a wall of nearly naked women between them. He pulled yet more money from his wallet, tucked it into the tiny string holding up the almost-too-small-to-bother bikini gyrating in front of his face, and thought about how he'd never once expected to find himself in this position.

It wasn't that Asher was opposed to nudity—far from it. But the female form wasn't what did it for him. Not that any of this mattered to Oliver, as evidenced by the fact that the man had dragged him to this place.

"A selfish asshole is the perfect description for a guy who can't let me enjoy my last weekend of freedom." Oliver's voice floated over across the sea of flesh. "It's my bachelor party, Asher. Quit making it all about you, as usual."

Asher threaded his fingers together and pulled his hands

up, cracking every knuckle. After endless weeks of his old friend's needling, he had agreed to come to this ridiculous bachelor-party weekend and sealed his own fate. Okay, so the unfortunate decision was his own fault, but that didn't mean he couldn't kick the crap out of Oliver for nagging him into it.

Oh, that little image made him feel a whole lot better. He leaned back in his chair and stretched out his long legs, hoping to discourage future lap dances, and thought of how he could use his broad, muscular, six-foot-four-inch frame to inflict the most pain on his friend without leaving marks that would show up in wedding pictures. No reason to upset Shirley on her big day, even if she was making a remarkably bad decision by marrying Oliver.

Predictably, thinking of inflicting pain managed to do what two hours' worth of wiggling tits and grinding hips had not, and Asher's cock hardened against his thigh. It was Thursday afternoon and he was stuck in Vegas on Oliver's madcap adventure until Sunday. Maybe he could escape for a few hours and find his kind of bar—one with hard bodies covered in leather kneeling at his feet. Yeah, that would make the trip almost bearable.

He moaned out loud at the thought of a tight ass raised and spread, waiting for him to take his pleasure. Oliver claimed he was selfish, but the subs Asher had been with hadn't ever complained, so no harm no foul as far as he was concerned. Well, maybe there was a little bit of harm, but that was kind of the point.

"I'm not selfish," Asher muttered defensively, more to himself than to Oliver, but the women who had been dancing between them had moved on to other customers, so his friend heard him.

"Oh, yeah? What do you call a guy who gets his rocks off by hurting other guys?"

"They get off on it too, Oliver," Asher growled. "That's the whole point. Just because I'm not into vanilla sex doesn't mean I'm selfish."

Oliver rolled his eyes. "You whip 'em, beat 'em, fuck 'em, and leave 'em. It's the last one that makes you selfish."

Asher's body temperature went up and he tried to keep himself calm. He tightened and relaxed his fists repeatedly and then ran his hands up and down his pressed, dark-washed jeans.

"I just haven't found the right guy yet. That's all. I'd be happy to have a relationship if I ever found someone compatible outside of the...bedroom." That wasn't exactly an accurate description of the place he most frequently had sex, but saying sling, club, or dungeon wouldn't help make his point. "And, by the way, I don't need commitment advice from a guy about to embark on his third marriage. You might want to try my approach and wait for someone compatible before you walk down the aisle next time."

Oliver's usually jovial expression changed, and he looked truly offended. "Shirley and I are compatible. She's great.

This one's going to work out. You'll see."

One blood-inducing tongue bite later, Asher nodded his shaved head with as much sincerity as he could muster. "I'm sure it will," he said, not meaning a single word. "And Shirley is great." That part he actually meant. As far as Asher could tell, Shirley's only flaw was crappy taste in men.

"Seriously, though, Asher. You're, what, forty-four, forty-five now?"

"I'm thirty-nine and you fucking well know it, you piece of shit."

Oliver chuckled. "Right. Thirty-nine. So you've had about two decades worth of dating, and in all that time, not one guy was good enough to be with you if he had his clothes on. Think about that, my friend. Think about it." Oliver tapped his index finger against his temple as he spoke. "The department has that shrink on staff and you can go to her anytime, even if it isn't ordered. You might—" Asher's hand clenched into a fist and flew out on its own initiative, making solid contact with Oliver's bicep. "Ow! What the fuck, man? I'm not one of your little boy toys, Asher. Keep your damn hands to yourself or I'll show you that a real man knows how to defend himself."

Coming in at just a couple of inches shy of Asher's imposing height, with the same muscle mass, just covered with an extra layer of padding, and looking every day of his forty-two years, Oliver certainly wasn't what anybody would describe as little or a boy toy.

Asher laughed out loud at his friend. "You think just

because a man enjoys pain he can't defend himself? I have news for you, Ollie—staying still on your knees while a cane connects with your back isn't something a weak person can handle."

"You beat them with a cane?" Oliver shuddered in horror, his brown eyes going wide. "Jesus! I'll never understand why that gets you off."

"It's not the beating, at least not for me. I'm not a sadist," Asher said, trying to articulate why he enjoyed, no, why he *needed* something nontraditional in his sex life. "The power exchange is what's important. Inflicting pain is secondary. The cane, the whip, the rope, they're just tools to demonstrate that I can do anything I want to him, and he'll take it. That for those few minutes, I own him."

Oliver looked stricken, so Asher let the subject drop. He wasn't ashamed of his needs, wasn't ashamed of who he was. But he realized that even the most open-minded people, like Oliver, would never be able to understand what made him tick. Hell, most of the guys he knew in the scene didn't really get him, so he shouldn't expect more from an outsider.

"So what's on the agenda for the rest of the day?" he asked, changing the topic. "Are we gonna hit the tables?"

"Uh, I guess that depends on what the rest of the guys want to do," Oliver replied. "They should be getting in soon. Let's settle up and go to the hotel, and then we can figure out a game plan."

"Sounds good." Asher raised his glass to his mouth and

drained the last of his beer. Then he unfolded his large body from the less than comfortable chair and waited for Oliver to do the same. "So remind me, again, who else is joining us on this"—various adjectives were considered and rejected as being unnecessarily harsh before he gave voice to them— "uh, trip?"

They began weaving through the tables, making their way to the exit.

"Well, most of the guys I know said two bachelor parties was their limit, so they aren't coming this weekend." Oliver frowned as he spoke, clearly frustrated with the fact nobody seemed to be giving much thought or respect to his third marriage. "But a couple of single buddies from the service can make it and so can my little brother. It's probably better this way, anyway. We can all fit at one table when we go to dinner."

Asher decided to go along with Oliver's attempt to whitewash the situation.

"I still don't understand how it is you've never once mentioned you had a brother in the ten years I've known you, and suddenly the guy is coming to Vegas to celebrate your marriage. Or, as you so promisingly called it, your last weekend of freedom."

Oliver rolled his eyes, but didn't verbally acknowledge the dig. "We have different mothers, just like with all my sisters. And he was raised on the other side of the country, so it's not like we were close. He couldn't make it to my other weddings, but he's available now and he's my only brother, so I want him here."

They took a cab to their hotel on the Strip and walked into the casino, then made their way to the lobby. They hadn't even gotten to the elevator before two men called out to Oliver.

"Ollie! Hey, dude, we're ready to parteeeee!"

"Hey!" Oliver shouted and hurried over to his friends, where they exchanged fist bumps. Asher managed not to snicker. He trailed behind, not feeling in any kind of hurry to join the rowdy group that was starting to draw attention. And that was really saying something, considering how some people in this city chose to dress. By the time he caught up to the guys, they'd said their hellos and apparently made plans.

"My brother should have been here by now, but he hasn't called." Oliver checked his phone and shook his head. "Well, since the rest of us are here, we may as well hit a few more clubs before dinner. You need anything from your room or are you ready to go, Asher?"

Was there a third option available?

"You know, how about I let you guys catch up and we can all meet for dinner? I could use a little rest." *From the naked women and the grown men acting like frat boys.*

Thankfully Oliver agreed and the three men laughed their way out of the hotel, leaving Asher sighing with relief. He collapsed onto one of the couches in the lobby and enjoyed the relative silence of the space. Sure, he could hear slot machines, music, and the combined hum of many conversations, but at least he didn't have to deal with Oliver's annoying friends, unwanted advice, and overall intrusiveness.

Asher's eyes drifted shut for what felt like only a few seconds, but could have been longer, when one voice from the crowd somehow penetrated through the others.

"Oh, I'm sorry! Sorry. Oh, shoot! Sorry about that."

He raised his eyelids slowly and turned toward the source of that almost panicked litany of apologies.

Messy hair, golden blond with streaks of light brown, a ridiculously huge sweatshirt weighing down what looked like a slight build, and jeans that, based on the frayed hems and torn pockets, had seen better days. This was the vision Asher saw spread out on the marble floor of the richly appointed lobby. Toppled luggage and grumbling people surrounded the red-cheeked man. By the time Clumsy managed to get himself back onto his flip-flop-covered feet, the people had retrieved their fallen suitcases and walked away. Huge brown eyes blinked rapidly, creating a dazed expression on an intriguing face.

Asher got up and tugged at the sleeves of his crisp white button-down shirt, making sure it lay straight. Then he found himself following Clumsy through the casino and out the door. He stayed just a few steps behind. The streets were crowded in Vegas at any time of day, and this was no exception. Asher's stony expression managed to deter the dozens of people shoving pamphlets at the tourists, but the man in front of him seemed to be gathering a collection, thanking every person who handed him a piece of paper. Okay, clumsy and polite. One pamphlet seemed to catch the man's attention, because he stopped and talked to the solicitor.

"Do these run all the time?" Asher heard the timid voice ask. A nod was the only response the guy received and then the solicitor was off, handing out more pamphlets. Narrow shoulders slumped and Clumsy examined the piece of paper he was clutching carefully. He caught his bottom lip between his teeth and darted his head around before choosing a direction and walking down the Strip.

About twenty minutes and two outdoor escalator rides later, the man was walking back the way they came. Skinny arms shot into the air and fisted hands pumped excitedly as he approached a kiosk. Asher couldn't hold back his smile as he watched the small man celebrate his victory in taking almost half an hour to locate a building that had been right behind him when he'd accepted the brochure.

If Asher didn't know better, he'd think the man had taken the most circuitous route possible because he was trying to evade him. But there was no way Clumsy had noticed him. First off, Asher had been in law enforcement long enough to know how to tail a subject without being noticed. And secondly, the number of times the guy tripped indicated he had enough difficulty being aware of his own limbs to be able to focus on anybody else.

After dropping his wallet not once but two times and

halfheartedly trying to chase after dollar bills that blew away, the man finally approached the kiosk. Asher tore his gaze from Clumsy, which was incredibly difficult for no discernible reason, and looked up at the sign above the kiosk—Double Decker Bus Tours.

"I'd like a ticket for the next bus tour, please," the quiet voice said to the salesperson. Asher heard a pause, a deep sigh, and then the man looked down and shifted from foot to foot. "Just one," he croaked.

A bus tour. Asher thought it over and then shrugged. Why not? It wasn't as if he had anything else going on. Not that this explained why he felt the urge to follow a stranger around Las Vegas, but he wasn't in the mood for self-analysis. Besides, he didn't have time. Clumsy had already walked away clutching his ticket and not looking at anything but his own feet. Asher needed to buy his own bus pass if he wanted to follow the man on what was sure to be the longest journey possible to the bus stop, which was adjacent to the exact opposite side of the kiosk from where Clumsy was headed.

As much as Asher enjoyed the impromptu tour of the Strip as the man he was tailing walked from Paris to Treasure Island, a quick glance at his gleaming metal watch told him that if they didn't turn around, they'd miss the bus tour's departure time. For a person who liked to arrive at airports at least two hours before takeoff, this was already cutting it close enough that Asher should have been well past frustrated and deep into ticked off. But oddly, he didn't feel either of those things. If anything, he was amused by the direction-challenged stranger. Still, amusing or not, the man clearly needed help or he'd never find the bus stop.

When his unwitting companion stopped on top of a walking bridge to buy a bottle of water from a vendor, Asher got a little closer, trying to come up with an opening.

"Shoot! I could have sworn I had a few ones in here." The guy looked inside his hemp wallet long enough to make Asher wonder whether he thought money would magically appear. Then the bus ticket dropped from Clumsy's hand, just as the money had at the kiosk, and Asher saw his opportunity. He squatted down and picked up the ticket.

"You dropped this," Asher said, then glanced down at the ticket nonchalantly. "Oh, you're doing the double decker tour too?"

The man turned his head and fixed soulful brown eyes on Asher, causing an unfamiliar sensation in his stomach. Asher smiled and the guy blushed, dropping his chin and shifting from foot to foot.

"Yes, I was planning on it." He lowered his voice even further. "Course I'm having trouble finding the bus stop."

Honest. Not trying to hide a shortcoming. Fucking adorable. Where had that last thought come from? Asher had always been attracted to tough, not *adorable*. And besides, since when did someone with holes in his barely-managing-to-stay-up jeans and various stains on his stretched-out sweatshirt meet the definition of adorable, or anything else positive?

Asher couldn't hold back a small grin when the guy quickly looked up at him. It turned into a broad smile when that fair skin flushed and the gaze dropped back to the ground. Turning to the vendor, Asher pulled his wallet out of his pocket.

"Two waters, please."

He handed over the cash and twisted open one bottle, handing it to Clumsy before opening his own water.

Those brown eyes did that confused blinking thing and a long-fingered hand reached for the bottle before hesitating. Asher covered the distance and pressed the water into his hand. "Should we?" he asked.

The man immediately nodded and then furrowed his brow. "Should we what?"

Knowing Clumsy had agreed with him without knowing what he was being asked caused an involuntary hardening in Asher's pants. Damn, but did he ever like a guy who could follow orders. What else would the stranger agree to do?

"I thought we could walk to the bus together," Asher explained. "Let's go." He smirked when the guy followed him without hesitation. "So, what's your name?"

Clumsy turned in his direction. "Daniel. Daniel Tover."

CHAPTER 2

"Well, hello, Daniel Tover. I'm Asher Penaz. It's nice to meet you."

Daniel looked into Asher's eyes and smiled gently. "It's nice meeting—" The man's words were cut off when he tripped over his own feet. Thankfully, Asher managed to catch him before he hit the ground.

"Are you okay?" Asher put his hand on the small of Daniel's back and rubbed circles on it, instinctively trying to soothe, and then wondered which rock that particular instinct had been hiding under for his entire life.

Instead of pulling away, that thin body nudged a little closer to him. "I'm fine. Just a little, uh, distracted sometimes."

Asher didn't mention that he'd already noticed that trait. They kept walking, with Asher's hand remaining on Daniel's back, subtly leading them toward the bus stop and avoiding the solicitors handing out pamphlets with pictures of remarkably well-endowed women who were naked from the waist up with the exception of tiny, strategically placed stars.

Were the stars supposed to add allure or were they

actually pretending to cover something? Whatever. Naked women weren't as interesting as the badly dressed man next to him.

"So, tell me about yourself, Daniel. Are you in school?"

Daniel graced him with another shy smile. Melted chocolate. That was what came to mind when Asher looked into those brown eyes.

"Just how young do you think I am?" Daniel asked.

Asher stopped walking and raked his gaze over Daniel, from head to toe and back again. He smirked when he saw the other man flush. Those jeans were annoyingly baggy, but Asher was pretty sure the bulge in the front looked a little fuller than it had before his appraisal.

"Well, we are in Vegas, so I'd say you've got to be at least twenty-one, maybe twenty-two."

In other words, way too fucking young for anything other than a little bondage, or a spanking, or maybe a quick fuck. So why was Asher interested in talking to the guy? In joining him on a tourist attraction?

"I'm thirty-three," Daniel said and then laughed at the shocked expression on Asher's face. "Yeah, I know. Older than I look. I get that a lot."

Shaking his head, Asher chuckled and then started walking again, putting his hand on the nape of Daniel's neck instead of his back and giving him a little squeeze. "I'm usually much better at this type of guessing game and figuring out all sorts of stuff about people. Thirty-three. Really?"

"Yeah, really." Daniel laughed again and pulled his wallet out of his pocket. He took his driver's license out and handed it to Asher. "There you go, Officer. Proof that I'm legal."

Asher coughed and looked at Daniel in surprise. Was that a figure of speech or had the younger man somehow figured out what he did for a living?

"Does the long silence mean I've already blown it?" Daniel looked down at his wallet as he asked the question, studiously avoiding Asher's gaze while he put his license away.

"Not yet you haven't, but if you're interested, that can be arranged."

Oh, hell no. Asher cringed at his own words. Had he actually made a lame-ass double entendre or pun or whatever? What the fuck was wrong with him? Maybe it was prolonged exposure to Oliver and titty bars.

"I don't fool around with a guy unless we're in a relationship," Daniel said, his voice quiet but steady.

Asher didn't know how to respond. It was the first time anyone had ever drawn that particular line with him. One of the advantages to meeting guys at leather clubs meant they were both usually there looking for the same thing. Of course he had friends who had dating rules—no making out on the first date, no full-on sex until the third, blah, blah, blah, so Asher was familiar with the concept. But then again, those friends hadn't met the guys they were dating during long weekends in Vegas.

"So now I really did blow it, right?" Daniel asked resignedly.

"No." Asher surprised himself with his own answer. "Nothing's been blown." He winked at Daniel. "Let's just...see where this goes, okay?"

Asher wondered what the fuck his own words meant. He had literally just met this man. He was leaving on Sunday, and he had to spend most of the weekend on the straight-guy bachelor party caravan of torture. Where exactly could this thing with Daniel go other than a round between the hotel sheets?

But then Daniel flashed him a brilliant smile and Asher felt that weird sensation in his stomach again. Yeah, they'd see where this thing could go.

"Here we are." Asher pointed toward the tall red bus. "Looks like we're right on time."

If right on time meant late enough to have almost missed the bus. That should have bothered Asher, given how much he valued punctuality. But, oddly, it didn't.

He paused at the entrance to the bus and let Daniel step ahead of him, keeping his hand on the man the entire time. They gave their tickets to the driver and climbed to the top of the open air bus, finding two empty seats together. Daniel took the seat at the end and Asher settled into the aisle seat, letting his long legs stretch into the walkway.

They remained quiet while the tour guide went through her introductory remarks, but then Daniel twisted his body so he was facing Asher and folded one leg underneath his ass.

"Have you been a police officer for a long time?"

Okay, so that answered Asher's earlier question. He didn't usually tell his pickups what he did for a living. Then again, Daniel had taken sex off the table, so the man couldn't exactly be classified as a pickup.

"I went to the academy right after high school. That was twenty-one years ago, so, yes, I've been doing it a long time. How did you know I'm a cop?"

"I don't know." Daniel shrugged. "I'm pretty good at reading people, I guess."

"You sure are. Maybe you should look into a career as one of those fortune-tellers."

Asher was kidding around, but Daniel nodded thoughtfully.

"I'm sort of between things right now." That plump bottom lip got pulled between Daniel's teeth once again. "I may go back to school, but I don't know what to study right now so... Yeah, I'm, uh, between jobs." He furrowed his brow. "But I'm not psychic or anything, so a fortune-teller gig probably wouldn't work out. It'd be fun, though, wouldn't it? To be able to tell people's futures and read their minds and all that?"

Asher actually thought that would suck. He knew firsthand from what he saw at work every day that the future often held devastating news for people. And as far as reading minds, the world was full of jackasses. No reason to want to get into those heads. Besides, if Daniel could read minds, he'd know Asher wanted nothing more than to get Daniel naked and...

"So am I bent over something or on my knees?" Daniel asked, his eyes sparkling and a happy smile taking over that cute-as-hell face.

"What?" Asher asked, dumbfounded.

"In that fantasy sequence you've got playing in your head right now, am I bent over some piece of furniture or am I on my knees?"

Asher swallowed hard and shook his head. "Neither, actually."

"Oh." Daniel's cheeks reddened and he gestured his chin toward Asher's packed crotch and the obvious erection trailing down his left thigh. "I just thought since you were turned on that maybe..."

"You were on your back. I was lying on top of you. And we were, um, kissing."

Big brown eyes met his.

"Kissing?"

Asher nodded.

It was true. He was actually fantasizing about kissing instead of fucking, which was especially weird because Asher didn't kiss even when he *was* fucking. He had always been of the opinion that mouths felt better around his dick than on his lips. Plus, he saw no point in wasting time on first base when a home run was guaranteed. Of course, Asher had left out the part of his imaginary scene involving Daniel's hands and feet being bound to the bed, putting the man completely at his mercy.

He almost groaned out loud at the thought. Damn, what would that be like? If he had the smaller man tied to his bed, under his control, what would he do? He thought about stroking Daniel until he came all over his hand and then making him lick his own cream, thought about straddling Daniel's chest and stabbing his cock into Daniel's mouth until he unloaded all over his face, thought about bending those skinny legs until Daniel was folded in half and then slamming his cock home.

Oh, fuck. Now he was trapped on a ninety-minute bus tour with a wiry, messy, and devastatingly beautiful human equivalent of Viagra who wouldn't put out. Asher was insanely horny. And, paradoxically, happier than he could remember being in a very, very long time.

"Tom Petty?" Asher asked in surprise.

Daniel nodded. "Yes. Best musician around, as far as I'm concerned. His old stuff is just as good as his new. And he's never put out a bad album. Not solo. Not with the Heartbreakers. And not with the Traveling Wilburys." Daniel paused and then shot up from his leaning position in the chair. "Oh! Have you ever seen him live?"

Asher shook his head and stared at Daniel. The little man was practically vibrating with excitement as he talked about his favorite musician.

"I'm telling you, he's amazing live. Definitely not one of those studio-produced sounds, you know? He gets up there, talks to the crowd casually, and plays his stuff. No big theatrics. Just the music." Daniel closed his eyes and swayed as if remembering a concert. "The harmonica riffs are my favorite. One summer, I followed his tour. Went to five shows in a row."

"You followed his tour?"

Dark lashes fluttered open, and Daniel pushed his too-long hair off his forehead and tucked it behind his ear.

"Uh-huh. I didn't have anything else going on so I drove around the country and watched his shows. It wasn't as much fun as following Phish, though, because there aren't as many people doing it. With Phish, we all used to caravan, share food, and hang out. I did that for almost a year. It was amazing."

Asher tried to decide whether he should ask what Phish was. From the context, he assumed he was a singer or maybe it was a group. He'd Google the name later and listen to some of the music so he'd have a better understanding of what Daniel enjoyed. Although why he wanted to know that information about a man he'd just met and who he'd never see again after that weekend, or maybe even that hour, was beyond him.

"I learned to braid necklaces on that tour. I can make all kinds of designs, weave in beads. I couldn't keep up with the demand for them after a while..." Daniel stopped talking and got a faraway look on his face.

Asher didn't like the thought of Daniel being away from him, even if it was only in his own mind. He put his arm around Daniel's shoulder and gave him a squeeze.

"Everything okay?"

Daniel's eyes snapped over to his. "What? Oh, yeah fine. I guess I just lost my train of thought." He smiled gently and shrugged. "It happens sometimes." He paused and then cleared his throat and focused all of his attention on Asher. There. That was more like it. "Tell me about what it's like to be a police officer."

Asher waited for the question that always came after that one—Have you ever shot somebody?—but it didn't come. Instead, Daniel asked, "I bet you get to save lots of people, huh? That must be pretty cool."

Two decades of police work, and not one person had ever uttered that particular thought. It took Asher off guard, which was a rare occurrence. Asher prided himself on always staying at least three steps ahead of others, always being prepared for any outcome. That way, he'd be able to steer things in whatever direction he chose. But, oddly, Asher didn't mind being caught unprepared by Daniel's comment. How could he mind when Daniel sounded so sincere and had those huge brown eyes focused on him like he was the most interesting person in the world?

"I have gotten to help a lot of people over the years, and, yes, it is pretty cool." He chuckled. "I'm a captain now, run my own squad, so I'm not on the street as often as I used to be. I don't like the paperwork or the politics but..." How much of an asshole would Asher sound like if he told this relative stranger what he liked most about his position—being in control, being the one who told others what to do? And since when did he care what he sounded like to anybody? "But I'm the head honcho." Asher ended the sentence simply, letting Daniel draw his own conclusions.

Daniel nodded, his wavy hair flopping back into his face. "Yeah, I could see that. You definitely strike me as the guy in charge."

Asher reached over to Daniel and rubbed his way up Daniel's back and over to the nape of his neck. Then he met Daniel's gaze and circled his big hand around until it was wrapped around Daniel's throat, not constricting, just petting gently, but making sure Daniel could feel the pressure against his windpipe.

"Yeah," Asher said, noticing how husky his own voice sounded. "I like being the guy in charge."

Daniel shuddered and swallowed hard, but his eyes didn't leave Asher's intense gaze. And he didn't pull away from Asher's touch. Oh, damn, that was such a turn-on. Asher wanted to get off the bus and take the younger man to his hotel room, where they could really play. It took all his control to let that desire go.

First off, he'd have to join Oliver and his merry band of mischief makers for dinner as soon as the bus trip ended, so there wasn't enough time for fun with the intriguing stranger. Plus, Daniel had set a limit—he didn't have sex unless he was in a relationship. And whatever else anybody could say about Asher—vicious with a whip or a cane, almost over the edge with ropes, and just generally pissed off and cantankerous— nobody could say he didn't respect hard limits. Oh, and the relationship thing wasn't his bag either. He sighed.

"I..." Daniel's voice broke on just that word, so he cleared his throat, still making no effort to extricate himself from Asher's hold. "I'm a little hot, so I, uh, think I should take off my sweatshirt."

The man's cheeks were rosy, and Asher could believe it was from heat. Of course, he was pretty sure the heat was generated from their conversation and the way he was touching Daniel rather than the outside temperature. Asher rubbed his thumb against the vein on the side of Daniel's neck for a full minute before releasing his hold. And in all that time, Daniel didn't complain or pull away.

Oh, yeah. The man was a natural sub. No doubt about it in Asher's mind. And the Dom in Asher responded to that on a fundamental level.

But Asher also recognized it wasn't just the dominant part of him that seemed to have developed an unusually quick and not particularly logical fixation on the disheveled, direction-challenged man. Strange as it was, Asher found he enjoyed talking to Daniel, liked listening to his stories about the many adventures he'd managed to squeeze into his thirty-three years, and loved seeing him smile. Since when did he give two shits whether a guy was smiling?

Asher was distracted by his own mental musings, so he was taken off guard when he saw Daniel standing in front of his seat with his arms and head tangled in the huge sweatshirt he was trying to pull off his body. Even worse, his twists and turns with the offending garment somehow caused him to lose his balance. So by the time Asher focused on what was going on right in front of him, he saw Daniel stumble and fall against the bus railing, his torso completely over the edge and his legs following.

"Ah, damn, Daniel. Don't move!" Asher shouted as he leaped from his seat and wrapped his arms around Daniel's waist, pulling him back down. Then he gently shifted the sweatshirt and pulled it over Daniel's head and arms. Daniel curled into Asher's body, and Asher felt him trembling and gasping for air as he tried to calm his too-rapid heart rate. The man was clearly terrified.

"Shhh, it's okay. I've got you. Maybe next time you can let me help you take your clothes off. I promise you'll be perfectly safe." He hoped the humor in his voice was clear, and that he wasn't coming across as a letch.

Daniel lifted his head and met Asher's gaze. "You saved

my life," he said in awe. "I was going to fall and you saved me." Those enormous brown eyes blinked several times and Daniel poked his pink tongue out of his enticing mouth and licked full lips. "You know what they say happens when someone saves your life?"

No, Asher had no idea what *they* said about such things. Superstitions played absolutely no role in his life. If he couldn't see it and touch it, then it wasn't worth his time or thought. Taking Asher's silence as acknowledgement that he did not, in fact, know the answer to this particular riddle, Daniel kept talking, his tone barely higher than a whisper, and his trim body still trembling.

"If someone saves your life, then your life belongs to him."

CHAPTER 3

Asher didn't respond to Daniel's comment, at least not verbally. His body, however, was another story and Asher wondered whether the smaller man practically sitting on his lap could feel what the thought of owning Daniel did to him. Because that was exactly how Asher's now fully erect dick interpreted Daniel's words. He had an almost overwhelming compulsion to order the younger man to strip naked and kneel at his feet.

He raised his hand and gently combed it through Daniel's hair, trying to calm the still frightened man. Daniel leaned into Asher's touch and then turned his face and nuzzled Asher's palm, looking up at him from underneath his lashes timidly. He was clearly making sure his action met with Asher's approval and there was no way for Asher to hold back his moan in response.

As the bus kept driving and the tour guide droned on about Al Capone and Vegas history, Asher looked down at the man snuggled in his arms in wonder. Asher Penaz didn't snuggle.

He thought back to the last time he'd brought a man

home instead of just playing around at a club. The cum hadn't been dry on the man's chest before Asher started feeling claustrophobic, so he'd gotten out of bed and taken a long shower. He fully expected the guy to be gone when he came out of the bathroom, but instead, he was greeted by the unwelcome sight of his hookup still in his bed, with no apparent plan to leave.

"Why are you still here?" he had grumbled. Three minutes later, the trick was out the door and Asher had made an internal vow not to bring guys back to his place. It was much easier to end an evening when he was the one with the keys and the ability to leave.

But maintaining a tight hold on Daniel seemed like a good idea. At the very least, it'd prevent the man from taking an inadvertent nosedive off the top of the bus. So Asher held onto the slender body, dipped his head and smelled some sort of citrusy shampoo in those messy locks, and sighed happily.

"Okay, so I know about your musical tastes," Asher said once the tour guide was finally, blessedly silent. "How about TV shows or movies? What are your favorites?"

"Um." Daniel shifted a bit and pulled back just enough to be able to look Asher in the eyes as he spoke. Asher had no intention of letting the other man move any farther than was absolutely necessary. He really enjoyed the weight of Daniel in his arms. "I don't watch a whole lot of TV and I almost never go to the movies. Books are more my thing. When I read, I can create images in my mind to go with the stories."

He shrugged and chewed on his upper lip as he furrowed his brow in thought. "Reading is more interactive, which keeps things interesting, you know? Keeps me from getting bored or distracted. How about you? Do you like to read?"

Asher nodded. "Yeah, I do. Mostly nonfiction—historicals, biographies, that kind of thing."

The conversation continued, with intermittent breaks when the tour guide spoke. Asher kept his hold on Daniel for the rest of the bus ride and surprised himself by feeling disappointed when they returned to the bus stop and he had to let go of the man in his arms.

"Do you have plans tonight?" Asher asked once they were back on the sidewalk in the middle of the Strip. "Because if you don't, I'd love it if you came to dinner with me. Well, me and a few friends."

Daniel smiled in that stomach-flipping way and reached over to touch Asher's face, then gently traced his ear. "Thanks for the invitation, but I don't think I can. I'm supposed to be meeting some people and I'm already late." He looked around and squinted. "Assuming, of course, that I can find the hotel."

Asher chose his words carefully, not wanting to scare Daniel off by admitting that he'd been following him since he left the hotel. Even to himself, it sounded creepy as hell. "I'm staying at the Bellagio," he said and then paused, hoping that Daniel would jump in.

"Oh, that's perfect! I'm going there too. We can walk together." Daniel beamed, making Asher grin.

"Great. It's this way," Asher said as he flattened his palm on the small of Daniel's back and guided him toward the hotel.

It was difficult to keep up a conversation as they moved through the loud, crowded streets, but when they reached their destination, Asher looked over at the man his body didn't want to relinquish.

"I want to see you again, Daniel. What's the rest of your schedule while you're here?"

"Asher! You found Danny. That's perfect!"

Asher frowned when Oliver's slurred words interrupted his conversation. His friend was smiling as he approached them and pulled Daniel into a hug. It was all Asher could do not to growl and yank Daniel up against his side while yelling something absurd, like, "Mine!"

Holy fuck, what was wrong with him?

"Hi, Oliver. You know Asher?" Daniel's confused tone cleared the fog in Asher's mind.

"Of course. We work together. I'm the assistant district attorney assigned to Asher's precinct." Oliver sounded like he was talking in cursive, which didn't bode well for the rest of the night. He turned toward Asher. "I see you met my little brother."

Little brother? Daniel was Oliver's brother? Asher groaned and hoped nobody else heard him.

Just great. He had a raging hard-on for his friend's brother. That probably violated multiple clauses in the guy code.

Asher suddenly regretted every piece of information he'd ever shared with Oliver about his private life over the past decade. Friend or not, there was no way Oliver would be supportive of Asher dating a member of his family given what he knew about Asher's proclivities.

Wait, dating? Since when did Asher date? Oh, this internal mental wrestling match just got better and better.

"Sorry I'm late, Ollie. I missed my flight so I had to wait for the next one and go on standby. I forgot to charge my cell. It's totally dead, and that's where I have your number so I couldn't call to let you know," Daniel rambled.

Oliver was clearly feeling no pain. He smiled and wedged himself between Asher and Daniel, flopping his arms over their shoulders and leading them through the casino to the sofas in the hotel lobby, where the bachelor party dream team was waiting.

"No problem, Danny. Are you all checked in? 'Cause we're all starving and we were waiting on you for dinner," Oliver asked.

"Oh," Daniel sighed. "Yeah, about that..." He cleared his throat. "I could have sworn I made reservations, but when I tried to check in, the hotel said they didn't have me down and they were all booked up for tonight. I was able to get a room for tomorrow night, and they said they'd call a few other hotels to see if they could fit me in tonight."

"You're welcome to share my room." Asher heard the

offer being made, and it took a few seconds to realize he was the one making it.

Oliver looked at him in confusion and Asher pointedly ignored him.

"I'm sure I can get a room somewhere." Daniel smiled shyly. "Vegas is like the hotel capital of the world or something. I don't want to put you out."

Smile, nod, and move on. You made the offer, which was polite, albeit weird. Anything else would be pushing it too far. Asher didn't bother listening to his own mental advice.

"It wouldn't put me out. And it'll be easier for us all to stay in the same hotel." Asher looked past Oliver's body and smiled at Daniel, hoping the other man could see how happy he'd be to share his space. "Plus, it'll be fun."

Daniel beamed. "Yeah, it will. Thanks, Ash. I'd love to stay in your room."

"Ash?" Oliver squeaked. "Dude, I highly recommend against nicknames for my man over here." He tipped his head toward Asher as he spoke. "He goes by Asher or Captain Penaz. That's it."

That actually wasn't it. Asher also went by "Sir" or "Master," but now didn't seem like the time to point out that little tidbit.

"Oh!" Daniel cried out. "Sorry. I didn't mean to, uh, I didn't—"

"Ash is fine, Daniel," Asher said in what he hoped was a reassuring tone. The damn thing was rusty from lack of use.

"I like the nickname," he added hastily, wanting to remove the nervous, uncomfortable expression from Daniel's face. He much preferred the man's bright smile and twinkling eyes.

"Oh, you *like* it? Since when do you like nicknames, *Ash*?" Oliver put emphasis on the name.

Damn it, but Oliver had managed to get more annoying with every drink. Asher wasn't sure he'd make it through the night without punching his friend. He stepped forward and forced Oliver to drop his arm off his shoulder.

"Watch it, Ollie," he growled. "I said I liked it when *Daniel* called me Ash. I didn't say you could use the name."

He glared at Oliver, daring him to get in his way as he moved between him and Daniel, taking back his place by the man's side where he belonged and hoping to alleviate any concerns regarding the adorable nickname.

And there he went again with the weird thoughts. Asher Penaz *belonged* in his orderly San Francisco apartment, not at a stupid bachelor party in Las Vegas. He *belonged* at the precinct, making sure every case was handled properly. He *belonged* in a dungeon, pushing subs up against their boundaries. But *belonging* next to a guy he'd just met? That was—Asher sighed and hooked his arm through Daniel's as they continued walking. Yeah, he felt like that was where he belonged, like the other man needed him.

"So, where are we going for dinner, Ollie?" He directed the question to Oliver but didn't stop looking at Daniel. Those brown eyes blinked at him and seemed to take over the open face.

"Prime," Oliver answered. "Tell me again how you two met."

"Out on the Strip," Asher answered absently. "Daniel, do you need to go change or anything before dinner?" he asked.

Daniel looked down at his faded T-shirt, frayed jeans, and flip-flops. Asher could see a blush creep up Daniel's neck and his shoulders seemed to hunch together, but when he looked up and met Asher's eyes, his gaze never wavered.

"I've got a bag with several changes of clothes, but it's all pretty much the same stuff." He chewed on his bottom lip for a few seconds. "This is me," he added quietly.

"You look fine, Danny," Oliver said. "Don't mind Asher—he's a neurotic perfectionist. Nobody can measure up to his standards."

Remembering what Daniel had said about being between jobs, Asher figured he couldn't afford new clothes. Not wanting to embarrass Daniel, he didn't respond to Oliver's antagonistic comment and just let the conversation drop.

"So, Danny." Oliver glared at Asher as he spoke. "Is your boyfriend going to join us for dinner?"

Asher's entire body stiffened. Daniel had a boyfriend?

"Chase has a show tonight, Ollie. I told you that," Daniel responded. He looked at Asher as he continued talking to his brother. "And he's my *ex*-boyfriend. I told you that too."

"Oh, did you?" Oliver asked, the lack of sincerity clear in

his tone. "Guess I forgot. Did you hear that, Asher? Danny's ex is a dancer. I hear they're really flexible. Is it true, Danny? Is Chase flexible?"

Daniel didn't raise his voice, and his stance remained loose and nonthreatening, as he answered his brother. "Yeah, he's flexible. Not quite as flexible as me, though."

Asher groaned in reaction to that comment. There was no way for him to hear about Daniel's flexibility without thinking of all the positions they could try out in bed. Hell, he didn't need anything fancy—just the thought of pinning the man's ankles to his ears was enough to make Asher want to skip dinner and say whatever he needed to convince Daniel to get naked.

"Thanks for reminding me to point out that little tidbit about myself, Ollie." Daniel winked as he continued speaking to his brother. "I think you may have just cinched things for me with Asher."

Oliver scowled and stomped away to catch up with his buddies, who were a few steps ahead of them. A small portion of Asher's brain managed to stop thinking about consuming Daniel's body long enough to recognize the significance of that accomplishment. He chuckled.

"I didn't think that was possible," Asher said, staring at Oliver's tense retreating form as they followed the other guys to the restaurant.

"What?" Daniel asked.

"Getting Ollie to shut the fuck up when he's trying

to annoy people into going along with his plot to rule the universe."

"Is that what he was doing?" Daniel asked quietly.

"What?" Asher asked, looking away from Oliver and into impossibly huge eyes.

"Was my brother trying to rule the universe? 'Cause I got the sense his goal was keeping me away from you."

Asher's jaw dropped before he could stop it. He quickly closed his mouth and furrowed his brow. Though Daniel's words were barely audible over the loud slot machines and piped-in music, and his tone was completely even and nonaccusatory, Asher nevertheless felt as if he needed to defend himself. But he wasn't sure what he should be defending until Daniel spoke again.

"Do you know why that would be, Ash? Do you know why Ollie would be against us spending time together?"

They reached the restaurant shortly after Daniel asked the question, and Asher found himself unusually grateful for the distraction. He wasn't sure how he could tell Daniel his suspected reason for Oliver's behavior—that he didn't want his brother dating someone kinky, even if that someone was one of his closest friends. If he told Daniel the truth right off the bat, there was a chance the man would want nothing to do with him. And even though they'd just met, Asher wasn't willing to take that risk.

For the first time in many years, Asher felt uncomfortable about what he enjoyed and uncertain about how to go about getting what he wanted. Hell, he wasn't even sure what it was he wanted from Daniel. His body pulsed with desire for the man next to him, that much was clear, and he wasn't willing to lose the opportunity to sate that desire. So rather than answer Daniel's question, Asher clasped Daniel's hand and gave him a squeeze.

"Looks like you managed to get your brother to back off. That sort of miracle deserves a reward. Dinner's on me."

CHAPTER 4

As it turned out, offering to pay for Daniel's dinner wasn't much of a hardship. The man barely glanced at the menu, and when the waiter came to take their orders, he seemed genuinely surprised, like the idea that they'd ask for food at a restaurant hadn't crossed his mind.

"Oh, ah…" Daniel blinked at the waiter. "Water's fine for me, thanks."

"You're not hungry?" Asher asked him. "I've been with you for the past few hours and you haven't eaten anything. I know they're not serving meals on the plane anymore, so… did you grab a bite at the airport?"

"They still serve meals in first class," Oliver interrupted with this useless piece of information. Asher ignored him.

"Daniel, when was the last time you had something to eat?" he asked. *And when did I turn into somebody's mother?*

Not his own mother, because she'd waited tables during the day and bartended at night to support herself and her four boys after their father ran out on them. She hadn't had time to nag anybody about eating right. Nope, he'd turned into one of those fictional television mothers.

"Uh, I don't remember," Daniel answered. "But—"

"No, buts. You need to eat."

Oliver's mouth dropped open. Asher continued ignoring him. It was easy, seeing as how he was already ignoring the voice in his head asking him who the fuck had taken control of his mouth.

"Okay, I'll, um..." Daniel glanced down at the menu and up to the waiter, who was staring at him with a barely concealed grin. "I'll have the vegetable soup, please."

"Are you sure that'll be enough?" Asher asked him. "Won't you still be hungry?"

"Oh, come on!" Oliver practically shouted from across the table. "Is this some kind of joke?" His hands flew up to shoulder height, and he looked around the room as if expecting an answer from somebody. "Seriously, are there hidden cameras around here or what?"

"Shut up, Ollie," Asher growled. "Leave it alone."

The waiter scurried away and Daniel raised his glass. "To my brother," he said, obviously trying to change the topic and clear the tension in the air. "I haven't met Shirley, but I know she must be a special woman to capture Ollie's heart. I look forward to meeting her."

Everybody raised their glasses in a toast and Oliver's frat-boy buddies even hooted and hollered. Asher hoped Ollie wouldn't ruin the applause with a speech, but the hope was short-lived.

Asher was taking the first sip of his beer when Oliver

started talking. The man was still going strong by the time Asher had drained his glass. Admittedly, he'd gulped more than sipped, but still. Realizing that his friend wasn't anywhere near done, Asher rolled his eyes and got the waiter's attention. He raised his empty glass in the air and tilted his chin toward it in a silent request for another round. Hopefully some medicinal drinking would make the rest of the night bearable.

"Then on our third date," Oliver rambled on, "Shirley and I went…"

"Holy shit, he's going to take us through every single moment they've spent together," Asher mumbled under his breath. "There isn't enough alcohol in Las Vegas to help me get through this."

A hand gripped his knee underneath the table and gave him a gentle squeeze. A glance at Daniel melted his tension away. Daniel focused those warm, twinkling eyes on him, a knowing grin on his cute face. Asher raised one eyebrow in question.

"I don't get to see my brother much," Daniel whispered in explanation. "This is like getting an abridged rundown of his life."

"Abridged?" Asher asked incredulously, but he returned Daniel's smile, his frustration draining away, just like that. "He just told us what he ordered for dinner on his third date with Shirley, down to every last detail. When we know there was too much pepper on the Greek salad and that he asked for lime in his water instead of lemon, we're well past abridged and fully into extraneous detail territory."

"Maybe." Daniel shrugged. "But now I know Shirley doesn't like pickles. That tidbit might come in handy one day."

A snort somehow escaped Asher's mouth. "You're funny," he said under his breath.

"Don't sound so surprised." Daniel's eyes shone as he spoke. "I'm not just a pretty face." He batted his eyelids in an exaggerated fashion.

Asher realized Daniel was making a joke and going for campy, but he had incredibly long lashes and the sweetest smile and… Asher considered taking himself outside and kicking his own ass. Was it possible that Oliver spiked his drink earlier that day? There seemed to be no other explanation for the nauseatingly sappy thoughts infiltrating his mind.

"You wanna share with the class, Asher?" Oliver asked.

It took Asher several moments to realize a question had been directed to him. He had been well on his way to training his brain to consider Oliver's voice background noise.

"Huh?"

"You're scowling at my brother."

"Settle down, Ollie," Asher said. "I'm not scowling at him. I think your brother's funny. Go back to your story."

Well, shit. Now he had nobody to blame but himself. He had actually invited Ollie to continue sharing way the fuck too much information. Where was the waiter with that beer?

"Oomph!" The air rushed out of Daniel's lungs when Asher shoved him against the wall in the elevator. "What're you—"

"Damn, your body feels nice." Asher had just a hint of a slur. Not a surprise, considering how much he'd been drinking. "Why do you hide it underneath these baggy clothes?"

Large, strong hands roamed Daniel's body. First skimming, then squeezing his chest, stomach, hips, and ass. It was impossible for Daniel to keep his body in check, to keep himself from reacting to the pressure behind Asher's touch. He loved being manhandled, always had, and he'd never been with anyone who did it quite so forcefully. He gulped and tried to keep his mind clear of the haze of lust that suddenly overwhelmed him.

"I don't... I, uh... Not into clothes, I guess. Um, Asher—"

"I wish you weren't in clothes. Gonna get you out of these as soon as we get to the room."

Asher leaned down, his lips so close Daniel could almost feel them against his own. He should pull away, put a stop to what they were doing before he lost all his willpower. But the large man had him caged in, a thick erection pressed against his belly, and there was so much heat in those black eyes. Daniel feared he might have already lost the battle to maintain any control. The ding of the elevator saved him.

"We're here," he whispered roughly. Asher didn't stop touching him, grabbing at his ass, pinching his nipples through his shirt. "Asher," he said as he flattened his hands on Asher's chest and tried to push the man back. It was like trying to move a brick wall. "Ash, we're on our floor."

A discontented grumble made Asher's feelings about the interruption clear. Nevertheless, he backed off and grasped Daniel's elbow, leading him out of the elevator and through the winding hallway.

"I've been waiting to get you alone all night," he said. "I thought your brother would never stop droning on with those boring stories. Each one was more painful than the one before."

Daniel grinned, feeling his mind clear now that he wasn't in a small space being pawed at by the large man.

"Oh, come on. It wasn't that bad. I know you enjoyed the story about the time he locked his keys in the car with the engine running and Shirley had to come rescue him."

"Fine," Asher conceded. "That one was good. So that's, what? Maybe three minutes of good material out of three hours of talking? Not worth it."

"Oh! I forgot," Daniel said. "I need to go back downstairs to—"

"You're not going anywhere," Asher insisted. He tightened his hold on Daniel's elbow. "I get you to myself for the rest of the night."

Daniel gulped and shifted his stance, trying to get comfortable. He was so hard he ached, and Asher's aggression and possessiveness were just making things harder. Literally.

"I need to get my duffel from the concierge," he croaked.

"Already handled," Asher responded. "I had them bring your bags up to my room while we were at dinner."

They got to the room and Asher dug into his back pocket for the keycard. He found it, slid it into the slot in the door, and then turned the knob and pushed the door open with his shoulder, never once loosening his grip on Daniel. After that, Asher moved more quickly than Daniel thought possible for a man of Asher's stature. In the blink of an eye, Daniel found himself pinned to the door, a muscular thigh pressed against his groin and strong fingers clutching his ass and pulling him forward.

"Want you," Asher breathed against him, lowering his mouth toward Daniel's. "Damn, your mouth...so pretty." He brushed a square-tipped finger over Daniel's lower lip, and Daniel had to fight the urge to suck on it.

"Asher, we need to slow down. Remember we talked about—"

When Asher leaned down and started licking the spot beneath his ear, Daniel realized banking the fire burning between them wasn't going to be easy. Especially when the half of "them" with the seventy-pound weight advantage was lit. With that thought in mind, Daniel decided a diversion would be his best tactic. And if the diversion he chose included running his hands over all those delicious muscles... well, lucky him.

He let Asher maneuver him toward the bed and worked open the buttons on the man's starched shirt as they moved. A firm tug had the shirt pulled out of the waistband of Asher's dark jeans. When he had the entire front open, he pushed it to the sides and slid his hands from Asher's waist to his pecs and back down again.

"You have an amazing body, Ash." Daniel loved the feeling of hard muscle, hot skin, and thick hair beneath his fingertips. "Let's get the rest of your clothes off and I'll give you a massage. How does that sound?"

"Massage?"

Well, based on Asher's tone, Daniel gathered it sounded unexpected. He wasn't sure whether that was because Asher didn't enjoy massages, wasn't offered them often, or had a beer-induced language gap making him forget what the word meant.

"Mmm hmm."

He worked on Asher's belt, jeans button, and zipper with nimble fingers, while raising himself up on the balls of his feet and tilting his chin up, aiming for a kiss. Just as his lips were about to connect with Asher's, the man turned his head and bit down on Daniel's shoulder. Any disappointment over the missed opportunity to taste Asher vanished when Daniel had Asher's pants and boxer-briefs pushed down to his ankles. His jaw dropped and his eyes widened at the sight of Asher's naked body.

Asher was tall, broad, and thick *everywhere*. The hair that had so intrigued him on Asher's chest trailed down his belly and surrounded a heavy cock and full balls. His legs were muscular tree trunks. His biceps were the size of Daniel's thighs. And his cock... Daniel shuddered just thinking about that heat pushing into his body, splitting him open. He whimpered with need. It had been so long since he'd been with a man and he didn't think any of his previous boyfriends had been built like this.

Asher cupped his chin with long fingers and raised it, closing his mouth and saving him from drooling.

"Like what you see?" Asher asked him, that deep voice sounding scratchy and sexy as hell. "'Cause, you know, the angle of the dangle is in direct proportion to the booty of the cutie."

Asher waggled his eyebrows and gave him a goofy grin with that last comment and Daniel's stomach flipped over. He had been prepared for demanding and horny, not adorable and corny. The latter was much harder to resist. So much so, that if Asher had been anywhere near the cross streets of with-it and sober, Daniel would have thrown his relationship requirement out the window and begged the man to bend him over the edge of the bed and pound him into the mattress.

He dropped to a squat and looked up at Asher from

underneath his lashes. "Sit down, please," he murmured quietly. "I'll get your shoes and socks off."

Asher flopped gracelessly onto the bed, lying back with his forearm over his eyes. Although horny had been holding the lead up to that point, Daniel could see from Asher's relaxed form and slow breathing that tired and drunk were catching up. As soon as he removed Asher's shoes and clothes, he stood and pulled the side of the comforter down.

"Ash, why don't you scoot up here and lie on your belly. I'm going to get some lotion and I'll give you a backrub."

Asher moved that strong arm off his face and peered at Daniel with cloudy eyes.

"I don't take orders," Asher growled.

It was hard for Daniel not to smile at that comment, but he managed it. The man was trashed, exhausted, well and truly out of it. But that wasn't stopping him from trying to exert some sort of dominance.

Asher didn't need to worry about Daniel fighting for control. He had no interest in it. At least not on the surface. But that didn't mean he didn't know how to get his way.

"I know," he said and dropped his gaze to the floor. "I just thought you'd be more comfortable without your legs hanging off the edge of the bed. I'll go get the lotion."

By the time Daniel returned from the bathroom, Asher was lying on his stomach with his head on the pillows and his tall body stretched across the bed. Daniel pulled his sweatshirt off, and pushed his loose jeans down to his ankles without unbuttoning them. Then he stepped out of his jeans and flip-flops and crawled up the bed wearing his boxers and T-shirt.

He straddled Asher's ass and poured lotion onto his skin, eliciting a deep moan. Asher's eyes were closed, his expression relaxed and easy. Daniel put his hands on Asher's wide back, letting the lotion ease his glide as he added pressure with the base of his hands and his thumbs.

"Feels good," Asher sighed, his breathing slowing even further, all the tension gone from his face. "You have amazing hands."

"So I've been told," Daniel said with a smile.

"Mmmm, seriously." Asher sighed deeply. "Where'd you learn to do that? 'S incredible."

"New Mexico."

"Huh?" Asher asked, apparently no longer able to articulate words.

"I once worked as a masseur at a spa in Santa Fe."

Asher gave a halfhearted grunt in response. It wouldn't take long to soothe the big man into sleep. And then Daniel would curl himself up against the hottest person he'd ever had the pleasure of meeting and join him in dreamland. So far, his brother's bachelor-party weekend was turning out much better than Daniel had anticipated.

CHAPTER 5

The first thing Asher noticed when consciousness seeped in was that he felt sore all over, and not in a "hard workout at the gym" kind of way. The sharp pain behind his eyelids and foul taste in his mouth confirmed the cause of his aches— hangover. He groaned, feeling way too old to be recovering from a bender. What had gotten into him?

That was when the memories started landing—Oliver's bachelor-party weekend, an event seemingly sponsored by the liquor companies because surely it had been engineered to lead him into alcoholism. He shifted and tried to piece together the previous day. Just then, he heard a quiet whimper and a slender arm flung itself across his chest.

He opened his eyes and looked at the man sharing his bed. Oh, damn. Daniel Tover. Heat immediately pooled in Asher's groin. The details of the night before came back to him. He remembered meeting Oliver's brother, remembered enjoying his company despite the annoying dinner with Oliver and his buddies, remembered going back to the hotel room and...

Asher furrowed his brow. He was nude in a hotel room

bed with another man, but he couldn't remember having sex with him. The level of wrong there bordered on criminal, and he needed to rectify it before Internal Affairs started an investigation. Speaking of investigating internal affairs... Asher ignored the throbbing in his temples and concentrated on the previous night. The only memory he had was of Daniel's awed expression when he stripped off Asher's clothes and stared at his cock.

Mmm, Asher had enjoyed seeing lust in Daniel's eyes and knowing he was the cause. He knew that he had a great dick. Many men had commented on it and Asher could see it for himself, obviously. Still, there was something particularly pleasing about seeing Daniel's appreciation of his body.

"Morning," Daniel mumbled and scooted closer. He tightened his grip around Asher's chest, swung his left leg over Asher's and rested it between his knees, and nuzzled Asher's throat. "Did you sleep okay?"

He smiled at the other man, reached up to stroke his hair, and suddenly realized what he was doing. Asher's smile was replaced by a scowl in the blink of an eye. He wasn't accustomed to sharing a bed with anyone, wasn't comfortable with the level of familiarity Daniel was exhibiting even though they'd just met, and he plain didn't like feeling as if he wasn't in control of the situation. In this case, *the situation* seemed to be his own thoughts and feelings, which had been out of whack since the moment he'd seen Daniel in the hotel lobby the prior day.

Right as he was about to push Daniel off him and scurry out of the bed, he heard the man make a contented little sound and felt him somehow burrow even more tightly against his chest and side. Though he'd never admit it, Asher enjoyed the idea that Daniel wanted to be close to him. Without his permission, his scowl morphed back into a tender smile.

"I can't remember the last time I slept so soundly," Daniel said.

Asher realized the same was true for him—he didn't know when he'd last slept so peacefully. It was odd, because he usually hated having anybody touch him when he was sleeping. He also didn't appreciate sharing covers, feeling the mattress move when somebody else tried to get comfortable, or hearing the toilet flush in the middle of the night.

Okay, fine, so there wasn't a whole lot of question as to why he was still single. He'd told Oliver he just hadn't found the right guy, but the truth was, Asher hadn't been looking for Mr. Right. He wasn't interested in making compromises or having conversations or limiting his sex life to one man or anything else having a boyfriend would entail.

What he *was* interested in was getting into Daniel. He wondered whether he'd fucked the other man or been sucked off the night before. Well, there was one way to find out. Two, really, but asking seemed rude, so Asher was going with door number two. He reached for Daniel's ass, planning to caress it as a ruse to feel for any residual lube, but then he encountered fabric.

He bent his neck and looked underneath the blanket. Why was Daniel dressed?

"Why are you dressed?" he asked, not one to shy away from speaking his mind.

"Hmm?" Daniel responded sleepily, making Asher feel a bit sheepish about waking him up. "'M not dressed. Just in my boxers."

Yeah, boxers and a T-shirt—two things that fell under the category of clothing. But Asher wasn't interested in arguing over semantics.

"Okay, why aren't you naked?"

There. No room for confusion with that question. He'd made himself clear.

Daniel pushed himself up and got onto his knees. Sure enough, the man was wearing his T-shirt from the night before along with white boxers covered in brightly colored polka dots. There was nothing sexy about that ensemble. In fact, the choice in underwear was bordering on ridiculous. And yet, Asher's heart rate increased and his cock filled. It shouldn't have been arousing, true enough, but even with bedhead, bleary eyes, a baggy T-shirt, and those stupid boxers, Daniel somehow managed to turn his crank.

"I, uh, always sleep in my underwear and a T-shirt, and uh..." Daniel chewed on his bottom lip. "I thought it'd make it easier for us to not, uh, you know," he finished in a whisper.

Hangovers and optimal mental function weren't exactly bedfellows, so Asher had some trouble following Daniel's awkward rambling.

"Oh, God," Daniel whimpered.

Asher darted his eyes to Daniel's face and saw the direction of his gaze. The man was completely focused on Asher's dick, which was rigid and pointing toward his chest. Apparently, seeing Daniel flustered had ramped up Asher's arousal. Whatever. It wasn't worth thinking about at the moment. Not when he was hard enough to pound nails.

He reached for Daniel's hand and pulled it toward his dick. Some nice stroking would give him time to decide whether he wanted the man's mouth or his ass. Before he could contemplate his options, though, Daniel yanked his hand away and jumped off the bed.

"I'm going to shower," he announced, his voice tense. "We have to meet Oliver soon and, uh, yeah, so..."

The man practically bolted out of the room. Asher furrowed his brow and looked at the nightstand. They were supposed to meet Oliver and the rest of the guys for brunch at eleven. It was only a little after nine. That did not fall under his definition of "soon." Most definitely not so soon that his needs couldn't be met.

He kicked the blanket to the foot of the bed and swung his feet onto the floor. Then he slowly followed Daniel into the bathroom, rubbing the heel of his hand over his erection as he went. Apparently shower sex was on the menu. Fine with him. Getting wet and slippery with Daniel would help get the day off to a good start.

He got to the bathroom in time to see Daniel shake his pale ass as he stepped into the shower. The water had barely hit him before he started singing. His voice was surprisingly good. Asher wasn't really into music, but he leaned against the doorframe and listened for a full minute, deciding that even John Lennon would sit up in his grave and clap if he heard Daniel's rendition of the Beatles song he was belting out.

Daniel sang and bopped around in the steamy shower cubicle. When he tilted his face up under the spray to rinse off soap and shampoo, he opened his mouth, filled it with water, and then kept singing, but instead of words, he made a sound that was part hum, part gurgle. And he kept shaking his ass the entire time.

The whole thing was so damn adorable that Asher almost forgot why he'd walked into the bathroom. But then Daniel dropped the soap, bent down to pick it up, fumbled with it a few times as it slipped out of his hands, and then stood back up and bumped his head on the tiled ledge. Asher's fingers itched with the need to steady the other man and his dick throbbed with arousal.

"Ouch!" Daniel exclaimed. He set the soap on the ledge and rubbed the injured spot on his head.

Unable to stay away any longer, Asher strode to the shower, yanked open the glass door, and stepped inside. He had his hand on Daniel's head before the other man registered his presence.

"Asher! What are you—"

"Are you okay?" Asher stroked Daniel's head gently with one hand and put two fingers under his chin with the other, lifting his face and meeting his gaze.

"Oh, yeah. Fine. Just bumped my head." Daniel shrugged. "It happens."

Asher dipped his head and pressed his lips to Daniel's forehead.

"I'd better keep an eye on you to make sure it doesn't happen again. No more unattended showers while we're here, okay?"

Light teasing was unfamiliar to Asher, but he thought he was doing okay with it. And then Daniel flushed, looked at the ground, and started breathing heavily. He was close enough to the other man to feel his heart pounding furiously.

"Daniel? Are you okay?" he asked.

"You're naked," Daniel replied with a shaky voice. "Naked."

Asher chuckled. "Well, yeah. We're in the shower. I don't tend to shower with my clothes on. They get heavy and they're in the way of my skin. How can I wash if I don't have easy access?"

"Right, right." Daniel nodded feverishly. "That makes sense. I'll just go."

He tried to move around Asher to get to the shower door, but Asher didn't budge. Instead, he grasped Daniel's arm.

"Hey, why're you running off? The fun's just starting."

Asher's voice was rough as sandpaper. He wanted Daniel and saw no point in hiding it. Particularly not with an erection that couldn't be missed making his desire obvious.

"Asher," Daniel sighed. "Remember what we talked about yesterday? I don't do...*fun* outside of a relationship."

Right. Asher hadn't remembered, actually. And now that the memory was back, he disliked it even more than when he'd heard it the first time. Not that Daniel seemed any happier about the line he'd drawn. The man was trembling. While Asher wasn't certain whether it was from the chill of being out of the flow of the water, nervousness, or arousal, he was leaning toward arousal, because Daniel's prick was as hard as his.

"You want me." He tilted his chin toward Daniel's groin and moved his gaze in the same direction.

"Of course I want you!" Daniel said, exasperation clear in his voice. "I'm breathing, aren't I?"

There was no way for Asher to hold back a smirk. He rubbed his hand slowly down Daniel's ribcage to his hip and enjoyed watching the man tremble.

"Ash, please." Daniel's face was flushed, his pupils huge, and his bottom lip red and swollen from his constant chewing.

"Please what? Please touch me? Please keep going?" He was practically whispering now, his words ghosting over Daniel's face.

"You promised." Daniel's gaze met his. "Please."

Well, damn. It was hard to turn down a plea from Daniel,

hard to say no to those soulful eyes. But then again, Asher was hard. Really hard.

"Here's a question," he said slowly. "Do you beat off when you're not in a relationship?"

"Huh?" Daniel furrowed his brow.

"You said you don't have sex outside of a relationship. But does that mean you don't get yourself off either?" Of course Asher already knew the answer to his absurd question, but he wanted Daniel to acknowledge it.

"No," Daniel said. "I mean, yes, I beat off, but what does that—"

"Go ahead," Asher said so quietly his voice was barely audible over the sound of the water. "You take care of you. I'll take care of me. No rules being broken that way, right?"

Daniel's lips were parted, his eyes wide. Asher wanted to kiss the man, but he didn't. And it wasn't because of the no-nookie rule. It was because he wasn't into kissing, despite the repeated desire he'd had the previous day and even that morning to taste Daniel's mouth. Shoving that feeling down, he reached for the small bottle of conditioner, poured some into his hand, then wrapped his fingers around his cock and started pulling.

"Oh, God," Daniel whimpered.

Asher licked his lips, spread his legs, and thrust his hips forward, putting on a show. This was fun.

"Feels so good," he grunted.

And it did feel good. He was incredibly horny and

getting the attractive man in his shower hot and bothered was arousing in and of itself. Asher couldn't remember the last time he'd enjoyed the feel of his own hand quite this much. He increased his pace, adding a slight squeeze when he reached his glans, pushing down hard to his root, and then pulling back up again.

"I'm close, sugar. So fuckin' close." His stare was so hot, he felt like he was burning into Daniel, whose face was bright red. "Don't you want to join me? Come on," he encouraged. "Touch yourself."

He rocked his hips, helping propel his cock through his fist faster. He tightened his grip, threw his head back, and shouted as he pulsed ribbon after ribbon of cum onto Daniel's belly and chest.

Up until that point, the other man had remained stock-still. He had stared at Asher's body and his face, his gaze wandering between the two without taking his eyes away for even a second. But he hadn't made a move to find his own pleasure. The feeling of Asher's release against his skin seemed to break Daniel's resolve. He blinked for what seemed like the first time since Asher had started this little game, shoved his hand down his body, desperately reached for his dick, circled his fingers around it, and barely got one stroke in before he was crying out Asher's name and shaking as he came.

"Uh, uh, uh," Daniel grunted as his body shuddered with the force of his release.

Stunning. The man was positively stunning.

When he'd wrung himself dry, Daniel leaned back against the shower wall and stared at Asher. "You are temptation incarnate," Daniel accused, but the way he raised one corner of his mouth let Asher know the statement wasn't meant as a complaint.

"I must not be tempting enough," Asher teased back. "I can't get you to abandon the 'no sex without a relationship' rule."

Daniel ran a finger through a smear of Asher's release that had painted his hip and then sucked his finger into his mouth. "I have news for you, Ash. What we just did? That was sex under any definition, except maybe the presidential ones."

Maybe so. And Asher also had a niggling feeling that what he and Daniel had going between them was a relationship under any definition, including presidential ones. So that meant Daniel's rule hadn't been broken. Of course, Asher wasn't sure if his relationship-meter was reliable. He wasn't in the habit of having relationships. And even if it was reliable, what did it matter? After this weekend, they'd likely never see each other again. He'd be going home to San Francisco and Daniel would go back to...

"Hey, Daniel?" Asher asked.

Daniel looked at him and smiled, his eyes twinkling. He rubbed his fingertips along Asher's wrist. "Yeah?"

"Where do you live?"

"Live?"

"Yeah." Asher smiled at the perplexed look on Daniel's face. He wasn't sure what was confusing about his question, but he liked how Daniel scrunched his nose and furrowed his brow. "Live. As in, where do you call home?"

"Oh, uh, well, I grew up in New York, but I moved away when I was eighteen, so that's not really home anymore. And I've lived in a bunch of places since then, but never for very long, so, uh, I guess they're not home either. And right now I'm sort of between cities, trying to decide what I want to do next and where I want to live, so, uh…"

No job. No home. That meant Daniel was completely portable. He could follow Asher to San Francisco. The thought hadn't even had time to fully settle before Asher gasped in shock. Was he actually considering asking a man he'd just met to move for him?

Maybe they pumped something into the air in Vegas. After all, there were wedding chapels in all the hotels and along the Strip. Something had to be done to keep them busy. Yeah, that was it. The hotels were using some sort of chemical substance to turn guests into lovesick fools.

Clinging to that nonlogic, Asher stepped out of the shower and started getting ready for day two of the never-ending bachelor party.

CHAPTER 6

Daniel tugged his T-shirt down and stepped into his flip-flops.

"Ready when you are," he called out over his shoulder to Asher, who was still in the bathroom.

Asher walked out of the bathroom, a towel tied around his hips, and Daniel almost lost his breath. It was as if a compilation of everything he found attractive had been put together in one person.

Asher was so tall that Daniel had to tilt his head back to meet his eyes, and he was broad enough to surround Daniel's frame completely if he were to wrap his beefy arms around him. There was strength in every motion of that thick, muscular body, and there was a roughness to Asher— the shaved head, the piercing black eyes, the deep-bronze skin, the whiskey voice. Daniel felt as if Asher could engulf him completely, body and spirit, which should have been frightening, but instead gave him a sense of safety in the other man's presence.

"Aren't you going to dry your hair?" Asher asked.

"My hair?" Daniel asked, feeling distracted by all the

exposed skin covered by dark, silky hair. He clenched and unclenched his fists, fighting the urge to run his fingers along Asher's chest.

Asher walked over and his eyes gleamed when Daniel looked up at him. He stroked the back of Daniel's neck, his touch undeniably tender, and Daniel trembled.

"Your hair is dripping wet. It's drizzling down your back and soaking your shirt." Asher smiled. "Here, I'll take care of it."

He covered Daniel's head with a towel and gently rubbed it over his hair. Daniel bent his neck down to give the man more access and then realized where Asher had gotten the towel. He was now standing next to a completely naked Asher Penaz, looking right at his dick and balls. Even flaccid, the man's cock was impressive—thick, long. And beneath it—

"I'm not going to be able to keep my hands off you if you tempt me like this, sugar."

Daniel blinked up at Asher, not sure what the other man meant. Asher dropped the towel to the floor and ran his fingertips from Daniel's shoulder down his bicep, over his elbow, and across his forearm until he reached Daniel's hand, which was cupping Asher's huge, lightly furred balls.

"Sorry. I... I didn't realize I'd... I didn't mean to..."

Daniel stammered and blushed, but he couldn't seem to move his hand. Asher's body temperature felt higher than his, at least in that part of his body.

"Lick them," Asher said roughly.

Asher moved his hand to Daniel's shoulder, pressing downward. Damn, but did Daniel ever appreciate a domineering man. He let Asher guide him to his knees and leaned forward, nuzzling Asher's groin. He shuddered from the musky sent and groaned when Asher twined his fingers through his hair and tightened his grip, holding him firmly in place.

"Lick them," Asher repeated, and Daniel complied, darting his tongue out and swiping it over Asher's sac. The big man relaxed his hold on Daniel's hair, and with the increased freedom, Daniel moved his mouth from side to side, lapping at Asher's testicles and inhaling his scent.

With his free hand, Asher held his balls and guided them to Daniel's mouth. He rubbed himself over Daniel's lips and pressed against Daniel's jaw with his thumb.

"Open, Daniel." He pressed harder. "Suck them."

It was an order, not a request, which just made it hotter. Daniel trembled and moaned. There was no way for him to resist. He didn't want to resist. Instead, he opened his mouth and took Asher's left testicle in.

"Yeah, that's it, boy. Suck my nuts. Suck them."

Being on his knees, Asher's words—the entire scene was seedy, and for a moment, Daniel hesitated. But then he looked up at Asher and met his gaze. While his words were rough, Asher's expression was awestruck and full of desire. And, most important to Daniel, there was nothing belittling in the way Asher looked at him; instead, the man's gaze was adoring.

As if sensing Daniel's concern, Asher released the hold he had on Daniel's hair completely and gently stroked his head instead. "That's good, sugar. You're doing so well."

Daniel relaxed and moaned, enjoying the taste and feel of this man who could be rough and gentle at the same time. Daniel was about to push his pants down so he could stroke himself while he mouthed Asher, but a banging on the hotel door startled him.

He fell back, resting his ass on his heels, and snapped his head toward the door. "Who's that?" he asked.

Asher took in a deep breath and sighed. "Your brother."

"Oliver? But I thought we were going to meet him at the restaurant." Daniel stood and adjusted himself, hoping his arousal wasn't too evident.

"We were, but I'm guessing he wasn't thrilled about us being alone together."

"Yeah." Daniel laughed. "He wasn't your biggest fan last night, was he?"

Asher grimaced at the understatement. Daniel patted his shoulder.

"I'll deal with Oliver while you get dressed, okay? I'm sure I can get him to tone down the protective-brother shtick."

Daniel shook his head and chuckled as he turned to walk toward the door. Asher stopped him with a hand on his waist.

"Daniel?" Asher said. Daniel looked back over his

shoulder. "I was having a good time," Asher continued, his voice quiet and his tone even, but Daniel could hear the question in it.

"I was too," he responded, assuring the other man and himself at the same time. "I'm, uh, sorry we got interrupted."

"Stay here with me again tonight."

Smiling, Daniel nodded and said, "Okay."

Asher opened his mouth, as if to say something else, but then the banging on the door got louder and they separated, Daniel heading toward the door to deal with Oliver and Asher walking to the dresser.

Daniel opened the door just enough to slip outside and then closed it behind him.

"Morning, Oliver," he said and smiled brightly at his scowling brother. "Come on now, let's turn that frown upside down." He poked Oliver's waist and belly playfully. "It's your bachelor-party weekend; you're supposed to be happy!"

Oliver pushed Daniel's hands away and glared at the closed door. "Where's Asher?" he grumbled.

"Getting dressed," Daniel answered.

"Why isn't he dressed?"

"Because he took a shower and that tends to be a clothes-free activity."

"And why did he need a shower?" Oliver demanded.

Daniel rolled his eyes. "Oh, come on, Ollie. Cut it out. Your friend and I are interested in each other. Is that what you want to hear?"

"No! That's exactly what I *don't* want to hear." Oliver's voice was getting louder.

"I thought he was supposed to be your friend. That should mean that you like him, right? So why're you being so weird about this?"

"Because you're my brother and Asher's dangerous." Oliver crossed his arms over his chest.

"Dangerous?" Daniel scoffed. "What's he do, Ollie? Step on cracks? Walk under ladders? Open umbrellas indoors?" Daniel fake-shuddered. "Sounds scary."

"I know what I'm talking about, Danny. Asher, well, he's into some weird shit. He, um, you know, uh…"

It was ridiculous to see a man in his forties stumbling for words, so Daniel put a stop to it. "Are you talking about sex?" Daniel asked. Oliver actually blushed in response to the question, and Daniel's anger dissipated. It was sweet, really, the whole brotherly concern bit. "Look, Ollie, I realize we don't spend as much time together as we should, but you've got to know I can take care of myself. I've been doing it for a long time."

Oliver shook his head. "The things Asher's into… You don't understand."

"I understand enough to know that I'm attracted to him and the feeling's mutual. Anything else I need to know, I'd like to hear from Asher himself. Look," Daniel said, sighing, "I appreciate your concern, but I have no interest in talking to my brother about my sex life. I'm not a kid and you're going to need to trust that I know how to handle myself."

"I do trust you."

"Good. Then will you please back off of Asher?"

Oliver snorted. "I wasn't doing anything to Asher."

"Oh, please!" Daniel laughed. "The way you rode his ass last night, you could've at least bought him dinner first, you know?"

"Jesus, Danny!" Oliver coughed and his eyes bugged out. "That's disgusting. I don't need an image in my head of Asher doing...*that*."

"Yeah, I know what you mean." Daniel nodded solemnly. "I like it the other way around too. There's nothing more disappointing than thinking you've found yourself a good, hard top only to learn that he's actually a—"

"Not what I meant!" Oliver was bright red now. He waved his arms in front of Daniel's face frantically. "*So* not what I meant."

"No?" Daniel raised one eyebrow. "Whatever." He shrugged. "Just as long as we're done talking about sex now. What Asher is into, or what I want going into me, or—"

Oliver thrust out his hand in a "stop" motion. "We're done. Totally done."

"Excellent." Daniel looped his arm with his brother's. "I knew I could get you to see things my way."

"Holy hard-on, Batman."

"What?" Daniel asked his dancer friend Chase.

"Seriously hot bear at three o'clock checking you out."

Daniel glanced away from the slot machine he was playing and followed his friend's gaze. He beamed.

"That's Ash Penaz."

"And who, pray tell, is Ash Penaz?"

"He's the guy I'm staying with," Daniel answered Chase while keeping his eyes locked on Asher. He pressed the button on the slot machine absently, not bothering to look at whether he got good numbers.

"Staying with? Does he live here?"

"No." Daniel shook his head and finally tore his gaze away from Asher. "He's my brother's friend and he offered to let me share his room because the hotel was sold out last night."

"Is that right?" Chase raised one eyebrow, planted his hands on his hips, and tapped his foot. "One bed or two?"

"What?"

"The hotel room," Chase said. "Does it have one bed or two?"

Daniel rolled his eyes. "One bed, and before you ask, we shared it. Is that okay with you, Mom?"

"Hey!" Chase looked hurt. "Don't snap at me because I care. Last I heard, you were on another one of your celibacy kicks, looking for Mr. Right, and suddenly you tell me that you're shacking up with the Latino version of Mr. Clean. I just want to make sure nobody takes advantage of you."

"Oh, Christ, not you too. I've already had to tell my brother to back off today; I don't think I can handle your meddling this soon. You haven't even met Asher. Why do you automatically assume he's going to take advantage of me?"

"Seriously? Have you met you?" Chase asked incredulously.

"What's that supposed to mean?"

"It means, Daniel, that every guy you meet wants to take advantage of you."

"You're ridiculous." Daniel shook his head and laughed. "Come on. I'll introduce you to Asher. I think once you stop drooling, you'll actually like him."

"Uh-huh. I'm sure I will," Chase said, disbelief clear in his tone.

Daniel stood and picked his baseball cap up off the top of the slot machine.

"You've got another credit left in the machine," Chase pointed out.

"Oh, right." Daniel pressed the button and the machine lit up and played a sound meant to resemble coins dropping, an attempt to make the modern machine have the character of traditional slots.

"Holy shit!" Chase said with a laugh. "You just won five grand. Looks like Lady Luck is still on your side."

Daniel darted his gaze toward Asher, who hadn't taken his eyes off him all night.

"Yeah." He smiled wistfully. "It sure seems that way."

"I've been to that dim sum buffet you're looking at. *Delicious*."

Asher's jaw ticced at the sound of that voice way too close to him. Daniel's friend, ex-boyfriend, whatever. Chase Rhodes. What the hell kind of name was that?

Plus, the guy was all long eyelashes, rosy cheeks, tight pants, and an even tighter sleeveless shirt, over a body that had not an ounce of fat anywhere. Asher hated him on sight.

"Congratulations," Asher said, not moving his eyes from where he was tracking Daniel as he looked at food in the buffet line and then put some on his plate. Good thing, too, because the man hadn't eaten all day. "It's thrilling to know you've been here before."

"I wasn't talking about the restaurant." Chase was standing next to his chair and bending down so close Asher could feel his breath against his cheek. His elbow tingled with the need to jab out and put some space between them. "I was talking about Daniel."

Well, now. That got Asher's attention. Was this guy trying to get under his skin? Seriously? Asher had just under a foot and a good ninety pounds on him. He turned his head slowly and glared murderously.

"Are you wearing makeup?" he asked, running his gaze

over Chase's face, contempt clear in his voice and expression.

The other man didn't step back, didn't flinch, hell, he didn't so much as blink. Asher would have respected him if he wasn't so busy hating the guy's guts.

"Why, yes, I am," Chase said with a wide grin, batting his eyelashes. "A little liner, some blush, and gloss. Thanks for noticing."

"It wasn't meant as a compliment," Asher grumbled.

"No." Chase laughed. "I imagine it wasn't."

Before he could respond, or hit something, Chase stood and Asher was looking at the bastard's groin instead of his face.

"Hey, Danny Boy," Chase said joyfully.

Asher twisted his head and saw Daniel approach their table, a plate in one hand and a bowl in the other. He sat between Asher's and Chase's chairs and set his food in front of him.

"Where're you going, Chase?" he asked.

"Nowhere." Chase walked back to his seat and sat down. "I was just stretching my legs. You know how I like to move around." He winked at Daniel.

Asher told himself not to take the bait. He took a deep breath and focused on Daniel. There, that helped calm him. Then he noticed the food on Daniel's plate and frowned. "That's what you're eating?"

Daniel blinked in surprise, looked down at his food and back at Asher, and then answered. "Uh-huh. It's soup and salad."

"Yum, I love their chipotle-lime tofu salad," Chase said. He picked up his fork and started eating from Daniel's plate.

Asher bit the inside of his cheek. If he said anything, he'd look like a possessive freak. He'd known Daniel all of one day. One day. He wasn't in a position to complain when the man shared his food. Even if there wasn't enough food there to fill one person. Besides, he knew Chase was trying to goad him and he wasn't going to give the annoying prick the satisfaction of succeeding at any level.

CHAPTER 7

Three hours and twice as many drinks later, Asher had the uncomfortable feeling that a dancer was besting him in a mind game. And he didn't even know the reason for the game or what they were playing.

Chase was all bright smiles and loud laughs, whispering in Daniel's ear, bringing up stories from the good old days, and constantly finding reasons to touch him. It wasn't anything overtly sexual—a shoulder squeeze here, an elbow grab there—but it was almost nonstop and it was driving Asher crazy.

It was that Vegas chemical-infused air thing. That had to be the reason for Asher's behavior. There could be no other rational explanation. He didn't normally get drunk, didn't normally obsess over skinny guys who needed a haircut, didn't normally notice, much less care, about whether someone should be wearing a jacket or at least a long-sleeved shirt. But there he was, slamming back one drink after another and watching Daniel—who was wearing a baseball cap so old that the emblem wasn't recognizable and a shirt so thin and threadbare he might as well have been nude—

shivering and rubbing his hands up and down his arms, but still smiling and talking with every person in the room except for him.

Well, that wasn't exactly true. Daniel had talked to him, but between Chase and the slew of strangers who made a beeline for Daniel and started chatting him up, Asher felt like he was playing second fiddle for Daniel's attention, something he didn't appreciate. So he decided to get a drink, hang out with Oliver, listen to music, do something else mature and reasonable and in no way resembling a temper tantrum. But apparently sometime during the night, logical thinking had vacated the premises and Jack Daniels had taken over the lease, at which point the only thing Asher seemed capable of doing was getting drunk off his ass and sulking.

"What's up with you?" Oliver asked as he sat down on an empty barstool next to Asher.

"What do you mean?" Asher barked. "I'm just having a drink. We're in a bar. That's what people do in a bar. You have a problem with that?"

"Damn, Asher. Chill out. You're wound tight, even for you."

"You're the one accusing me of being jealous," Asher snapped defensively.

Just then, Chase leaned close to Daniel and whispered something in his ear while he moved his hand to the small of Daniel's back and looked at Asher with a smirk. Asshole.

"Jealous?" Oliver asked, but Asher was too distracted

to respond. "Uh, Asher, nobody said anything about being jealous."

That comment filtered through and Asher finally looked at Oliver. He tried to replay their conversation in his mind, but he hadn't been focusing. He had been watching Daniel talk with Oliver's friends, mingle with strangers in the bar, smile and laugh, and bump into just about every table and chair in the place. It was adorable, actually. Or it would have been adorable if Chase hadn't been attached to Daniel at the hip.

Thankfully, Oliver kept talking so Asher didn't have to respond to his question. At least he could count on his old friend to be consistent in his inability to shut up.

"I just asked what was going on with you. Are you drunk?"

"No," Asher said, somehow managing to slur the one-syllable word. It was as if Oliver had the power to make his accusation a reality merely by the power of suggestion.

"Yes, you are. You're drunk. You never get drunk and suddenly you're getting wasted two nights in a row. Something is definitely up with you. And what did you say about being jealous?"

"Please." Asher rolled his eyes and then hated himself for acting like a twelve-year-old. "I'm not jealous of *Chase*." He spat out the name. "I mean, come on! Look at him. He's wearing makeup and giggling. And is that a scarf around his neck?"

With that comment, he grasped his glass and tilted it back, not realizing it was empty until he was looking up at the ceiling and still had a dry mouth.

"You are such an asshole." Initially thinking Oliver had made the comment, since they'd been talking, Asher was surprised when he realized it wasn't Oliver's voice he'd heard. It was Chase's. "I have no idea what Daniel sees in you," Chase continued.

Asher slammed his glass on the bar and drops of liquid flew out. How that was possible when no liquid had been available to go into his mouth, Asher didn't understand and he didn't have time to think about it. He had to deal with Daniel's annoying gnat of a friend.

"He sees a man. Am I actually supposed to believe you're his ex? What were you two, girlfriends or something?"

"Wow," Oliver gasped.

Chase scowled. The bright smile and guileless expression he had been wearing all evening vanished. He squinted and leaned close to Asher. With Chase standing and Asher sitting on a barstool, they were face-to-face.

"Go ahead, tough guy. Keep it coming," Chase said. "Thump your chest, glare at me, drink until you throw up in an alley. I have news for you: none of that's going to impress Daniel. Oh sure, he's enamored with you now. But I've seen your type before. You'll pay him attention as long as he does things your way, and as soon as he steps out of line or you get annoyed, you'll toss him out without a second look." He turned to walk away and then seemed to change his mind, because he glared at Asher again and kept talking. "Oh, and I'm a *man*. Makeup, giggling, and all. You can ask Daniel if you want confirmation. He's seen every inch of me naked. I know where he likes to be touched and his favorite positions in bed. I know what makes him moan and what makes him cringe. And I'll be there when he realizes that you don't give a damn about any of it."

With that, he stormed away, shaking his ass and holding his head high.

"Well, then," Oliver said with a smirk. "I guess we can end that debate forevermore. My brother's ex-boyfriend is a guy. And you're an asshole. Well played, my friend, well played."

"I hate you," Asher said.

"No, you don't." Oliver elbowed his ribs gently.

"Yeah, I do." Asher sighed. "And I need another drink."

"No, you really don't," Oliver said.

"Yeah, I really do."

Oliver looked at Asher and seemed to study him.

"Oliver." Asher sighed and rubbed his big paw over the back of his neck. "I went to a titty bar for the second day in a row, I was just told off by a guy wearing lip gloss for something I haven't done to a man I just met, and I'm giving serious thought to asking that man to come stay with me after this weekend is over. I've lost my fucking mind and I think a goddamn drink is in order here."

"Bartender," Oliver yelled as he leaned over the bar.

"We'll have another round."

Daniel was a light sleeper, always had been, so he knew the moment Asher returned to the hotel room.

Daniel had left the bar with Chase and walked him to his car to say good night before going back to the room. He figured Asher would already be there, but the place was empty. He was too tired to party anymore, so he took a shower and crawled into bed, falling asleep the minute his head hit the pillow.

The sound of the keycard in the slot and the handle being pushed down woke him. He heard the door swing open and debated about whether he should stay in bed and let himself fall back asleep or get up to help Asher. Based on the amount of alcohol he'd seen the other man consume that night, Daniel was pretty sure Asher would have difficulty standing, let alone taking off his clothes. The shoelaces alone were bound to be trouble.

"Did you have fun tonight?" he asked quietly, opening his eyes and looking around the dark room.

"How'd you know I was here?"

"Well," Daniel said, chuckling, "it was either you or a grizzly bear trying to keep the noise down while he undressed. I figured you were the more likely choice because grizzlies don't like to ride in elevators."

"They don't?" Asher turned toward the bed and rubbed his eyes. Daniel guessed he was still adjusting to the low light. "Are you fucking with me?"

With a laugh, Daniel sat up and then knelt on the bed. "Come here," he said to Asher. "I'll help you."

Asher walked over to him and Daniel slid his jacket off and tossed it onto the armchair in the corner. He worked on Asher's shirt next, carefully pushing each button through its slot and then tugging the shirt out of Asher's jeans. Once he had the entire garment open, he pressed his hands onto Asher's chest and enjoyed the feeling of hot skin, hard muscle, and silky hair.

"Mmm," Asher moaned. "Feels good."

Daniel bent forward and kissed Asher's nipple as he unfastened the buttons at Asher's wrists and pulled his shirt completely off. That kiss led to a lick, then a nibble, and then Asher twined his hands in Daniel's hair, holding him in place while he suckled at the man's nipple and unzipped his pants. He slipped his thumbs into Asher's waistband and paused. He could either remove Asher's jeans and leave him with his briefs, or he could push both the jeans and the underwear to Asher's feet.

"Naked," Asher said. When Daniel didn't move, he tugged Daniel's hair back, forcing him to look up at Asher's face. "I want to be naked."

Rough, demanding...even drunk, the man was sexy

as hell. There was something about Asher's conviction, his decisiveness about what Daniel should do, that made Daniel feel incredibly free.

Grateful that he'd have the pleasure of Asher's hot skin pressed against him all night, Daniel followed Asher's instructions and pushed his jeans and briefs down his thighs. They dropped to his ankles and caught on his shoes. Asher took a step back without letting go of Daniel's hair. He moved his piercing gaze from Daniel's eyes to the floor and back again. The message was clear—Asher wanted Daniel to help remove his shoes. Daniel scooted off the bed and squatted at Asher's feet, unlaced the shoes, pulled them off Asher's feet, and then peeled off his socks.

Asher loosened his fingers in Daniel's hair and then seemed to be petting Daniel as he knelt before him and helped him undress. When Daniel was done, he started to get up and found himself on his knees with Asher's groin in his face. A gentle pressure on the back of his head told him without words what Asher expected, and he was perfectly willing to comply. More than willing, actually. Daniel's heart slammed against his ribcage and his dick tented his boxer shorts.

He moved his face closer, wanting to smell Asher's musk, taste his skin. But a sudden grasp of his hair held him in place. He winced and looked up questioningly. Asher rubbed his fingers on Daniel's scalp in apology for the unexpected pain.

"You're coming home with me," Asher said. Daniel was

still a little groggy from sleep. Add in his intense arousal from the scent and feel of the man before him, and he was having trouble following the conversation. "On Sunday, when we leave Vegas," Asher clarified, apparently sensing Daniel's confusion. "You're coming home with me."

"I am?" Daniel asked, not that he was opposed to that plan. It meant being with Asher, and Daniel couldn't remember ever wanting a man with this level of intensity.

"Yes. You said you aren't working right now and you're trying to figure out what to do next. You'll come live with me and I'll take care of you while you figure it out."

"Oh, I... I don't need you to take—"

"You'll come live with me and I'll take care of you," Asher repeated, his tone leaving no room for argument.

"Okay," Daniel said, his voice breaking as he gulped in air. He wondered if he could come just from the sound of Asher's deep voice telling him how things were going to be. At that moment, it seemed possible. He was so turned on.

"That's a relationship," Asher said and then hesitated, almost as if he wasn't sure whether his statement was accurate.

Daniel made a mental note to ask him about his past relationships. He wanted to learn more about Asher's past, wanted to see all the details that went into forming the strong man standing above him. He was distracted by Asher's hard dick being dragged across his cheek and over to his mouth. He moaned in approval, somewhat surprised Asher could get it up, given how much he'd been drinking that night. Asher took the opportunity to paint his lips with the slick head of his cock.

"We're in a relationship," Asher said again. "Suck me."

It was an easy order to follow. Daniel licked his lips and opened his mouth, letting Asher hold his head in place and push inside, not stopping until he hit his soft palate. Daniel loved giving head, always had, but it'd been a while since his last boyfriend and that man hadn't been as well hung as Asher. Plus, being on his knees in front of Asher wasn't the best angle for deep-throating. The combination of those things resulted in what should have been an embarrassing amount of gagging.

But Asher didn't seem to mind; if anything, he looked turned on. He stood above Daniel, wrapped one hand around the base of his dick and gripped the back of Daniel's head with the other as he fed Daniel his length and gazed down at him. Every time Daniel made a choking sound, Asher's eyes heated and he groaned. The saliva pooling in Daniel's mouth became too much and he couldn't swallow around the thick rod thrusting into him, so the liquid drizzled past his lips and down his chin.

"Fuck, you're gorgeous," Asher said, his whiskey voice husky with arousal. He moved his hand from his dick to Daniel's cheek, petting him gently before swiping his thumb across Daniel's spit-slick chin. "Look at you. On your knees, drooling for me."

Daniel would have blushed, but all the extra blood in his body had pooled in his groin. He reached into the fly of his boxers and fished out his dick, moaning in pleasure as he pushed into his fist.

Asher's eyes were on fire. He increased his pace, thrusting his hips hard, his grunts sounding loud in the room. Then he twined his fingers in Daniel's hair, yanked his head back, and stroked himself two times before long ropes of white ejaculate shot out and landed on Daniel's cheek, his nose, his lips, and his chin.

"Ash!" Daniel cried out and came hard, his body shaking with the rush of pleasure. "Ash," he said again, quieter this time, and then he sighed contentedly. He dropped his forehead onto Asher's hip, his muscles feeling languid, his limbs heavy.

Floating in his relaxed state, Daniel's eyes drooped shut. He didn't realize Asher had gotten them into the bed until he felt thick fingers brushing across his cheek and then pressing past his lips.

"Mmm," he moaned when he tasted Asher's seed and realized the man was wiping it off his face and into his mouth.

"You like that, sugar?" Asher's husky voice made his whole body shudder. "Like the taste of me?"

Daniel blinked his eyes open, gulped, and then nodded. "Yes."

He was lying on his back and Asher was propped above him, his elbows on either side of Daniel's shoulders and his knees spread, straddling Daniel's legs.

"Good." Asher smiled down at him, his expression unexpectedly tender when only moments before it had been rough. "Good," he repeated and then leaned down and licked the rest of his release off Daniel's face. If he wasn't so tired, Daniel was sure he'd have gotten hard again.

It wasn't until twenty minutes later, when Asher was sleeping soundly with Daniel curled around him, that Daniel realized why Asher had made a point of telling him they were in a relationship. Unlike Daniel, who had thrown his convictions out the window when faced with a hot man, Asher had remembered what he'd said—no sex outside of a relationship.

Oliver was wrong about Asher being dangerous. A dangerous person wouldn't make it a point to follow his rules when he didn't bother to enforce them. And a dangerous person wouldn't look at Daniel the way Asher had while he was falling asleep, his eyes full of warmth and affection. Daniel drifted off with a smile on his face, feeling unaccountably fortunate to have found a man who pushed all his buttons and respected him at the same time.

CHAPTER 8

"Ash?" Daniel croaked and cleared his throat. He reached across the bed and encountered cold sheets. "Asher?" he tried again.

"I'm right here," Asher answered, his belly warming at the knowledge that Daniel's first thought upon waking was him. Daniel's first desire, to reach for his body.

He got up from the small desk wedged into a corner of the hotel room, walked over to the bed, and sat next to Daniel. A sleepy smile greeted him.

"Hey," Daniel said. He scooted a couple of inches so he could rest his cheek on Asher's thigh and sighed happily when Asher began petting his head. "Why're you up so early?"

"It's ten o'clock. I don't think we can classify that as early."

"Sure we can," Daniel said with a yawn. "We were up 'til after four."

"I don't need much sleep," Asher responded. "And I'm usually up by six every day so I can hit the gym before work."

"Mmm," Daniel murmured. He reached up and caressed Asher's firm pecs and bulging biceps. "I can tell. But what were you doing now?"

"Getting you a reservation on my flight home."

"You didn't have to do that. I would have taken care of it."

"Yeah?" Asher smiled down at him. "The same way you took care of making your hotel reservation?"

Daniel blushed. "I get distracted sometimes."

"I've noticed." Asher caressed Daniel's cheek and cupped his jaw.

"Thanks for taking care of the flight, Ash," Daniel said. "I'll pay you back."

"No, you won't. I want you to keep your Vegas winnings and let me take care of the flight."

"Asher, I don't need—"

"You have freckles."

The nose housing those freckles scrunched up.

"Yeah. They're pretty light, but in some lighting...yeah, freckles."

Asher moved his finger across the bridge of Daniel's nose and over his cheek bones. "I like your freckles. They're cute."

"Cute?" Daniel asked, raising one eyebrow.

"Yeah." Asher chuckled. He gripped Daniel's chin and tipped his face up. "Cute," he said.

"Okay." Daniel blinked owlishly at him. Then his gaze dropped from Asher's face and he seemed to notice Asher's state of undress for the first time. "You're naked."

"Yeah, I am. I was planning to hop in the shower, so there

seemed to be no point in putting something on only to take it off again." He gave Daniel a devilish grin and then continued. "And I know how much you like to look at me, sugar."

Daniel dragged his gaze over Asher's body—his chest, his stomach, and then his groin. "Yeah," he said with a nod, seemingly unable to tear his gaze away from Asher's hardening cock. "Yeah, I like it."

"Show me." Asher cupped the back of Daniel's head and urged him forward. "Show me how much you like it."

"Are you always this horny?" Daniel murmured as he nuzzled Asher's balls.

He liked sex, sure. Who didn't? But there was definitely something about Daniel that made his libido run at full tilt. He twined his fingers in Daniel's hair and tugged hard, wanting to see the man's reaction. There was no moan, no shiver, nothing to indicate Daniel was turned on by the hint of pain. So Asher gentled his hold and massaged the back of Daniel's head and his nape.

"Mmm," Daniel sighed happily. He licked his way from the base of Asher's cock to the flared head and then dropped his mouth over it and sucked hard.

"Daniel!" Asher shouted and bucked. He glanced down and met Daniel's chocolate eyes before the man looked back away, his entire focus centered on Asher's dick. That hot mouth felt so good that Asher couldn't think about investigating Daniel's reactions to pain, not while he was so consumed with appreciating the pleasure he felt from

Daniel's ministrations.

Later, he thought briefly. He'd think about what Daniel was into and how to tell him what he himself was into later.

"Tell me how you met Chase. Were you guys together a long time?"

Asher hoped his questions didn't sound as awkward out loud as they did in his head. After all, why should he care where Daniel met his ex and how long they were together? It wasn't as if it was his business or impacted him in any way. But Asher's curiosity needed to be sated and the questions slipped out.

"Mmm," Daniel sighed and pressed his lips against Asher's skin. "I'm glad you like to cuddle."

They were lying in bed together, the shower plans forgotten. Daniel was resting his head on Asher's shoulder; he was combing his fingers through the hair on Asher's chest and belly and rubbing his calf against Asher's knee. Okay, so Asher could understand how their current positions might look like they were cuddling to the untrained eye, but in reality, they were just suffering from postorgasmic melted-bone syndrome. He was about to correct Daniel's misimpression of him being *cuddly* when Daniel kept talking.

"Chase and I met on a cruise. We were both working on

board and we were assigned as roommates, which was great because we really hit it off."

Daniel kissed Asher's chest again, this time darting his tongue out for a fast taste.

"So you were living together?" Asher asked, his words coming out too fast, voice sounding too loud and high-pitched. What the hell? He took a breath. "Sounds serious."

There, that sounded better. Less panicky. Still nosy. Why was he asking these questions? Asher usually didn't ask for a last name, sometimes not even a first name, and here he was taking a dating history. Damn that Vegas air.

"Well, we were together during the year we were on board, but we were more friends than lovers, so when we moved on to other jobs, it was understood that we were moving on personally too. He's still one of my best friends, though. It's not like there were hard feelings or anything."

That description relaxed something in Asher's gut. Maybe it was indigestion. Had to be. Nothing else made sense.

"He seems like a nice guy," Asher said magnanimously.

"Oh, please," Daniel scoffed. He raised his head and met Asher's eyes, chuckling. "You can't stand him. If looks could kill, I'd be down one friend today. And from what I saw, he wasn't treating you any better."

Asher raised one side of his lip in what started as a snarl and ended as a snort. "Yeah, okay. So Chase and I didn't make a love connection."

Daniel crawled on top of Asher, propped his forearms on

Asher's chest, and peered into his eyes.

"Or even a like connection."

Asher smacked his hand down on Daniel's naked ass. It wasn't meant as a punishment, just a tease. But when the brown eyes that had been looking at his with a melty, half-lidded gaze suddenly widened in surprise, Asher thought he might have stepped over an unknown boundary.

That was, until he felt Daniel's cock harden against his thigh. He smirked knowingly.

"You like that, do you? Want me to give you a spanking?"

Daniel stared at him, seemingly trying to gauge whether he was kidding. Eventually he must have realized it wasn't a joke, because he shook his head. "I don't, uh… Let's get in the shower, okay?"

Asher decided to let it drop. He didn't want to push Daniel too far too fast, didn't want to scare him away. That realization was like a kick to the gut, and it had Asher hesitating, catching his breath and rubbing a hand over his stomach while Daniel climbed out of bed and started walking toward the bathroom.

What was going on with him? He'd just met this guy and he was, what, going to go vanilla?

"Ash?" Daniel said with one hand on the hallway wall, his head turned so he was looking back at Asher over his left shoulder. "You coming?"

Asher raked his gaze over Daniel's body and paused at his pert, white ass. White, that was, except for a pink mark the shape of Asher's hand. He groaned. No, he wasn't going vanilla. He was just biding his time. He got out of bed and strutted up to Daniel, cupped his left ass cheek and gave it a rough squeeze, knowing it'd be a reminder of the slap that was still smarting. When Daniel inhaled sharply, Asher smirked and sauntered past him into the bathroom.

"With you on your knees, I'm sure I'll be coming real soon. Let's go, sugar. It's time to get wet and slippy."

"You look bored, Ollie," Daniel said to his brother. Oliver shrugged, just adding veracity to Daniel's observation. "Which is weird, 'cause there are naked women and all, and I know you're into that kind of thing."

"Yeah," Oliver said blandly, reaching for his soda. "What is this, like the fourth strip club we've been to?"

"Seventh," Asher replied.

"They're all starting to blend together or something." Oliver shrugged again and then squirmed in his chair. "Plus, these wood chairs are really uncomfortable and there's not enough room to stretch my legs. It's like they furnished this place for hobbits."

"I have a suggestion that might help with all those things," Asher supplied helpfully.

"What's that?" Oliver asked.

"Let's get the fuck out of here and never come back," Asher replied dryly.

"But it's our last night in Vegas," Oliver whined. "It's too early to go home yet. I'm all out of gambling money. We've already eaten dinner. And I'm pretty sure we'll all die of alcohol poisoning if we go to another bar." Oliver sighed dramatically and slumped in his chair. "There's nothing else to do."

Daniel hopped up, knocked over a glass, which was, thankfully, empty, and almost tripped over the table leg before getting his balance and beaming down at Oliver. "I have a great idea," he exclaimed. "Let's go dancing."

"I don't know, Danny. None of us is really into that." Oliver gestured at the other men around the table.

"Speak for yourself," Oliver's service buddy said. "I love cutting a rug." He stood up from the table.

"Me too," the other man agreed. "Let's dance."

Asher climbed to his feet. "And I'm happy to go anywhere that isn't here." He looked down at Oliver, who was the only man still sitting. "Come on, Ollie. Let's go make all those single ladies eat their hearts out when they see you move and then hear you're off the market."

He gave himself a metaphorical pat on the back for successfully making that compliment sound completely insincere with nothing but the power of voice inflection. Sometimes it was the little things that made life worth living. After three straight days frequenting titty bars, insulting

Oliver most definitely qualified as one of those times.

"Fine," Oliver grumbled. "But I've got two left feet, so one of you is going to have to show me how to dance."

"I'll teach you, Ollie," Daniel said excitedly. "You'll be dancing like a pro in no time. Come on." He reached for Oliver and knocked down yet another glass, then snapped his arm back and elbowed a stranger at the next table.

Daniel apologized profusely and Asher turned his head so he wouldn't see him laughing. The last thing he wanted to do was insult Daniel, especially since his desire to go dancing was liberating them all from that strip club, but the idea of Daniel, who could barely walk without tripping, teaching anybody how to dance was hilarious.

"Hey." Oliver leaned over Asher's shoulder and spoke directly into his ear so he could be heard over the thumping music. "What do you say we call it a night?"

Asher twisted around on his barstool so he could see the dance floor. As he'd been the entire night, Daniel was there, laughing with his latest dance partners and moving gracefully. The current song had a fast techno beat and Daniel somehow rolled his body with the sound, one hand in the air and the other on his chest while he gyrated his hips.

Asher sighed deeply and glanced back at Oliver. The

expression on Oliver's face indicated that he was well past ready to go. No real surprise there. It was three in the morning and they'd been out all day and night. Half of the bachelor party brigade had already gone back to the hotel and it was apparent that Oliver was itching to join them.

"'S not last call yet," Asher slurred.

"We're in Vegas, Asher. There's no such thing as last call."

"That's right. We're in Vegas, baby! I'm just getting started."

"Oh, God. I'm so embarrassed for you right now. You sound like a jackass. I have no idea what's gotten into you on this trip."

"Your brother, that's what."

"My brother has gotten into you?" Oliver smirked and raised one eyebrow.

"Shut up. You know what I mean."

Asher thumped his forehead on the bar and Oliver sat down next to him.

"Yeah, I know what you mean. And I think Danny's better off without you, but he doesn't seem to agree."

"Gee, thanks, Ollie. I appreciate the support."

"Hey, we've known each other too long to start lying now. Can you blame me for wanting my brother to be with a guy who knows how to have a relationship that lasts after sunrise and doesn't involve bruises?"

Asher rolled his head to the side and tried to land his bleary gaze on Oliver. He was more tired than drunk. Or maybe he was both.

"There's something there, Ollie. Something about Daniel that clicks with me. It's like he needs me to look after him or something." He closed his eyes and groaned. "Is that strange?"

"Honestly? Yeah. As Danny pointed out to me in no uncertain terms yesterday, he can take care of himself. And you can't even take care of a houseplant. Didn't you manage to kill that cactus garden I gave you for Christmas?"

"Shirley gave me the cactus garden," Asher mumbled.

"Well, I signed the card."

"She signed your name on the card."

"Same difference," Oliver replied.

Asher raised his head and tried looking for the bartender. The room spun.

"Asher, come on. I'm tired. Your blood alcohol level is .85 for the third night in a row. My brother asked if you were ready to go back to the room two hours ago and gave you a look that clearly meant something I refuse to articulate or I'll throw up. Why are we still at this club?"

"I'm not drunk anymore, just tired and buzzed. Did you notice how he can't walk across the room without bumping into at least three people and every piece of furniture?"

"If you're tired, Asher, then let's leave. Come on." Oliver was officially whining.

"But then put him on a dance floor and suddenly his body moves like liquid or fire or something," Asher continued. "Seriously. These past three days he couldn't even take two steps without endangering himself. Made me feel like I should put him on a leash to keep him out of trouble, and now—"

"He's had a lot of experience dancing. Used to do it professional—Wait. That was metaphorical, right? You're not actually thinking of putting my brother on a leash."

"What do you mean he danced professionally?" The way Daniel moved his body was like sex personified, and Asher suddenly had visions of Daniel taking the place of the strippers he'd seen on this trip. It was hot as hell, but it pissed him off to the point that he wanted to put his fist through a wall. "Like a stripper?"

"Nooo, like a dancer. On Broadway and shit. From what my father said, he was big-time or was about to be big-time or something." Oliver shrugged. "I don't remember the details. It was a long time ago. Now about that leash comment, you didn't really—"

Asher pushed his stool back and stood. "All right. Let's go."

Oliver still seemed worried, but he followed Asher to where Daniel was dancing without asking more questions, which was a testament to the man's exhaustion. Good thing too, because Asher didn't want to lie, and Daniel in a collar, tied up and under his control, seemed like a very good idea.

CHAPTER 9

Daniel's gaze landed on Asher as soon as he and Oliver got to the edge of the dance floor. A huge smile took over his face and he waved them over excitedly.

"No way," Oliver grumbled. "My knees are already killin' me from being dragged around up there half the night. I'm done dancing."

Asher couldn't use that excuse because he'd refused to move from his seat. He'd originally planned to dance, but as soon as he saw Daniel move to the music, he'd changed his mind. It wasn't that Asher was uncoordinated, and when there'd been occasion to dance in his life, he had always felt like he had held his own. But Daniel... The man was in another league and Asher would look like a fumbling oaf in comparison. So he'd begged off dancing, found a spot at the bar, and parked his ass there all night. Again.

When Daniel realized that Asher and Oliver weren't going to join him, he kissed his dance partner on the cheek, making the girl blush and giggle, and then bounded over to them.

"Hey!" he said when he was close enough for them to

hear him over the thumping music. He stepped right into Asher's personal space, rested a hand on Asher's upper arm, and raised himself on his toes to kiss the side of Asher's neck.

Asher was way too manly to blush and giggle like the girl on the dance floor, or so he told himself, but he understood her reaction. Having Daniel close by, smelling him, did things to Asher's chest. Unfamiliar things. Things that might or might not have been welcome. The jury was still out.

"Hi," Asher said roughly. "It looked like you were having a good time out there."

Daniel nodded. "I love dancing and I don't get to do it as much anymore."

"Your brother said you were a professional dancer. Why'd you stop? You get injured or something?" Asher asked.

"No." Daniel shook his head. "Just bored. I'd been at it for a while, started out when I was a kid and pretty much did what there was to do, so I figured it was time to move on. You guys want to have a go on the dance floor?"

"No more, Danny. You got all the dancing genes in our family and I'm beat," Oliver said. "Let's go back to the hotel."

Asher pushed Daniel's sweaty hair off his forehead. It looked darker than usual because of the moisture. He leaned down and spoke into his ear. "How about we go back to the room and you give me a little private lesson?" He rubbed his hand over Daniel's arm, up his shoulder, and over to his nape, where he massaged his slick, hot skin. "I'd like to see you making some of those moves naked."

Daniel licked his lips and bobbed his head excitedly. "Yeah, okay. Let's go."

The three of them made their way through the sea of bodies and onto the street. As soon as they stepped out of the hot club, Daniel started shivering. His shirt was stuck to his chest and back, and his sweat-damp hair curled over his collar.

"Here, put this on." Asher handed Daniel his jacket.

"I'm okay," Daniel said.

"Now that you're not expending all that energy, you're freezing. That shirt you're wearing barely protected you from the elements when you were dry. At this point, it's practically soaked, so it's doing more harm than good." Asher frowned when Daniel didn't respond. "I don't want you to get sick," he growled. "Put the jacket on."

Daniel stood perfectly still and locked his gaze with Asher's. After several long seconds, he nodded. "Okay," he said through chattering teeth and reached for the jacket. "Thank you. It's sweet that you're worried about me."

Sweet? Asher's frown intensified to a full facial scowl. But then Daniel took the jacket from him, pulled it over his left arm, and waved his right arm in a windmill trying to get it through the sleeve. There was no way for Asher to do anything but laugh at that charming display.

"Honestly, sugar." Asher shook his head and smiled fondly at Daniel. "You were practically doing somersaults out there tonight and now you can't even get your jacket on." He steadied Daniel's arm and slipped the jacket on him, tugged the bottom and then buttoned it up. Then he cupped Daniel's cheek and ran his thumb over the man's lips. "I've never met anybody like you."

"This is all very romantic, but I'm tired. Get in the cab, *sugar*," Oliver said. He was standing at the curb, holding a taxi door open.

Asher flipped him off. "Calm down, we're coming," he said and led Daniel over to the cab.

The light seeping in from around the edges of the curtains indicated that it was morning or maybe early afternoon. The pounding in Asher's head indicated that he was hungover. Again. This trip had been murder on his liver. He was well past ready to get out of Vegas.

Come to think of it, he was leaving today, or rather, *they* were leaving today. He'd gone to Vegas for the weekend, seen more silicone than he'd have previously thought possible in one location, picked up a stranger with holes in his clothes, and now he was taking the man home. No part of that made sense, and Asher made an internal vow to never drink again. Well, not drink that much, anyway.

"What time is it?" Daniel's voice was thick with sleep. He scooted into Asher's side, burrowed his face under Asher's chin, and threaded his fingers in Asher's chest hair. Asher tried not to smile and failed. He glanced at the bedside clock.

"Almost eleven. Our flight is at two. We need to get up and get going."

As close as their bodies were to each other, Asher could feel Daniel's heart rate increase and his limbs stiffen.

"What do you want to do this morning? Maybe we can, uh..." Daniel shot up and wiggled off the bed. "Dance! You said you wanted to see me dance and then you fell asleep. I can dance for you now."

Asher tried to keep up with Daniel's change in mood from snuggly to fidgety while trying to remember the previous night. Had he really fallen asleep when there was a private nude dance on the table? That was so wrong, he would've denied it, but Daniel was wearing yet another huge shirt and boxers loose enough that they reached his knees, so he knew it was true. No way would he have let the man wear that ensemble to bed had he been conscious. No way would he have let Daniel wear anything to bed.

"We don't have time for dancing right now. Sorry I crashed, sugar. It's been a long few days, but we really need to get going or we'll miss our flight."

"We have lots of time," Daniel insisted as he stumbled around the room. "I'm sure there's a radio or something around here or, uh, I think my phone is charged, right? 'Cause I have some good music on there."

Asher pushed the sheet down and climbed out of bed.

He slowly stalked over to Daniel, who was searching the top of the dresser, clasped his bony shoulder, and pulled him against his chest. He cupped the back of Daniel's head with one hand and placed the other at the small of his back, forcing him to still.

"Shh, what's up with you? You're twenty kinds of jittery all of a sudden."

At those words, Daniel deflated and melted against Asher. "I hate flying," he confessed quietly. "I know it's perfectly safe, that, statistically, driving is much more dangerous and all that other stuff, but I still hate it, which is ridiculous considering how much traveling I've done. I mean, you'd think it'd get easier, right?" Daniel sighed deeply. "But it still scares me."

Daniel was trembling in his arms, he could feel the man's hot breath fan across his chest, and suddenly Asher was achingly hard. He grunted and thrust against Daniel's belly. Daniel gasped and pushed long fingers between them, trailed them across Asher's hip, and then curled them around his erection.

"I can take care of this for you," Daniel whispered.

"Oh, you'll definitely be taking care of it," Asher replied. "But not right now. We're going to grab a shower, get dressed, pack, and head out." He clasped Daniel's shoulders and moved him an arm's length away. "I told you I'd take care of you and I meant it. That means you're not missing a flight on my watch."

"Yeah, okay," Daniel relented. He took in a deep breath and gave Asher a shaky smile. "I didn't intentionally miss my flight out here, you know? I just dread getting on the plane, so I put it off and sometimes..." He shrugged.

"I understand. But you've never been on a plane with me, right?" Asher cupped Daniel's chin and ran his thumb over the man's bottom lip, wondering how it'd feel pressed against his own. "I'll take care of you."

It was, Asher figured, an easy promise to make. After all, it wasn't as if the plane was going to crash. But the way Daniel looked at him when he said it, the complete trust and awe in his eyes, made Asher feel like he'd do anything to make sure this flight experience would be better for Daniel than merely not crashing to earth in a fiery ball. Speaking of fiery balls...

"You know, sugar, if we get in the shower right now, we may just have enough time to make sure you're good and relaxed before this flight."

Daniel yanked his shirt over his head and tossed it onto his duffel bag, which was wedged next to the dresser. His boxers followed right after.

"Let's go," he said eagerly.

Asher raked his gaze over Daniel's body. The man was gorgeous, all pale skin and lanky limbs. But he was too thin.

He trailed a finger down each of Daniel's protruding ribs.

"We need to get some protein into you."

"Ugh." Daniel crinkled his nose. "I can't even think about food right now. My stomach's all topsy-turvy."

He dropped his towel on the bathroom floor and walked out. Asher shook his head, picked up the towel, and placed it on the counter next to his own. Then he threw out the travel-size shampoo and conditioner bottles from the shower and wiped everything down. He answered Daniel as he walked out of the bathroom.

"Well, how about a protein drink for now, and then when we get home, I'll grill you a big steak and a baked potato with all the fixings?"

Daniel was bent over his bag, his tight, white ass tilted upward invitingly. Asher had never wanted to get inside something so badly.

"Oh, God. Seriously, Ash. Just the idea of putting something in my mouth right now makes me want to throw up." Daniel found a pair of underwear and stepped into them. It was the first time Asher had seen anybody wear boxer briefs that didn't hug every curve.

"You didn't seem to have so much as a gag reflex ten minutes ago when I was filling your mouth and your throat," Asher reminded him.

Daniel turned around. "Oh, is that what you meant by a protein drink?" He darted his gaze from Asher's face to his sated cock and gave him a saucy smile. "You're already ready to go again? That's some refractory period you've got, old man."

Asher strode over to Daniel, cupped his ass, and lifted him off the ground. "You're a little shit," he said with a laugh.

Daniel smiled at him, his eyes warm and twinkling. He looked from Asher's eyes to his mouth and back again, the question clear. Then he stretched his neck and tilted his face up toward Asher's. Instead of moving away, which was his normal response when a guy tried to kiss him, Asher licked his lips and thought about how much he wanted to kiss the person he held in his arms. Then he moved one of his hands back and let it fly, giving Daniel's globes two smacks in short order.

Huge brown eyes blinked at him, and Daniel's jaw dropped, leaving his lips in an enticing O shape.

Asher arched one eyebrow. "You like that, do you?" he asked, his voice sounding rough to his own ears.

"I don't—" Daniel swallowed. "I don't know."

Asher lowered the man to his feet and then palmed his erection. "This says you do, sugar. And when we get home, after I've fed you, I'm going to show you how much you like it."

"I don't," Daniel said again and licked his lips. "I'm not sure about that, Ash."

Something in the way he said it, or maybe it was something about Daniel in general, made Asher anxious. He knew how to wield a single tail so he could leave a man's skin covered in red welts and never break his skin. He had planned complex, public scenes and garnered applause and admiration from his contemporaries. But somehow pulling off a mild, private spanking had him questioning himself. This was ridiculous.

"You don't need to be sure. I am." There. He'd said it. Now he needed to see how Daniel would react. Asher peered at the other man and waited.

Daniel reached for him, his hand moving slowly, long fingers tracing Asher's eyebrows, the outer curve of his ear, his jawline. There was tenderness in Daniel's touch, desire in his eyes. The way Daniel looked at him warmed Asher's stomach and made his chest constrict. Asher's heart melted a little, and without conscious thought, he turned his head into Daniel's hand and kissed his palm.

Daniel let out a shaky breath. "I'll try."

Asher grinned in triumph.

"It's a short flight, sugar. We won't even be in the air two hours," Asher said.

Daniel bobbed his head in agreement, but his eyes were wide, he was chewing on his lip, and he was frantically pulling at the threads in his jeans, expanding one of several holes. Clearly, logic as an approach to calm the man wasn't succeeding.

Asher wasn't a fan of public displays of affection, or, if he was being completely honest, affection in general unless it led directly to him busting a nut. But he was willing to make an exception in his case. After all, there were extenuating circumstances. Namely, Daniel's near panic and Asher's desire to protect the man from any harm, both real and perceived. Weird, but true.

He reached for Daniel's hand, prying it from the ruined jeans and holding it tightly. "Just close your eyes and relax." Asher rubbed his thumb back and forth over the back of Daniel's hand, the gesture as unfamiliar as it was instinctive. "We'll be landing before you know it."

Daniel nodded again, less frantically this time, squeezed his eyes shut, and burrowed his face under Asher's chin. It made no sense, but he was clearly petrified. Asher continued holding his hand as the plane taxied down the runway. As soon as the wheels left the ground, Daniel lurched up and gripped both armrests so hard his knuckles turned white.

"Shhh, sugar," Asher said. "It's okay. Promise."

Scared, needy eyes looked up at him. "Ash?" Daniel said.

"Yeah?" Asher once again put his hand on top of Daniel's and stroked it.

"Will you—" Daniel licked his dry lips. "Will you kiss me?"

All the reasons Asher normally had for avoiding that type of intimacy escaped him in that moment. He cupped

Daniel's cheek with one hand, gripped his nape with the other, and leaned down, touching his lips hesitantly to Daniel's. A sigh was his reward as Daniel melted against him, and Asher decided maybe he didn't hate kissing as much as he'd thought. He increased the pressure of his mouth against Daniel's, darted his tongue out and swiped it across Daniel's lower lip and then pushed it into his mouth when the man parted his lips on a sigh. All right, so maybe he more than didn't hate it.

CHAPTER 10

"Did you just move here?" Daniel asked as he looked around Asher's great room.

Asher looped his keys on the stainless steel peg next to his front door and hung his jacket on the gleaming hook above it.

"No. I've been here for about..." Asher stopped, seemingly thinking about the answer to the question. "I'd say close to five years now."

"Oh." Daniel couldn't hide his surprise. "It's really... clean."

Tightly looped white carpet, showing some wear around the center of the space, but still in decent shape. Bright white walls. Asher must either keep a can of paint somewhere for touch-ups or he meticulously avoided the walls, because there were no smudges anywhere. A black leather sofa with shiny chrome legs, a matching chair, and a glass coffee table. Everything was in its place.

"I like order," Asher explained. "Come on. I'll show you the bedroom." He walked ahead of Daniel down the short hallway. "There's a washer and dryer in that closet," he said, gesturing with his chin toward a door on their left, and then he walked into the room across from it.

A king-size bed took up most of the space. It was made of black iron, with posts on every corner and bars connecting those at the head to each other and those at the foot to each other. Like in the great room, there weren't any pictures on the walls, no knickknacks on any surfaces or, really, many surfaces to speak of. Two nightstands, one dresser, both glossy black. That was it.

Asher put his suitcase and Daniel's duffel down. Daniel set his laptop case down next to the bags.

"There's an attached bathroom through that door," Asher said as he pointed toward a door at one end of the room.

Daniel put his hand on his stomach and rubbed it. He felt just as sick as he had in anticipation of the flight. He looked up at Asher and licked his lips. When Asher's face seemed to fade out at the edges of Daniel's vision, Daniel blinked his eyes rapidly and tried to focus. He swayed and suddenly felt light-headed.

Asher's expression, which had been neutral, morphed immediately. "What's wrong?" he asked, concern evident in his tone and in the way his eyebrows furrowed. He cupped Daniel's cheek and rubbed his thumb over Daniel's bottom lip. "You look like you saw a ghost or something and"—Asher moved his hand to Daniel's nape, put the other at this waist, and tugged him close—"you're pale as a sheet."

Daniel darted his gaze to the bed, taking in the crisp

white sheets. Had anybody even slept in that bed? He was sure he could bounce a quarter off the mattress and...were those hospital corners? "I don't... I don't..." Daniel sucked in huge gulps of air.

"You don't what, sugar?" Asher looked down at him, his expression tender, the look in his eyes full of worry. He pulled Daniel's head against his chest and rocked them both from side to side. "Shhh," he whispered into Daniel's ear. "Shhh. Talk to me, sugar. I'll take care of it. Whatever has you so upset, I'll take care of it. Talk to me."

Daniel relaxed at the comforting words and gestures. He pressed himself as close as he could to Asher and clutched his shirt tightly.

"Daniel?" Asher said. "Talk to me."

With his eyes squeezed together to shut out his surroundings, Daniel took in a deep breath and answered. "I don't fit here. I thought—" He licked his lips again. "I thought it'd be different this time, but it's not... I don't—"

"Oh, is that what has you so worked up? I know the apartment isn't big, but don't worry. I'll clear out room for you in the closet and in the dresser. Everything will fit just fine."

It took a moment for Asher's words to register, and then Daniel started shaking with laughter. He was in the midst of an existential panic attack and Asher was going to solve it by emptying a drawer.

"Hey, come on now. Are you... You're not crying, are

you?" Asher asked, sounding horribly uncomfortable. "There, there," he said and patted Daniel's back awkwardly.

That was all it took for Daniel to let out a deep belly laugh. Big strong man, terrified of a few tears. He leaned back and looked at Asher's face. "I'm okay. Sorry about that. I, uh, get a little worked up sometimes but..." He darted his eyes around the room and took a calming breath. "A couple of drawers would be great." He looked at his duffel bag. "Don't worry about making space in your closet; I don't have anything that needs to be hung."

"Okay. Good," Asher said with a nod. He sounded relieved that the emotional episode was behind them. "Not good about the closet, good about the, uh, other, uh... When the rest of your things get here, if we need more space, we'll figure it out, okay?"

Daniel chuckled. "The rest of my things?"

"Well, yeah." Asher walked over to the bags he'd set down and started unzipping his suitcase, separating dirty clothes into piles. "I mean, you're staying here now, right? So you should have, uh, whoever has your stuff send it." He paused and looked back at Daniel over his shoulder. "Who has your things?" It sounded less like a question and more like an accusation.

Was Asher jealous? Daniel rubbed his lips together to hold back his pleased smile. He knew he shouldn't like that, but he couldn't help himself. He had a thing for possessive men. Always had. Chase was forever giving him a hard time about it. "My clothes are in that bag. All of them. There's nothing to send and nobody to send it."

"Uh." Asher looked down at the duffel bag and then back at Daniel. "All your belongings are in this bag?"

"Sure." Daniel nodded and squatted next to Asher, unzipped his duffel, and added his dirty clothes to Asher's pile. "A couple pairs of jeans, a couple pairs of shorts, some T-shirts, and a couple sweatshirts. I don't need anything else, and besides, I like to travel light. Makes it easier to go wherever, whenever, you know?"

It was quiet for a couple of minutes, and then Asher pulled Daniel's bag a bit closer to him and snatched clothes out, slamming them down onto the piles. "Well, you're here now, so that wherever, whenever business is no longer an issue. We'll go shopping and get you more things."

"I'm fine, Ash." Daniel sighed. "I hate shopping and I don't need more clothes."

"I'll buy them," Asher grumbled. Daniel's bag was empty and Asher folded it and placed it into his own suitcase, zipped it up, and shoved it under the bed.

The man seemed angry and Daniel wasn't sure what he'd done to set him off. He laid his hand on Asher's upper arm, right above his elbow. "Ash," he said, choosing his words carefully. "I appreciate the offer, but it's not about who pays. I like my clothes just fine and I don't need more of them."

Asher raked his black eyes over Daniel's body, obviously cataloging his loose, worn jeans and washed-out sweatshirt.

Eventually, Asher spoke. "Depending on what job you decide you want, you may need to, uh, dress up a little more."

This wasn't the first time Daniel had heard comments about his clothes. Plus, he wasn't blind; he knew he wasn't the snappiest dresser around. But he was thirty-three, not thirteen, and he intentionally chose clothes that made him comfortable, outside and in.

He sighed. "I seriously doubt any job I'd want would require me to dress up, but if the need arises, I'll make sure to pick up something appropriate."

Asher stared at him and seemed to weigh his words. After a couple of minutes, he sat down on the floor, scooted against the wall and reached for Daniel, pulling him onto his lap. "I didn't mean to offend you. I just..." Asher shrugged awkwardly. He seemed oddly uncomfortable finishing his sentence, let alone having a conversation. And it was clear Daniel's show of emotion hadn't been par for Asher's course, either. Daniel once again wondered about Asher's past relationships.

Well, only one way to find out. He took a deep breath. "Is it out of line for me to ask about your exes?" he asked.

"My exes?"

Daniel nodded. "Yeah, you know, past boyfriends, guys you've lived with. Exes."

"Oh, uh." Asher stumbled on his words, but Daniel kept his gaze glued on the other man, waiting for him to share some information about himself, something to help Daniel understand the person who had suddenly become such a big part of his life.

"I haven't lived with anybody," Asher said. "Other than roommates, I mean. Of course I had roommates when I was younger, but, uh, other than that I haven't lived with anybody."

"You just weren't that serious about your ex-boyfriends? Or..." Daniel let his question trail off, waiting for Asher to finish it.

"I'm not sure I've been with someone who's qualified as what you'd consider a boyfriend."

"Really?" Daniel was surprised, which came through in his voice. "Why not?"

Asher furrowed his brow, and Daniel knew he was contemplating the question. "I guess I haven't wanted that. I like things a certain way. I've always enjoyed my space. I have a really busy, high-stress job."

Daniel's heart rate increased and his palms got clammy as he listened to the string of excuses. He wasn't so great with order, wasn't so great with space, wasn't a fan of busy jobs or stress. He already felt like he didn't fit in Asher's apartment, but now he wondered whether he fit with Asher at all.

"What am I doing here, Ash?" he asked quietly.

"I want you," Asher replied immediately. Asher's eyes held such warmth, and his expression was so tender, Daniel forced himself to push white carpets he was sure to stain and glass tables he was sure to break out of his mind. "I know it's crazy and fast and impetuous, but"—Asher shrugged sheepishly, quite a feat for a muscle-bound, bald-headed, rough-faced man—"it feels right in my gut, and in my line of work, I've learned to trust my instincts."

Fast and impetuous didn't bother Daniel. That was how he lived his life. But his instincts didn't have the same track record as Asher's, and what his gut felt was fear that he'd get attached only to have Asher realize all the reasons he'd remained single up until then still applied. After all, why would four decades of history change after meeting him?

"Why me?" he asked, not one to hold back his feelings.

"Well," Asher said, dragging the word out. He ran his fingers through Daniel's hair, massaging his scalp. It felt so good Daniel wanted to purr. "There's something about you, sugar. Something that makes me feel like we fit together. I can feel it right here." He took Daniel's hand and placed it on his firm belly. Daniel usually went for feelings that came a little higher; in fact, the ache in his chest told him he was already experiencing those feelings. "I'm new to this, so I hope it isn't coming out all wrong, but I want you here with me. I know you're trying to figure out what to do with your life right now, but I think you could be happy here with me."

Daniel snorted. "I'm a pretty easy guy, Ash," he said. "A peanut butter sandwich and a blow job is about all it takes to make me happy."

Asher turned up his lips in a cocky grin. "Well, I'm not sure I have any bread right now, but I can take care of the other task."

"Yeah? We've never... I mean, you haven't... I know we've only known each other a few days, but I have and..." Daniel let out a little moan and pressed his mouth to Asher's, stealing one kiss after another, nibbling and licking at Asher's lips until he opened and let Daniel in.

Asher looked at the man in his lap. Daniel was shaking and panting, his cheeks were red, his pupils wide. He was the picture of arousal, and Asher thrummed with need in response. He bent down and kissed Daniel again, hungry for more. The taste of Daniel's mouth was so arousing, the small motions and whimpering noises he made so erotic it took Asher longer than it should have to put together what Daniel meant. He was reaching down to the button on his own jeans when it hit him—Daniel was talking about *receiving* a blow job, not about *giving* one.

But that didn't make sense. Asher topped. Always and in every way. He never let another man use his mouth, well, at least not in years, not since he'd started getting involved in the leather scene. And Asher was about to say exactly that when Daniel's heated breath hit his neck. "You have me so worked up already," he said quietly, his voice husky, his thin body trembling against Asher's. "I'm dying to feel you but I just know I won't last. I've..." He gulped and blushed. "I've wanted to feel you going down on me since we met."

Well, damn. Asher closed his eyes and considered his options. At least he tried to consider them. The truth was, he was hard and horny and he wanted Daniel with a desperation he'd never before experienced and seemed unable to control. He moaned quietly, the noise almost sounding like a whimper. Nobody would know about this, he justified to himself. What could it hurt?

He snapped his eyes open when Daniel's weight left his lap. He reached up instinctively, wanting the warmth, the man, back where he belonged. Daniel stood in front of him, yanking his shirt off and pushing his jeans and boxers down. And suddenly, Asher was sitting on the floor with a nude Daniel standing above him, his cock at eye level, hard and heavy and clearly wanting.

Asher raised his gaze to Daniel's face. His eyes were wide and expectant, he was chewing on his bottom lip anxiously, and Asher knew he couldn't refuse him anything. It wasn't Asher's thing, but it sure seemed to be something Daniel wanted. All right, so he was going to suck dick. But not like this.

Asher got to his feet. "Get on the bed, sugar," he ordered.

Daniel's body shook, but he nodded and stumbled to the bed, crawling across it and giving Asher a view of the most perfect ass he'd ever seen and a little pink pucker he had yet to breach. That would change soon. But first, Asher would take care of Daniel, would give the man what he needed.

"Like this?" Daniel asked. He was lying on his back, his head propped on the pillows, hands clenched in fists at his sides, and legs spread. He looked like a feast, just waiting for Asher to consume him.

"Yeah," Asher answered thickly. "Just like that."

He planted his hands on the bed on either side of Daniel's legs and lowered his head slowly, keeping his gaze locked with Daniel's as he licked at his calf and then gave him a sharp bite. Daniel cried out but didn't move away; he just breathed harder and released and clenched his fists. Enjoying the reaction, the unexpected power he felt in having this type of control over Daniel's pleasure, Asher smiled wickedly. He continued to make his way up Daniel's body, continuing the pattern—darting tongue, followed by bites and nibbles, all along the fair skin exposed to him. He tasted Daniel's knee, his hip, his thigh in the spot so very close to his groin that Asher felt the man's balls brush against his cheek.

"Ash!" Daniel shouted. Asher chuckled and soothed his tongue over the bite he'd inflicted to the sensitive skin on Daniel's inner thigh. "I can't..." Daniel gasped. "I'm gonna... Ash, Ash, I..."

Asher shot his hand from its perch on Daniel's knee and circled the base of his cock, squeezing lightly. "Not yet. That's for me and you'll wait until I'm ready before you give it up," he growled, surprising himself. If he wanted to avoid going down on the other man, he could do it, could make Daniel spend himself without Asher ever taking that ruddy cock into his mouth. But that wasn't what Asher wanted.

It was unexpected, but Asher was enjoying this. He was enjoying the taste of Daniel's skin, the way the man gasped and trembled for him, the need pouring out of Daniel, all for him, all because of what he was doing. As he swiped his tongue up Daniel's balls and along the vein on the underside of his dick, Asher didn't feel a hint of submission within himself. It was a new type of control, to be sure, but he was in charge of the interaction, of Daniel's body, of his pleasure, of his orgasm. And with that in mind, Asher circled the head of Daniel's cock with his tongue and dropped his mouth over the flaming skin, taking Daniel in as deep as he could before applying strong suction and pulling up.

"Ash!" Daniel keened, tossing his head from side to side, arching his back. "Please, please," he begged, completely undone.

If Asher's mouth hadn't been so full of dick, he would have smiled in satisfaction. Oh, damn, he was so turned on he ached. So much so that he was seconds from losing it just from the feeling of Daniel's cock on his tongue, his musky scent, his trembling body, and breaking voice.

He pumped Daniel's cock, his hand meeting his lips at the midpoint of that rigid pole, for a couple of strokes, and then he pulled off with a pop. "Come," he demanded, and then, without giving it any thought, he dropped back down, taking Daniel into his mouth instead of pulling away. He wanted to taste the intoxicating man's seed.

Daniel cried out his name like a benediction as shot after shot of bitter liquid pulsed into Asher's mouth. When Daniel was done, Asher scrambled to his knees and tore at his pants, wanting to free his cock before he came in his jeans. He never would have imagined that he'd be so turned on by giving someone else pleasure, but there it was.

Before Asher realized it was happening, Daniel was sitting up, lowering Asher's zipper and reaching for his dick, his movements just as desperate, just as hungry. Asher tangled his fingers in the man's hair, tipped his face back, and then dipped his own head down, smashing their mouths together. Daniel whimpered when Asher thrust his tongue into Daniel's mouth, allowing the man to taste his own semen.

With his free hand, Asher pulled on his own dick, using rough, fast strokes. Daniel whined and pressed closer, and that was all it took—Asher yanked Daniel's head back and grunted as the orgasm racked his body and he shot hot, white ejaculate on Daniel's chin, neck, and chest.

"Fuck," he grunted once he could breathe. That had been intense. Crazy intense.

Daniel wrapped slender arms around his hips and clung to him. He pressed his cheek against Asher's groin, his hot breath threatening to get things started all over again. Asher gently stroked his hair and rubbed the back of his neck.

"Good?" he asked, even though he knew the answer.

Daniel looked up at him, his face relaxed and sated, and

he nodded. "Yeah."

"You see?" Asher said. "You fit just fine with me." Not in the way Asher had expected, but, yeah, Daniel was going to fit just fine into Asher's life.

CHAPTER 11

A knock on Asher's open door distracted him from the interminable stack of paperwork on his desk. He looked up in relief. "Yes?"

Oliver was leaning against his office door. "Time to go," he said.

Asher darted his eyes to the clock on the wall. It was five o'clock, and much as he wished his job actually ended at that hour, it didn't. Which was something Oliver knew full well, seeing as how he he'd been the assistant district attorney assigned to Asher's precinct for over ten years. "We don't have plans, do we? Because I've got another hour, at least, and..."

He stopped himself before he admitted that he was itching to get home to Daniel. He'd left the house at seven that morning and had suffered through a pile of post vacation work all day, but Daniel had never drifted far from his mind. He'd even called the man at lunch just to check in. It was ridiculous and he couldn't come up with any chemicals to blame, airborne or otherwise.

"We have that computer training meeting today,

remember?" Oliver said. "You signed up for it after you missed the one last month. And the one before that. Aaaand the one before that. Let's go."

"Fuck," Asher growled. "Can't do it today. I have to catch up on the real work I've missed since Thursday. You know how hard the first day back from being away is. There's not time to waste on—"

"Save it, Asher. I don't make the rules and I'm suffering through this just like you just so I can have the privilege of logging in on your computers. I don't want to hear your bitching; let's go."

Asher pushed his chair back and yanked his jacket off the back. "I don't understand why you're all excited about these fuckin' trainings," he grumbled. "Do you think they're going to blow us?"

"Yeah, right," Oliver scoffed. "I don't even think we're going to get our balls tickled. And I'm just as pissed as you, but this computer-training shit is mandatory and you've missed the last three, so unless you want to face a suspension, we're going."

"Fine, whatever." He waved his hand in frustration. "Just give me a second to let Daniel know I'll be later than I said."

He got his phone out of his pocket, dialed Daniel, and had the device next to his ear before he looked up and saw Oliver staring at him with his jaw hanging open. The expression was becoming disconcertingly familiar.

"Hello." Daniel's voice distracted him from wondering

about Oliver.

"Hey, sugar. Listen, I forgot about this computer-training thing I have to do, so I won't be home until closer to eight tonight."

"No problem," Daniel said, sounding like he meant it. "I figured I'd try making dinner tonight so that'll give me more time. Do you have any favorites?"

"You cook?" Asher asked in surprise. Not that he was complaining. His chest warmed at the thought of Daniel making a meal for him. Which was a weird as shit reaction, but Asher was getting used to his strange responses when it came to Daniel Tover.

"Well, no, but I can learn. I saw that you have pots and pans and stuff and I can look up a recipe online."

"Asher, let's go." Oliver was tapping his fingers on his wrist, not that he was wearing a watch. Asher glared at him.

"I'm sure whatever you come up with will be great," he said to Daniel. "I'll see you in a few hours."

Oliver didn't say anything as they walked out of Asher's office and made their way to the elevator bank.

"Aren't you going to call Shirley?" Asher asked him.

"What for?" Oliver's brow was furrowed in confusion.

"To let her know you're going to be late. Or did you already tell her about the training?"

"Uh, no, I didn't," Oliver responded. "But she won't care."

"Shit, Ollie, show some consideration. That woman is way out of your league, and if you're not careful, she's going to figure it out."

Oliver shrugged. "So, how's my brother?" he asked.

"You saw him yesterday," Asher grumbled. "Nothing's changed since then."

The elevator opened and both men stepped inside.

"Sure it has. He's living in your apartment now. I'd say that's a pretty big change for you and for Danny."

Fair enough. Asher hadn't had a roommate in years. Not since the first moment he'd been able to afford a piece-of-shit, four-hundred-square-foot studio in the Tenderloin. The neighborhood was crappy, his apartment a shoebox, but it had been worth it to him because it had given him a place to escape at the end of the day where nobody could bother him or get in his way. He'd moved to a bigger neighborhood and a nicer apartment since then, but his space had always remained his own.

The fact that he'd moved Daniel in days after meeting him was way outside Asher's normal comfort zone. So, as much as he hated having anybody butt into his business, Asher understood why Oliver was asking about Daniel. And besides, Oliver wasn't just anybody. He was Daniel's brother and Asher's friend.

"Daniel is doing fine, Ollie. I'm not going to hurt your brother, okay?"

"Is that right?" Oliver said drolly, disbelief clear in his tone.

"Yeah, that's right." Asher's jaw ticced in annoyance at

the implied accusation. He crossed his arms over his broad chest, spread his legs, and glared at Oliver. "You have my word on it."

Oliver raised one eyebrow, his expression stoic at best, indicating to Asher that his promise didn't erase Oliver's concerns. But then the elevator opened, depositing them in the training room, and time for conversation, and anything else except brain-piercing boredom, was over.

With Asher at work, Daniel had time to get acquainted with his new neighborhood. He'd spent time in San Francisco, visiting friends or vacationing, but he didn't know the area well. Asher lived in Bernal Heights, not an area that Daniel remembered frequenting.

Daniel pulled on his warmest sweatshirt, slipped the strap of his messenger bag across his chest, and walked out of the apartment. It was chilly, but not uncomfortable, and he enjoyed his walk. He thought he was miles from the apartment when suddenly he saw it at the end of the street and realized he'd been walking in a circle. On the plus side, he was standing next to a cute little coffee shop. Deciding it was a nice time for a break, Daniel brushed his hair out of his face with one hand, and pushed the glass door open with the other. He inhaled deeply as soon as he stepped inside. Mmm.

Nothing beat the smell of fresh coffee.

He yanked his sweatshirt off, no longer needing it in the cozy space, and walked up to the counter. "Medium vanilla latte, please," he said. "And is the Wi-Fi open or do I need a code?"

The woman at the counter turned around, moved her gaze from his face down his chest, and then back up again. Then she raised a pierced eyebrow and grinned. "Well, aren't you a pretty one?"

Daniel blushed, dipped his head so his hair fell back over his face, and dug through his messenger bag for his baseball cap, pulling it on so it sat low and covered his face.

"Hey, now, don't worry, pretty boy. I was just yanking your chain. I like 'em with a little more on top." She grasped her breasts and winked. "No need to hide."

He wasn't hiding. Okay, well, maybe he was. He lifted his chin and found a smile for the woman. "How much do I owe you?"

She finished making his latte and slid it across the counter. "This one's on the house," she said.

"Oh, no. I can't let you do that." Daniel shook his head and opened his wallet.

"I insist. You're a new customer and I want to make sure you come back. Didn't mean to make you uncomfortable. Most of the boys that look like you soak up the compliments."

Daniel shrugged. What could he say? He knew how he looked, had been hearing it all his life. Plus, he had access to a mirror. He wasn't going to complain about being attractive, but the come-ons didn't appeal to him.

"I, uh, thanks for the latte."

"I'm Lindsey." The woman held her hand out.

Daniel looked at the huge chalkboard hanging on the wall with the menu. The coffee shop's name was scrawled across the top: Lindsey and Anita's.

"Lindsey as in *Lindsey*," he said with a grin.

"That's the one. Owner, barista, cashier extraordinaire. Anita's my partner. I keep her in back chained to the oven. Oh, and her name's the password for our Wi-Fi. Very high security operation we're running." She winked at Daniel again and picked up a cloth to wipe the counter. "Enjoy your coffee, pretty."

It turned out that the latte was good, the Wi-Fi connection fast, and the seats plush and comfortable. Daniel had his headphones on and was engrossed in the work he was doing on his computer when a guy slid into the empty seat at his table. Daniel glanced up. There were plenty of empty tables in the coffee shop. He took off his headphones and looked at the guy expectantly.

"Hi," he said. "That's a great-looking laptop you got there." He tapped Daniel's MacBook. "Almost as good-looking as its owner." Daniel snorted out a laugh. The guy smiled broadly. "Yeah, I know. It's a crappy line. Still working out the kinks." He held his hand out to Daniel. "Name's Marc Dorey. I think I saw you leaving my building this morning. You just move in?"

Daniel took his hand. "Daniel Tover. Yeah, I'm, ah, living with Asher Penaz. You know him?"

"Know him? Not so much. Drooled after him a lot, though. He's got that dangerous vibe going. It's hot."

"Yeah." Daniel grinned and nodded. "He's definitely drool-worthy."

"So what do you do? That looked like some sort of keyboard on your screen."

Daniel closed his laptop. "Oh, yeah, that's a program I have. Uh, why? Do you play?"

"No." Marc shook his head. "I cook. I'm the head chef at Salvador's. You heard of it?"

"No, but I've lived here for about two minutes. Actually, I was thinking about taking up cooking. Asher works crazy long hours and I've got time during the day."

"I'm jealous. I need to find a man to take care of me so I can do the whole Suzie Homemaker thing, but until then, I have to slave away," Marc said dramatically. Then he smiled and picked up his coffee as he got up. "Seriously, though, I was getting my coffee on the way into work when I saw you, so I stopped to say hi, but I'll be late if I don't get going. If you want any tips in the kitchen, come by. I live three doors down from Asher and I'm usually home in the mornings."

"I'll definitely take you up on that," Daniel said. "Thanks for the offer."

CHAPTER 12

The hallway smelled off, but it wasn't the first time odors from the street or the neighbors had permeated the air outside of Asher's apartment, so it didn't strike him as particularly unusual. In fact, it didn't do much more than register vaguely in the back of his mind. Back behind what he was going to do about an officer who was too short-tempered and red-eyed lately, an arrest that wasn't going anywhere if they didn't find some solid evidence once they obtained a warrant the following day, the annual visit he had from the parents of a kid who was killed ten years ago and were still waiting for justice, and how Daniel kept his skin feeling so smooth, his lips always slightly red, and his ass so damn round that Asher wanted to sink his teeth into it and leave his mark.

That last thought was so vivid, so all encompassing, that Asher was almost distracted from the fact that the weird smell was getting stronger, not weaker, the closer he got to his apartment. When he opened the door and the air seemed just a little hazy, he snapped to attention.

"Daniel?" he asked worriedly. "Is everything okay? Daniel?"

"Hey, you're home!" Daniel walked out of the kitchen, wiping his hands on a towel. His baseball cap was on backward, his huge T-shirt was covered in new stains, and his jeans dragged on the floor behind his flip-flops, the hems tattered and frayed from the constant friction. Asher would have suggested smaller pants or a belt, but Daniel's smile seemed to have knocked the air out of his lungs, and he was having trouble breathing, let alone talking.

He'd been away from the man for more than twelve hours, hadn't enjoyed that happy expression all day, so having the full impact of Daniel's bright smile aimed at him made his chest ache with desire. Sexual desire, yes, but it wasn't just that. Asher wanted to do anything and everything in his power to keep Daniel looking as happy as he did at that moment. And to keep Daniel looking at *him* as the person responsible for that happiness, as the person responsible for Daniel.

He was rooted to his spot as Daniel walked up and slipped right into his arms. When had he opened his arms? He was pretty sure that was tomato sauce on Daniel's shirt, and it looked like it was still damp. That sauce was sure to transfer to his own shirt.

"I missed you today," Daniel said and wiggled against him, tucking his face under Asher's chin, kissing the base of his throat and running his hands from Asher's hips over his back to his shoulders, and then back down again.

Thoughts of stains on his shirt fled from Asher's mind as he clung to that skinny body, took Daniel's hat off, tangled his fingers in messy hair, and massaged Daniel's scalp. He had missed Daniel too, more than he thought was reasonable considering the fact that they'd known each other less than a week. But when he opened his mouth to tell Daniel how he felt, the words got stuck in his throat.

Instead he said, "What were you doing in here? It smells like—" He sniffed the air, then pressed his nose to Daniel's hair and inhaled. "Smoke? Is something on fire?"

"Not anymore," Daniel answered, the words muffled because he was still gliding his mouth over Asher's neck and jaw.

Asher gripped Daniel's shoulders and held him out at arm's length. "Not anymore?" he asked. "As in there *was* a fire? Here?"

"Yeah," Daniel said with a nod. "Just a little one. Turns out cooking is pretty complicated." He sighed. "But I'll get the hang of it. I just need more practice."

A glance toward the kitchen wasn't enough for Asher to get a handle on what was going on. From his angle, he could see a small portion of the floor and the lower cabinet. Nothing else.

Daniel tracked his gaze and looked weary. "Don't worry. I've got everything cleaned up. I didn't leave a mess in your apartment. I was just working on scrubbing the last pan when you got home. I've almost got the black off."

"Black? What happened?" Asher snapped. He immediately regretted the harshness in his tone, but the words were already out, so there was nothing he could do about it.

Daniel's face dropped, first his expression and then his angle. His chin almost touched his chest, his hair hung over his eyes, and he rubbed his foot in circles on the floor.

"I tried to make this chicken thing, but there was oil and it splattered and I didn't want your counter to be dirty, so I was wiping it up but I wasn't sure which cleaner to use and then I ran out of paper towels so I looked for more and I found them, so I was wiping the counter but then things were all smoky and I realized the chicken was burning and I was taking the pan to the sink but then I thought I once heard something about not putting water on oil, so I wasn't sure what to do, and then I opened the window and held the pan outside until my arm was tired and the smoke was mostly gone, but then when I got back to the stove I realized the water on the rice had boiled off and the rice was all black and crispy in the bottom of the other pan so I had to hold that out the window until it stopped smoking, and..." Daniel finally paused his babbling long enough to take a deep breath, and Asher used the opportunity to brush his hair out of his face and tilt his chin up.

He couldn't hold back his grin. The man was adorable.

Daniel raised his eyebrows when he looked at Asher's face and blinked in surprise. "I made spaghetti for you," he said slowly, carefully, as if he was testing Asher's reaction. "The sauce is from a jar but I bought fresh parmesan cheese."

"That's nice," Asher said. "Thank you."

"I...I'm sorry about your kitchen. It's mostly all clean. I swear."

"It's okay," Asher said, and surprisingly, he meant it. He'd had a fight with more than one roommate over leaving dirty plates in the sink or not taking out the trash when it smelled bad, so having someone set fire to his kitchen and stink up his apartment should have rankled. But it didn't. Maybe he was mellowing with age.

Yeah, Asher settled on that reasoning, pointedly ignoring the fact that this newfound calmness had started when he met Daniel and didn't seem to apply to anybody else. Some of his officers could definitely attest to that after being faced with Asher's loud and angry reaction to their sloppy documentation that very morning. One officer had walked away with his eyes looking a little wet. Another had grumbled under her breath about not needing that new asshole she'd just been ripped. And a third hadn't said a word or made eye contact with anyone for the rest of the day.

"It's okay?" Daniel asked. "You're not mad?"

Asher cupped Daniel's cheeks, holding his hair back with his fingers and stroking his jaw with his thumbs. Standing there with no distractions, just gazing at Daniel's face without the man looking away or using his hair as a shield, without Asher pushing him down to his knees in a haze of lust, without so much alcohol in his system that the room seemed to spin half the time, without the dark lighting in a bar or casino or hotel room; standing there gazing at Daniel's face, Asher realized how incredibly beautiful Daniel was. Not just cute or attractive. The man was positively stunning.

His heart slammed against his ribs, he was having trouble getting enough air, and his dick was so hard he ached. Holy shit. He had never experienced such a strong reaction to another man. Not ever.

"Do you have any idea how gorgeous you are?" he asked breathlessly.

Daniel's gaze lowered and he fidgeted uncomfortably. Asher couldn't have that.

"No, don't hide from me." He took Daniel's chin in his hand and forced him to look up and meet his gaze. "I mean it. You're the most beautiful man I've ever seen in real life."

He wasn't sure what to expect in response to those words because he wasn't usually one to shower guys with compliments. If they were particularly strong in a scene, he'd let them know they'd pleased him, but otherwise, he didn't say much. It wasn't that Asher was keeping anything back, he'd just never seen the point of flattering someone. Either a guy wanted to bend over for him or he didn't. And if he didn't, well, there was always someone else a few stools over who was perfectly willing to take his place without making any demands.

"Did you have a good day at work?" Daniel asked.

Well, that was a diversion if Asher had ever heard one. But Daniel was looking into his eyes, his expression sincere, like he really wanted to hear about Asher's day. Being the focus of Daniel's attention was heady, and Asher found he enjoyed the position. Daniel should always be looking at him. Just him.

"My day was fine," Asher answered. "Nobody got shot, which is always a good thing. Mostly I was cleaning up messes from when I was out last week and catching up on paperwork. What'd you do?"

"I walked around the neighborhood a little, discovered a good coffee shop, met some nice people, spent time on my computer, and then I worked on dinner. Speaking of dinner," Daniel said and dropped his gaze, "I hope you like your noodles extra limp because I may have overcooked them."

"You *may* have overcooked them?" Asher repeated, tilting one side of his mouth up in amusement. Daniel shrugged and chewed on his bottom lip. "I'm sure they'll be fine," Asher assured him.

"I'll do better next time," Daniel promised with conviction.

Whether he would or not didn't matter to Asher. There were a dozen takeout places that could have dinner at his door in less than thirty minutes. But the knowledge that there would be a next time, that Daniel seemed to be happy enough to want to stick around, those things mattered to Asher more than anything else he could remember, although he still wasn't sure whether that was a good thing.

Daniel already had the table set so Asher sat down without bothering to change out of his work clothes. He scooped some of what Daniel claimed was pasta onto his fork and took a bite.

"This is, uh..." He reached for his water glass and

swallowed down the food.

Daniel started laughing. "Oh God, it's awful, isn't it?"

"No, not awful, just..." Asher searched for some word that wouldn't be a complete lie and yet wouldn't be insulting.

"Awful. The word you're looking for is awful. I'll make you a sandwich." Daniel started to get up from the table. But Asher clasped his wrist.

"Seriously, sugar, it's fine. Not the best spaghetti I've ever had, but not bad enough to throw away. And I appreciate that you took the time to make it for me."

"Yeah?" Daniel gave him a shy, hopeful smile, and Asher would have agreed to just about anything in response.

"Yes." He took another couple of bites of pasta to prove his point. "Now, talk to me. Did you give any thought to what kind of work you want to do?"

"Not really." Daniel squirmed in his chair and shrugged.

"Well, when you were a kid, what did you want to be when you grew up? Maybe that's a good way to start."

"When I was a kid?" Daniel asked, confusion clear in his tone.

"Yeah. Like I dreamed of being a professional football player, Batman, a fireman, or a cop. You know, normal kid stuff. Didn't have the speed for football or the superpowers for Spiderman, not a big fan of not breathing, so I went with cop."

Daniel thought about the question. "I don't know if I had dreams like that. I mean, I've tried out a bunch of different jobs and they've mostly been fun. But what I dreamed of being?"

"Uh-huh." Asher nodded. "When you were in bed at night and you thought about the future or when you blew out candles on your birthday cake, what did you wish for? What did you want most of all?"

"Nothing complicated. Mostly I just wanted to be wanted or needed or whatever. Wanted to feel like I belonged."

Asher reached out and took Daniel's hand. "You didn't feel like you belonged?"

"No, don't look all sad like that." Daniel smiled at him. "I don't have a sob story or anything. My parents loved me. It's just, you know, my biological dad wasn't ever around much. He married Oliver's mom, but with mine, they split before I was even born and she married my first stepdad when I was a baby. There was a string of stepfathers and special *uncles* after that. My mom was a dancer and then a choreographer when she got older. We moved around a lot, depending on where she had a show or where whoever she was with at the time lived. She always made sure I was taken care of, her guys were pretty decent, and I met all sorts of people but..." Daniel shrugged. "There was so much motion, you know? People would come and go from our lives all the time. Made me feel alone, and I hated it. Just wanted someone to need me enough to stay around, I guess."

CHAPTER 13

"Hey, you okay?" Oliver asked as he settled into a chair in Asher's office.

"I'm ready for this fucking day to end already," Asher replied and rubbed his hand over the back of his neck.

A dead suspect. Two officers who shot at him. Somewhere along the way, one of the officers had taken a bullet to the shoulder. They didn't know whether it was from the suspect's gun or one of their own. The day was the very definition of clusterfuck.

"I bet. It's already water cooler fodder in my office. Is Davis going to be okay?"

"We don't know yet. Last I heard he was out of surgery, but they don't know if he'll have muscle damage."

"Hey, muscle damage is still alive, right? That's what matters," Oliver pointed out.

"Alive, yeah. Back on the street, no. It's his right shoulder, which means he may not be able to carry a piece again. That man is a fourth-generation cop. He's thirty-two years old. If he has to turn in his shield, he'll be crushed."

"Yeah, I see that." Oliver grimaced. "Fucking sucks, man.

How about his partner, the new guy?"

"Rogers. He's suspended until IA finishes their investigation. They need to run the bullet they pulled out of Davis through ballistics and interview a shitload of witnesses and fuck knows what else. But, honestly, I don't think the kid's coming back. When I got to the scene, he'd already puked twice and he was shaking so hard I was sure he was going to keel over."

Oliver leaned forward and rested his forearms on his knees. "Why was he throwing up and shaking? Is he on something?"

"Nah, dial it down, counselor. The kid was just scared out of his mind. His partner was down, there was a perp bleeding all over the place, and then they pronounced him DOA. Something tells me the reality of the job doesn't match whatever Rogers had in his head when he chose this career path. I just hope it wasn't his bullet in Davis. 'Cause if he shot his partner..." Asher shook his head. "There'd be a fuckin' shitstorm heading his way that I wouldn't wish on any of my guys."

Just talking about his craptastic day had Asher ready to go home and...huh. For as long as he could remember, that thought had ended with "crawl into bed" or "get drunk and crawl into bed" or maybe "change, go to a club and find a guy to fuck, then go home and do option one or two." But none of those endings entered his mind at that moment. Instead, all he wanted was to go home and see Daniel, feel that skinny body in his arms, bury his face in the man's hair and let his scent wash away all the stress of the day.

He quickly glanced at the clock. It was after six. Everything on his desk could wait until morning. He was done for the day. Asher pushed his chair back, stood up, and swiped his jacket off the back of his chair.

"I'm taking off, Ollie."

"Really?" Oliver sounded surprised. "You never leave before seven."

"Yeah, well, I…" Asher stopped short. It'd sound pathetic to say he wanted to leave work so he could be with Daniel. "I've had a long day," he explained instead.

Oliver grumbled a little, but he got up and walked out of Asher's office.

"So I got your e-mail. What's the deal with the wedding?"

"I don't know. Shirley said something about bad weather so we're going to push it back."

They lived in San Francisco. Aiming for predictably good weather was about as likely as winning the lottery. Not that a delay was a big deal. After all, Oliver and Shirley were just having a few people over to their place, where a judge friend would do the honors. Still, something about it seemed off to Asher. *Whathefuckever*. He rubbed his hand over his scalp. He had enough on his plate without adding Oliver's relationship idiosyncrasies.

They got to the stairwell, and Oliver headed up to his office while Asher started walking down the stairs. "See you tomorrow," he said and waved over his shoulder.

"See ya," Oliver replied.

The drive home didn't take long and then Asher was pounding up the stairs and rushing to his door. He wondered whether Daniel had managed to make dinner without setting something on fire or overcooking it. The spaghetti the night before had been the consistency of a casserole, not that he'd said anything about it. After all, his mother had taught him manners.

He remembered how pissed he'd been as a kid when his mother's boyfriends criticized her cooking or her appearance. She'd put on a good show, giving as good as she got, but when they were gone and she thought nobody was looking, he'd seen how sad she was, how down she'd get after those fights. So Asher knew an overcooked meal was still a meal. Besides, nobody but Daniel had made anything especially for him since he'd left home, and he found that he liked it.

"Daniel?" he called out as soon as he pushed the door open. He pulled his keys out of the lock and hung them on the hook by the door, then let the door close behind him. "Daniel?" he repeated when he didn't hear an answer.

The apartment was empty. He knew that before he'd taken more than two steps inside. It was quiet, dark, the air was still. Asher couldn't squash down the feeling of disappointment that washed over him. Half a decade living in that apartment on his own and it had never felt empty. Less than a week sharing his space with Daniel, and the man's absence was palpable.

He'd had a bad day. Wasn't the whole point of a relationship to be able to come home to somebody after one of those? Having him take your mind off it or make you feel better or suck your dick or something? He was pretty sure that was what he'd heard from the people who had tried to set him up over the years.

So why was he walking into an empty apartment? It wasn't like Daniel was working. He had nothing to do all day. Was it too much to expect him to be available when Asher was home?

He tossed his jacket over the back of the couch. He'd hang it up later. Then he paced across the great room to the kitchen and back again, getting more agitated with every step. Where in the fuck was Daniel? He got his phone out of his pocket and dialed.

"Hey, Ash," Daniel's bright voice chirped after a few rings. "How's your day going? Do you know when you'll be done working?" There was music in the background and some other sounds Asher couldn't identify. It didn't sound like street traffic, so he knew Daniel was indoors.

"Why?" Asher snapped. "You have somewhere you need to be or something? 'Cause I can pick up dinner on the way home if you already have plans." Okay, that didn't come out right at all. Damn it. Why was he yelling? He tried to calm down.

"No, I don't have anywhere to be," Daniel answered

quickly. "I have dinner ready for you at home."

Any attempt at curbing his anger was effectively halted by Daniel's lie. He was standing in his apartment. There was no dinner. There was no Daniel. "Is that right?" he asked slowly, carefully, dangerously.

"Yes." Daniel sounded out of breath, and Asher heard clanging noises. Lord knew what the man was bumping into this time. "Will you be home soon?"

"Are you leaving?" a male voice Asher didn't recognize said to Daniel in the background. "But I thought you were going to..." The phone rubbed against something, blocking out the rest of the sound, but Asher had heard enough. Daniel was with another man.

He should have known better. Who picks up someone in Vegas for anything more than a quick fuck? Not that he'd gotten a fuck out of Daniel. *Goddammit!* Asher felt like a fool. With his pride wounded, his already bad mood escalated. He threw his phone across the room and stomped into the bedroom, tearing off his shirt and then yanking his belt and pants open.

This was why he didn't bother with relationships. All the aggravation, all the effort, for what? To drain his balls? No need. Not for him. Some lucky bottom was going to have trouble sitting by the end of the night.

He was taking off his last sock when he heard the front door open.

"Ash?" Daniel's surprised voice filtered in from the front

room. "You're home?"

He didn't bother answering. It wasn't like he was going to be home for long. He stripped off the last sock and tossed it into the laundry basket. He usually showered before going out, but it wasn't necessary. In fact, shoving someone's face into his sweaty balls and making him lick them clean would be a good start to his night out.

"What happened to your—" Daniel stopped talking, and Asher heard him gasp.

He turned around to see Daniel standing in the doorway, raking his gaze over Asher's nude body. He was wearing mauve jeans, cut-off and cuffed just above the knee, a slim-fitting baseball T-shirt that looked like something he'd outgrown from his youth, pushed up past his elbows and hitting just above the waistline of his shorts. Although the clothes weren't falling off Daniel's body, which was a change, they still weren't what anybody would consider fashionable. They were old and washed out and...fuck it all to hell, why was Asher getting turned on just looking at the man?

Hiding an erection while he was naked was impossible, so his desire had to be obvious to Daniel, which just pissed Asher off even more. He squinted and crossed his arms over his broad chest. "Nice of you to make it," he said.

"Huh? I don't—"

Asher managed to drag his gaze away from Daniel's huge eyes and saw his phone in Daniel's hands. "What're you doing with my phone?" His nostrils flared as he stalked over to Daniel and ripped his phone out of the man's hands. "I'm not the one hiding things! You have no right to go through my things."

Goddammit! He closed his eyes and sucked in a deep breath. That sounded like an accusation. Nobody made accusations unless they gave a shit, and he wasn't going to give Daniel the satisfaction of knowing how much he'd gotten to him by lying, by not being home when Asher needed him.

"I didn't... I wasn't..." Daniel stammered. "It was on the floor and I was putting the battery back in. I wasn't snooping, honest."

"Like that means anything coming from you," Asher muttered under his breath. He put the phone down on his dresser and grasped the edges of the wood. His arms were stretched out, his head bowed, and he was having trouble calming his racing heart. Daniel's long fingers trailing over his shoulder was the last straw.

Asher snapped one hand out and gripped Daniel's wrist hard enough to leave a mark. He swung the man in front of him, pushed his ribcage against the dresser, and twisted his arm behind his back.

"Ash?" Daniel's voice was shaky, but quiet. "Are you okay? What's wrong?"

That sounded like concern, but Asher knew better. "I'm fine," he growled. "I just don't like being lied to."

"I wasn't lying. I didn't look in your phone." Daniel reached back with his free hand and stroked it over Asher's hip in a calming gesture.

"You weren't lying? Just like you weren't lying when you said you were home but you clearly weren't? Who were you with, Daniel?" he growled and moved Daniel's arm farther up his back, drawing out a whimper. Then he pressed his body against Daniel's. "And don't even think about lying to me again."

Daniel was panting and squirming. "Asher, you need to let go now." Asher didn't move an inch. "Look, I get that you're upset about something, and we're going to talk about it, but you need to let go because you're hurting me."

Asher was shaking with anger but he couldn't release his hold on Daniel, couldn't take the chance that he'd walk out on him and go back to whoever he'd been with that day. Couldn't take the chance that he'd lose him. "Who. Were. You. With." He was grinding his teeth so each word sounded like a growl.

"I was at Marc's house."

He knew it!

"Who the fuck is Marc?" he snapped. "And what the fuck were you doing there when you should have been here?" *When you should have been waiting for me. When I needed you.*

With all his wiggling and squirming, Daniel's shorts had started slipping, and Asher suddenly noticed that he wasn't wearing anything underneath. "Never mind," he hissed into Daniel's ear. "I know exactly what you were doing. Did it feel good, Daniel?"

"What're you—"

He didn't give Daniel a chance to finish speaking. Instead he shoved the man's shorts down past his hips and rubbed his groin against that tight ass. For the first time since he'd met Daniel, being close to him wasn't making Asher hard enough to pound nails. He circled his hips, hoping the friction would get him where he needed to be. It didn't. "Here I was being patient, giving you time. And it turns out all your talk of relationships was just a bunch of bullshit. I leave you alone for a few hours and you go out prowling for someone to fill your hole."

"Asher—"

"Tell me this, did he use a rubber or did you let him bareback you? I bet you get off on being a cum dump, don't you?" Asher moved his hand over Daniel's ass and wiggled his fingers into his crease, looking for the evidence of his betrayal, but a sharp elbow to the ribs took him off guard.

"Oomph!" The air pushed out of Asher's diaphragm, and he tried to suck in a breath. Before he could get himself together, Daniel had twisted around so they were face-to-face. He flipped his wrist and Asher lost his grip on it. Then Daniel pushed his hand up, folding Asher's wrist until his fingers touched his forearm. The resulting pain was so sharp that it dropped Asher to the ground. All of that happened in less than thirty seconds. Asher was reeling.

"I know this doesn't feel good and I want to let you go, but you need to tell me that you're going to calm down, because the first time you finger my ass, it's not going to be in the middle of a jealous rage." How Daniel could sound so calm when Asher felt like his head was going to explode was incomprehensible. "Are we clear?" Daniel added.

"You brought me to my knees," Asher said incredulously, looking up at the smaller man.

"I had to." Daniel cupped Asher's face with his left hand and loosened the grip he had with his right hand. "Otherwise you were going to do something you'd regret."

"I'm twice your size," Asher pointed out unnecessarily.

Daniel grinned. "I'm tougher than I look. Used to teach Taekwondo. Third-degree black belt. Now, are you relaxed enough to hold it together while we have a conversation?"

At that point, Asher knew he could get loose. Daniel had caught him off guard with that little self-defense move, but the man wasn't strong enough to keep Asher down for long. He shifted his weight so he tipped backward and landed on his ass. Then he grabbed Daniel's hip and pulled him down onto his lap. He expected Daniel to pull away, to be scared after the way Asher had been acting, but Daniel surprised him once again when he snuggled closer into his embrace and draped his arms over Asher's shoulders, looking perfectly at ease.

"Marc is your neighbor," he said. It took Asher a few seconds to catch up and realize Daniel was answering his earlier question. "He lives three doors down and he's a chef. I ran into him when I was going for a walk today, and he asked about yesterday's fire." Daniel's cheeks reddened. "I guess the smell traveled. Anyway, I told him what happened and he offered to teach me a few tricks. I was at his place putting the finishing touches on dinner when you called." Daniel smiled gently at Asher and traced his eyebrows with a long finger. "I figure if I can walk there without putting on shoes and we share the same roof, it counts as me being home. If I'd known you were here, I would have been more specific."

"How is it I've never met this neighbor?" Asher grumbled, not liking the sound of anybody teaching Daniel *tricks*.

Daniel's eyes twinkled. He dipped his head and skated his lips across Asher's jaw with a barely there touch. "He works nights, you work days. He's off tonight, which is the only reason he was able to help me this late. Any more questions?"

Yeah, Asher had more questions. He wanted to know if Marc was single, if he was good-looking, if he'd touched any part of Daniel that day. But adrenaline was no longer coursing through his body and he was mortified by what he'd said to Daniel, how he'd treated him.

"Fuck," he groaned and closed his eyes. "Did I hurt you?" He heard the catch in his voice, the regret overwhelming. He moved his hands over Daniel's arm gently, not wanting to be rough. "I'm sorry."

"I'm fine," Daniel assured him. "I know you weren't really going to hurt me, not that I'd have let you if you'd tried. But in the future, I'd appreciate it if you could, I don't know, maybe talk first and shoot later, yeah?"

Asher snapped his head back like he'd been slapped.

Damn, he'd been out of line. The things he'd said, the way he'd manhandled Daniel. So far out of line. And he wasn't nearly as sure as Daniel that he wouldn't have hurt him. He'd lost all semblance of control.

"I don't know why I said...what I said. I know you're not..." He couldn't bring himself to finish that sentence and repeat the words he'd thrown out in an attempt to hurt the man now curled on his lap as if it was the most natural place in the world for him to be.

"You were jealous," Daniel said matter-of-factly.

He opened his mouth to respond, but nothing came out. Really, what could he say? There was no denying it. "That's not an excuse," he finally said.

"No, it isn't," Daniel agreed.

Asher's heart sank. Fifteen minutes earlier, he'd been calling himself all kinds of stupid for thinking a relationship was a good idea, for asking Daniel to live with him. Hell, he'd been planning to find a stranger in a bar to fuck before coming home and throwing Daniel out of his apartment and out of his life. But the truth was, even when he was raging mad, he didn't really want Daniel to go. It was the last thing he wanted.

"Daniel, listen I..." Fucking hell, he had no idea how to finish that sentence. How do you call a man a cum dump, shove him against furniture, practically dislocate his shoulder, and then ask him to stay with you? That wasn't a scene. It wasn't sane or consensual. It was a fight. Even his mother's deadbeat boyfriends hadn't sunk low enough to use that kind of language when they'd roughed her up.

"I'm not bothered by jealous," Daniel told him. "But the arm twisting and the name calling—" He paused and looked straight into Asher's eyes. "That can't happen again."

Asher flinched in response to the mention of his transgressions, but he nodded in agreement.

Daniel's gaze softened. He leaned in close and whispered in Asher's ear, "You wanna know something weird?" He reached for Asher's hand and then moved it over to his exposed groin. "It turned me on," Daniel confessed. Sure enough. Asher held the proof in his hands. Smooth velvet over hard steel. He stroked Daniel's erection and trembled.

"Which part?" Asher's voice broke, arousal coursing through him, sudden and strong. He cleared his throat. "Which part turned you on?"

"When you... When you had me against the dresser and your whole body was covering mine. You're so strong." Daniel's eyes fluttered shut and he trembled. "I didn't like what you did with my arm. That hurt. And those things you said..." He shook his head. "But until then..." He sighed. "Felt like you wanted me so much you couldn't control yourself. God, yeah. Made me so hard."

Daniel enjoyed being held down, being made to submit. That was what he was saying. And that was something Asher sure as shit knew how to deliver. He trembled in anticipation. Holy fuck but did his day just look up.

CHAPTER 14

Asher bent forward, gently lowering Daniel's back to the floor. It wasn't his usual move. Normally, when he was going to fuck a guy, he bent him over the nearest flat surface, or pushed him against a wall, or had him get on all fours. He had better leverage that way; he could shove in harder, deeper, faster. But right then, he wanted...no, he needed, to see Daniel's face.

He planted a hand on either side of Daniel's head and looked into his eyes. Daniel grasped his wrists and met his gaze.

"Hey," Daniel said and grinned. "Whatcha doin'?"

Asher chuckled. Leave it to this man to lighten the mood. The tightness in his chest loosened, his muscles relaxed. "Well, I was thinking about doing you."

"Ohh," Daniel replied and wiggled, trying to get rid of the shorts that were bunched around his knees. "You have the best ideas."

Asher reached for the shorts and pushed them off. Then he scooted between Daniel's knees and stroked from his ankle over his calf, across his inner thigh, and around to his bare hip.

"Why aren't you wearing underwear?" Asher asked. He wasn't punch-a-hole-in-the-wall jealous anymore, but he still wanted to know.

"I ran out," Daniel explained. "I actually have a load of laundry going now. Does it bother you?"

He moved his palm over Daniel's belly and then cupped his balls, squeezing gently, rolling them. "It only bothers me if I'm not here to appreciate it and someone else is."

Daniel dropped his hands and visibly shivered in response to the possessive words. So fucking sexy. The man was heart-stopping lying on the ground, nude from the waist down, arms limp at his sides, legs spread around Asher, just waiting to be touched.

"I'll make you a deal," Daniel said. He smiled up at Asher and traced the curve of Asher's ear with his finger.

"What's that?"

"Well, I'll promise not to be naked around other guys if you do the same," Daniel said. He moved his hand to Asher's nape and rubbed it, still smiling, his eyes twinkling.

Asher looked at the happy man lying beneath him and realized it would be the easiest promise he'd ever made. "I'm in," he agreed.

"Well, not yet you're not, but I'm hoping we're about to get there." Daniel's tone was all camp, and he waggled his eyebrows as he spoke.

This was far and away different from any of Asher's past

fucks. It felt like they were playing, having fun together.

"Count on it, sugar," he said, moving his fingers from Daniel's balls over his perineum and then into his crease.

Daniel whimpered and tilted his hips up, giving Asher more room to play. Once again, Asher found himself out of his element. Fucking, he was used to, but this was not the type of foreplay that usually led up to the act. Whipping a guy's ass? Yeah. Fingering it? No, not so much.

Sometimes he'd plug a sub before he paddled him. Or he'd force him to finger himself while he sucked Asher's dick. But otherwise, Asher figured if they needed a little something in their hole before he got his dick in there, they'd take care of it before joining him. And if they didn't? Hell, it just meant a tighter fuck for him.

"Hey, did I lose you?" Daniel asked, snapping Asher out of his mental musings. "'Cause crashing after an orgasm is one thing, but I might get offended if I'm putting you to sleep *before* you get off."

Daniel was still smiling brightly, wiggling his ass against Asher's hand, stroking his neck, and Asher felt oddly light, like there was nothing for him to worry about or do but be with Daniel in that moment.

"You are so fuckin' cute," he said. Daniel pouted, scrunching his nose, making his freckles more pronounced. Asher burst out laughing. "Is that little expression intended to get me to change my mind? Because you're just driving my point home."

"At this point," Daniel drawled and arched one eyebrow, "your point is pressing against my belly. I'm pretty sure you can't drive it home from that angle."

"All right, that's it, sugar!" Asher curled his hands under Daniel's legs and grasped his ass, pulling the man up as he stood. "You're asking for it? Well, I'm going to give it to you." He walked over to the bed and tossed Daniel on it, laughing when he bounced and smiled. Asher crawled over him, curling a hand around each side of Daniel's waist and giving him a little tickle. Daniel giggled and then slapped his hand over his mouth, like the sound had escaped without his permission. Seriously, the guy was cute as fuck.

In his position, Daniel's hard cock was bobbing in front of Asher at eye level. It was just a bit darker than the rest of Daniel's skin, a little ruddy, smooth without many noticeable veins, topped by a perfect mushroom cap. Even the man's dick was adorable. Asher leaned down and swiped his tongue over that crown, enjoying the taste of Daniel's precum and no longer cataloging all the ways in which being with Daniel varied from his usual modus operandi.

"You have a pretty dick," he said, and then he sucked the head into his mouth.

"Mmm, damn, that's good." Daniel moaned. "It likes you too."

Asher popped off Daniel's cock and wrapped his hand around it, stroking gently. "Excellent. Because something tells me he and I are going to be spending a lot of time together from here on out."

Daniel laughed and Asher grinned up at him from between his knees.

"I have condoms and lube in the nightstand," he said.

Daniel twisted to the side, opened the drawer, and found the supplies. "Magnums, oooh. I'm a very lucky boy," he said.

Usually, Asher would have agreed with a statement like that. But in that moment, he felt like the lucky one. He ripped open a condom packet and suited up. When he was done, Daniel handed him the lube, so he drizzled some onto his palm. He was about to reach for his own dick, to get himself slick and then get himself buried in the tight ass in front of him. But then Daniel's earlier reaction to fingers playing with his ass popped into Asher's mind.

Daniel had seemed really into that, so Asher dipped his fingers into the lube, coating them, and then bent one of Daniel's legs up and out, leaving his trench completely exposed. He looked down at the man spread before him and couldn't hold back a deep moan.

Goddamn, Daniel had a fine fucking ass. He reached down to explore, no longer doing it just because Daniel had enjoyed it. Hell, Asher wanted to play with that tight ass just as much. He smoothed his fingers up and down the crease a few times and then rubbed the pink starburst, massaging and pressing lightly on it.

"Feels good, Ash," Daniel sighed at him. "Love having you touch me."

Asher bent down and pressed his lips to Daniel's, nibbling and licking as he continued massaging his entrance. "Turns out, I'm pretty fond of touching you myself," he mumbled into Daniel's mouth.

"Mmm, well, you can touch me anytime you want, for as long as you want." Daniel cupped the back of Asher's head and brought him even closer, opening his mouth and sucking on Asher's tongue, deepening the kiss. He dragged his calf up and down Asher's thigh and back, massaged Asher's nape, and rolled his hips in small circles, seemingly trying to get as much sensation as possible from the fingers Asher had pressed against his hole.

As turned on as Asher was, he didn't feel a huge rush to get inside the man beneath him. He was enjoying the touching, the kissing, the chatting. It was warm and relaxing, comfortable.

He moved his mouth away from Daniel's, kissed his way across the angular jaw to his ear, and took a minute to nibble and tug on his earlobe.

"Tickles," Daniel said with a quiet laugh. "But I like it."

Asher smiled against Daniel's neck, giving it a loud, smacking kiss, and then licked up his chin and back to his mouth. He lapped at Daniel's lips, expecting the man to open and resume their kissing. Damn, but did he enjoy kissing. But instead, Daniel darted his tongue out and flicked at his. Asher snorted in amusement but played along, licking Daniel's tongue in return.

Somewhere along the way, almost without thinking about it, Asher slipped one finger into Daniel's ass. As their tongues played, he moved his finger as far as he could into those warm depths and then pulled it back out. When he added a second finger, Daniel arched his back and slammed his mouth up at Asher's, sucking in Asher's tongue and whimpering.

Fuck, it was hot how much Daniel was enjoying that ass play. Asher slanted his mouth and returned the kiss, licking and sucking at Daniel's mouth as he increased the pace of his fingers' thrusts into his channel.

"I want you to put it in now." Daniel panted as he pulled away from the kiss. He licked at Asher's lips and gasped for air, continuing to roll his hips, continuing to encourage the action in his hole.

After a couple of failed attempts, Asher managed to snag the lube and slick up his erection, all without putting a stop to the messy kisses he was sharing with Daniel. He pulled his fingers out and lined his dick up.

"Ready?" he asked, for what might have been the first time in his life.

Daniel nodded. Their gazes locked together, and Asher was trapped, unable to look away as he slid his dick into Daniel. The farther he pushed, the faster Daniel breathed, until he was gasping for air and moaning almost continuously.

"Damn, Ash," Daniel said huskily. "You feel incredible inside me."

"Yes, I do," Asher agreed with a smirk.

Daniel beamed, smiling up at him. He twined his feet around Asher's torso, resting his heels on Asher's lower back and rocking up, trying to get Asher's cock deeper into his body. Asher planted his forearms over Daniel's shoulders, tangled his fingers in Daniel's hair, and rocked into him. He didn't look away, couldn't look away, from Daniel's smiling face.

They set up a rhythm, slow but good, their bodies moving together, their lips meeting for kiss after kiss. He could hear Daniel's sighs, his quiet moans melding with Asher's deeper grunts and groans. And it was good, so damn good, that Asher never wanted to stop.

But the friction on his dick, the scent of Daniel all around him, the vision of the man lying beneath him, all those things conspired to make the end game inevitable and Asher felt himself reaching the precipice.

"I'm close, Daniel," he warned. "Do you want to grab your dick?"

He would have taken Daniel in hand, but he didn't want to release his hold on the man's face. Their gazes were still fixed on each other, and the intimacy was heady and perfect.

"Don't need to." Daniel shook his head. "You can get me off like this."

"Yeah?" Asher was surprised. He'd never been with a guy who could come just from being fucked. Of course, he usually took them from behind. As he thought about it, he realized that in their current position, his stomach was constantly rubbing over Daniel's dick, so it was getting some attention. "Well, let's do it, sugar."

Daniel thrust his hips up as Asher pressed forward. They increased their speed, both of them grunting, until Daniel arched his neck and cried out Asher's name. Wet heat spraying between their bodies proved to be Asher's undoing. He pushed inside as deep as he could and stilled.

"Daniel!" he cried, looking into soulful brown eyes. "Daniel," he whispered. Then his orgasm took away the power of speech and he pulsed over and over into the tight body beneath him.

They lay together, both of them sucking in air, Asher combing his fingers through Daniel's hair, Daniel massaging Asher's nape. Eventually, Daniel lowered his legs, stretching them alongside Asher's body, and Asher pulled out, tying off the condom and dropping it to the floor before turning back to the man in his bed.

Looking sated, relaxed, and happy, Daniel gazed at him, eyes twinkling. He cupped Asher's cheek and leaned up, clearly wanting a kiss. And even with the sexual pressure released, Asher found he wanted to give it. He truly enjoyed kissing this man.

"Mmm," Daniel moaned as their lips met. "Thank you. That was fun."

And Asher had to agree. He didn't know sex could be like that. Light and warm at the same time. Passionate, but happy. They'd laughed together, smiled at each other, seen each other.

"Yeah," he agreed. "It was." He closed his eyes, took in a deep breath, and squeezed Daniel as tightly as he could. A thought suddenly occurred to him. "Did you say you used to teach Taekwondo?"

"Uh-huh," Daniel murmured. He kissed his way down Asher's neck and sternum, then over to his nipple. Then he licked around the areola and took the nub into his mouth, suckling gently.

Asher shuddered. Nobody had ever played with his nipples that way and he was surprised at how much he enjoyed it. Even though he couldn't get it up again, the feeling was arousing and relaxing in equal measures.

"When did you do that?" he asked, continuing their conversation.

"Umm, one of my mom's exes worked at a dojo in New York when I was a kid. I was pretty small, kinda flaming—" Daniel winked. "He said I needed to know how to protect myself, so he took me under his wing, let me sit in on all his classes. I kept up with it on my own after they broke up, but I didn't do it full time until I left Santa Fe. He had moved to Oregon and opened his own dojo, so I went there and worked for him. When I wasn't working, we were training. It was like full immersion, so..." Daniel shrugged as he let the thought trail off.

"And you're a third-degree black belt? That's what you

said, right?" Asher asked. Daniel nodded. "That's pretty impressive."

"It was fun for a while."

Asher rubbed circles on Daniel's back. "I can see how it would be. Why'd you stop?"

Another shrug. "I don't know. I guess it felt like I'd figured it out, you know? Like I'd done it so it was time to move on to something else." Daniel took in a deep breath and straightened his arms, holding himself above Asher. "Hey, you hungry?" he asked.

"Yeah, I am, actually. How about you feed me that dinner you made and we go at it again?"

Daniel laughed and patted Asher's ass. "Sounds like another good deal."

"So, what'd you make for me?" Asher asked as he walked into the great room. He had put on a pair of socks and sweatpants and he was pulling on a long-sleeved T-shirt.

"Pot roast with carrots on the side," Daniel answered. He was standing in the kitchen, scooping food out of a pot and onto plates. And he still wore only the long-sleeved baseball-style T-shirt he'd had on earlier. The shirt was short enough that his entire ass was exposed, and when he bent his leg to scratch his left calf with his right foot, Asher could see his balls swinging and a portion of his flaccid dick.

It would have come across as an attempt at seduction—not that anybody had ever tried to seduce Asher in that type of ensemble—but Asher moved his gaze from Daniel's ass to his face and noted that he was perfectly at ease, performing his task with no ulterior motive. Somehow seeing him in only the shirt was dirtier than if he had been completely naked. And if Asher hadn't shot his load minutes earlier, he was pretty sure he'd have bent Daniel over the counter and taken him right there.

"Is this enough or do you want more?" Daniel turned with a plate in his hand and held it out toward Asher, completely comfortable in his almost nudity.

The food looked and smelled delicious. The pretty dick swinging between Daniel's legs even better.

Asher walked over to Daniel and took the plate out of his hand. "This is great," he said. "You made it?"

"With very close supervision, yeah," Daniel said with a nod.

Before he could stop himself, Asher pressed his body to Daniel's, shot out his free hand, and cupped Daniel's package, holding it tight. "It better not have been too close," he rumbled.

Daniel ran his hands over Asher's chest. "You don't have anything to worry about." He inhaled deeply, like he was savoring Asher's scent, and then he trembled. "I don't cheat. Ever."

It wasn't that he didn't trust Daniel, it was that the more time he spent with the man, the more of him he saw, the more he got to know him, the more Asher realized how desirable Daniel was. And there was no way other people wouldn't notice. It was those other people that worried Asher. But after the fit he'd thrown an hour earlier, he figured he had used up his allotment of jealousy for the evening, so he kissed Daniel's forehead and sat at the table, ready to eat dinner.

CHAPTER 15

Coming home to find Asher in the midst of some sort of a jealousy-induced breakdown had made for an intense night. Plus, it had changed the order of Daniel's plans. He'd spent the day working with Marc on what he had thought would be a romantic dinner as a prelude to going to bed and having Asher top him for the first time. Instead, he was shoved against furniture and held down while Asher staked his claim, first with anger, then with passion. All before the salad course.

Not that Daniel was complaining. Being wanted desperately enough to make such a controlled person snap and manhandle him was much hotter than candlelight and soft music. Getting off by being overpowered was dangerous, Daniel realized. He'd only trusted a couple of guys in his life enough to leave himself that vulnerable. Unfortunately, neither of them had Asher's fierceness, his heat when they touched him. Or maybe they simply hadn't wanted him with the same intensity.

He rubbed the fingers of his left hand over his right wrist and felt a soreness that would probably last a couple of days.

Shivers racked his wiry frame as he remembered the look of frantic desire in Asher's eyes when they were in the bedroom and the tight grip of his big hands on Daniel's body.

"Daniel?" Asher's voice was hesitant, his eyebrows furrowed. "Are you okay?" He reached out and then stopped just short of Daniel's wrist, as if he wasn't sure of his welcome.

"I'm fine." Daniel flipped his hand palm up and moved it closer to Asher's, making the invitation clear. "Why?"

Asher ran his fingers over Daniel's palm from wrist to fingertips and back again, tender, barely there touches that left a trail of heat in their wake. "I'm sorry I lost control like that. I didn't mean to hurt you," he said mournfully.

Daniel closed his eyes and breathed deeply, relaxing under the gentle ministrations. "I'm fine, Ash, seriously. Like I said, I wouldn't have let you hurt me."

Asher scoffed, and Daniel's eyes fluttered open. He raised one side of his mouth in a wry grin.

"You don't believe me?" he asked.

"You got me with that move earlier, I'll give you that. But it was only because I was caught off guard."

Daniel decided it was pointless to argue about whether he could defend himself against Asher. He had a lot of experience winning matches against men just as big and with more training. But he didn't want to wound Asher's pride, so he decided to leave it alone. Besides, he didn't believe Asher would have hurt him when push came to shove. Not really.

"Well," he said quietly as he moved his arm down and

started mirroring Asher's gentle touches on his forearm. "Either way, I'm fine."

Asher moved his hand under Daniel's chin and tilted it up so their gazes met. "You sure?" he asked tenderly.

Intense emotion flooded through Daniel and the speed of his breaths increased. It was that gentle-rough dichotomy that did it for him in a big way. "Promise," he said thickly.

"Then why aren't you eating, sugar?" Asher asked. "This roast you made is really good."

"Oh." Daniel looked down at his full plate in surprise. "No reason. I just wasn't thinking about it."

"You weren't thinking about eating when we're sitting down for dinner and there's a full plate in front of you?" Asher asked skeptically. "Did you eat with Marc before I got home?" The last question came out in a harsh tone, and Asher winced after he said it.

Daniel chuckled. Yup, Asher was definitely the jealous type. It was sexy, and Daniel could feel his dick thickening against his thigh. "I didn't eat with Marc," he assured the big man.

Asher furrowed his brow and crossed his arms over his broad chest. "Late lunch? Giant breakfast?"

Suddenly Daniel felt like he was in the midst of a pop quiz and he had all the wrong answers. "Uh..." He picked up his fork and moved his food around the plate. Then he looked up at Asher from underneath his lashes and gave him an innocent smile. "I may have skipped those."

Asher rested his free hand on Daniel's thigh and then curled his fingers around it. "Daniel, you're too skinny to skip meals." He squeezed Daniel's leg and moved his hand up to his hip, across his belly, and over to his chest. "I can feel your ribs."

Damn, just that touch was enough to take him from a semi to a full-on erection. "I told you I get distracted," he panted. "And food's not big on my list of important things."

"Uh-huh, I can see that," Asher said. "Sounds like you need a keeper."

Daniel groaned. "Not sure how you expect me to eat when you say things like that." Asher continued caressing his chest, circling his nipple. "Or touch me like that," he groaned.

Asher leaned over until his mouth was inches from Daniel's ear. "Want me to stop?" he asked quietly, his breath hot on Daniel's ear.

Oh, God, he was so hard he ached. "N-n-no," Daniel stuttered. "Please don't stop." His fork slipped from his grasp.

Suddenly, the heat was gone. Asher had leaned back in his chair and moved both hands away. Daniel whimpered and looked at him, wide-eyed, trying to focus. "Why?"

Asher slowly moved his gaze from Daniel's face to his plate and back again. "You eat, I touch."

Why was that hot? Daniel whimpered and picked up his fork with shaky fingers, managing to scoop something onto it and put it in his mouth.

"Good boy," Asher whispered, scooting his chair right

next to Daniel's, leaning close once again. Daniel was sure he'd never been harder. "Keep going, sugar."

Asher squeezed Daniel's knee, caressed his inner thigh, ran fingertips over the crease where thigh met groin, cupped his sac, massaged his pecs, gently pinched his nipples. And the whole time, he kept his mouth close to Daniel's ear, nibbling on his lobe, licking the outer curve, whispering words of praise. "Such a good boy, Daniel. Love watching you obey."

How he managed to eat without breathing, Daniel couldn't say. But he didn't want those hot touches to stop. So he dragged his fork from plate to mouth, chewed and swallowed between whimpers and moans. He was in a daze, moving by rote memory through a fog of arousal and need so strong it made his lungs hurt and his balls tighten against his body. Before he knew it, the plate was empty.

Asher tangled his fingers in Daniel's hair and tugged him forward for a deep, all-consuming kiss. He tilted Daniel's head to the angle he wanted, put his hand on Daniel's jaw and forced it open, and then he bit at Daniel's lips before invading Daniel's mouth with his tongue, licking and penetrating with enough force to almost hurt, but in the best possible way.

Daniel keened. He gripped Asher's shoulders and climbed onto his lap, thrusting his exposed dick against Asher's belly. Early seed left him slick, and the contact felt so good he wanted to cry.

"Oh, God, Ash," he said when Asher pulled his mouth away and nibbled across Daniel's jaw. "Want you so much."

He couldn't stop rocking, needing the friction more than air.

Asher moved his left hand to Daniel's nipples, twisting each of them in turn. He cupped Daniel's ass in his right hand, pulling him forward, encouraging his motions. Then he dipped fingers into his crease, moved up and down, and circled the puckered skin of his entrance, giving a bit of pressure, but not penetrating.

Daniel arched his back, his head flew back, stretching his neck, and he grabbed his cock, stroking furiously as he shouted, "Oh, oh, oh! Put it in. P-p-please," he begged. "God, put it in. Put it in."

Asher shoved a finger into Daniel's hole, twisted it until he found his gland, and pressed down on it. That was the endgame. Daniel shot so hard his vision went black. The pleasure seemed to last forever, and he reveled in it.

When Daniel finally regained his focus, Asher had his pants open, dick out, and he was stroking himself with tight, hard pulls. He was grunting in moments, white cream streaming through his fingers and over his fist.

Daniel's balls ached in sympathy, trying to push out more fluid. "Oh, God," he said shakily, dropping his forehead to Asher's shoulder and rubbing his hands over Asher's chest, enjoying the feeling of all that thick hair. "How do you... That was... Oh, God."

"Yeah," Asher sighed. "I think that about covers it, sugar." He curled his big paw over Daniel's hand. "All right, I think it's safe to say that I'm going to need a shower." He grinned and looked down at Daniel's semen-covered hand. "Cum and chest hair aren't a comfortable combination."

Daniel blushed. Asher was meticulous about everything, cleanliness included. "Sorry," he said. "I wasn't thinking. I just like touching you."

Asher raised his cum-covered hand to Daniel's face and painted his jaw, nose, and finally his lips with sticky fingers, leaving a damp trail of his seed behind. "The feeling's mutual," he said in a husky voice.

A sharp feeling of arousal tightened in Daniel's belly. "Ungh," he moaned. "I can't get hard again, Ash. Jesus!"

"Is that a challenge?" Asher grinned wickedly, looking like a wild tiger who'd found his cage door unlocked.

Daniel's eyes widened. "Oh, shit."

Daniel woke the next morning to the feeling of firm lips trailing kisses up his spine, from the top of his ass to his nape.

"Morning, sugar," Asher's rough voice whispered in his ear. "How'd you sleep?"

He sighed and melted into the bed, finding just enough strength to open his eyes and meet Asher's gaze. "Slept great. When we weren't going at it."

It had been an amazing night—a sensual shower, followed by Asher pounding him into the mattress. They both passed out from exhaustion, but throughout the night one of them would wake and reach for the other, and then they'd join together again, kissing, touching, coming before falling asleep until the next round.

"Glad to hear it." Asher nuzzled his neck and nibbled on his ear. "I need to go into work, but I made you a protein shake."

Daniel raised one eyebrow and looked down toward Asher's groin. The man laughed. "Get your mind out of the gutter. I'm already dressed." He gestured toward the doorway. "It's in the fridge. Promise me you'll drink that first thing when you get up. I need to get some meat on your bones."

"Oh, you can bone me with your meat anytime," Daniel said, all camp. He chuckled for a minute and then he reached up for Asher's cheek and cupped it. "Seriously, though, thank you."

Asher turned his mouth into Daniel's hand and kissed it. "You're welcome. I'll see you tonight."

He snuggled into the blankets and fell back asleep for a few hours. He was up, showered, dressed, and had one hand on the door when he saw the note taped to it. Two words: Protein shake.

With a deep sigh, Daniel shuffled into the kitchen, swung the refrigerator open, and reached for the large glass waiting for him. He wasn't hungry, but he forced himself to chug it down before washing and drying the glass. Actually, it wasn't terrible. Chocolate and peanut butter.

He had planned to go back to the coffee shop that day, spend a bit more time on his computer. But as he looked around the apartment, he decided to do some shopping instead. He pulled out his phone and texted Asher while he walked out the door.

Thanks for the drink. Hope you're having a good day. Miss you.

Before Daniel reached the stairwell, his phone buzzed: *Miss you too, sugar.* He pulled on his baseball cap, slid his sunglasses on his face, and practically bounced out of the building. He couldn't remember the last time he'd felt so happy.

Asher had to go into work on Sunday morning, so Daniel took the opportunity to go for a run. He was walking out of the bedroom after his shower, wearing cut-off sweat shorts and running his fingers through his damp hair, when he saw Asher sitting at the end of the sofa, drinking a beer, and watching what sounded like a football game on the television.

"Hey!" he said happily. "That didn't take long."

Asher held his hand out in invitation. "False alarm. Ollie thought we'd lost a shirt he needs to use in a case, but it turned out the new guy working in the evidence room just couldn't find it. It's right where it's supposed to be, though, still sealed in the evidence bag, with the chain of custody intact."

Daniel straddled Asher's lap and wrapped his arms around his neck. "Bet that made Ollie's day." He leaned down for a few kisses, nuzzled Asher's neck, and then scooted onto the couch, lying across it with his head resting on Asher's lap.

"He's happy about the case, yeah. Hey, did you hear that they're postponing the wedding?"

"Again?" Daniel furrowed his brow. "This is the second time, right?"

"Uh-huh," Asher said with a nod. "They were supposed to get married three weeks after we got back from Vegas, then they pushed it ahead six weeks to next Saturday, but today Ollie said they're postponing again."

As he spoke, Asher buried his fingers in Daniel's hair and massaged his scalp. It felt so damn good that Daniel couldn't keep his eyes open.

He sighed, covered himself with the throw draped over the back of the couch, and wiggled closer to Asher's chest. The leather sofa stuck to his skin and he wished, not for the first time, that Asher had chosen suede instead. Once he was settled, he lifted Asher's shirt and kissed his stomach before pushing his hand between Asher's thighs.

"Did he say why they're postponing it?" he asked.

"Something about the wedding cake," Asher responded.

"Huh," Daniel said. "It's just a dozen or so people at their place, right? It can't be hard to find a cake. What's the problem?"

"Fuck if I know," Asher said with a shrug. He fingered the soft throw. "I don't remember this blanket."

Of course not. It was a wool knit in reds and purples. There hadn't been a single thing in Asher's apartment with those colors until Daniel moved in. The entire color palette seemed to have been inspired by zebras. Or prisons. Slowly but surely Daniel was rectifying that issue and adding some life into the spare space.

"I found it at a craft festival in the Mission on Thursday. I got the pillows there too," Daniel said, referring to the brightly colored pillows Asher was using to prop his arm up. "You like them?"

Asher looked at the pillows. "They're nice," he said. "And they look good with that lamp you picked up."

Daniel swallowed down his grin. He'd found the lamp at a flea market about a week after he'd started staying with Asher. It was raku with colors transitioning from red to green to blue to violet. The lampshade had faux marbling as a basecoat with checks around the top and bottom perimeter, a gold luster overlay, and beaded fringe trim. The whole piece was ornate, elaborate, and flamboyant. And it stuck out in Asher's apartment like a peacock in a penguin enclosure.

Though he hadn't said it in so many words, Daniel could tell Asher didn't like the lamp at first. But eventually he got used to it. And now, he'd sit in the armchair and turn the lamp on to read, leaving the ceiling lights off.

"Glad you're here, sugar," Asher said quietly, combing his fingers through Daniel's hair and relaxing into the couch. "You brighten the place up."

Asher kept petting Daniel—his hair, his cheek. He traced the curve of Daniel's ear, his eyebrow, his lips. Daniel sighed happily. They were quiet, the noise from the television the only sound in the room, until suddenly it was gone. Daniel blinked his eyes open and looked from the dark television to Asher. The man had a thoughtful expression on his face.

"Remember when we were in Vegas?" Asher asked. Apparently the question was rhetorical because he kept talking without waiting for an answer. "Your friend Chase said something to me." Asher looked down and met Daniel's eyes. "He said he knew your favorite position in bed."

"He did?" Daniel asked.

"Yeah. And I was just thinking that we've never talked about that."

Daniel shuddered and his breath came out faster. Asher leaned down and, with their faces upside down, somehow still managed to kiss him deeply, not pulling away until Daniel was breathless. "You love kissing, I know," Asher said, and then he pulled Daniel onto his lap and kissed him again, taking complete possession of his mouth. Eventually, he stopped and said, "Stand up."

Daniel trembled like a leaf, but he complied, climbing onto shaky legs. Asher put his thumbs in both sides of Daniel's shorts and pushed them down. His hard dick sprung up and Asher immediately wrapped his lips around it and drew him in. Hard to believe this man tried to tell him that he hadn't previously enjoyed giving blow jobs. Since that first time Asher had taken him into his mouth, he'd gone down on Daniel more times than he could count. And he always moaned as he did it, getting into the act as much as Daniel.

"Feels like you're about to fall over, sugar," Asher said with a self-satisfied smirk. "Lie down."

He tugged Daniel and lowered him back to the couch, arranging him so Daniel was lying across it, his head resting on the couch arm, one leg propped on the back, and the other flat on the floor. Then Asher dipped his face and started licking Daniel's dick like it was a Popsicle. He watched Daniel the entire time, his gaze never wavering, a sexy grin on his face.

"I know you like blow jobs," he eventually said, circling his tongue around Daniel's glans and then pulling it into his mouth with a strong suction before popping off.

"God!" Daniel gasped, arching off the couch.

"And I know you love it when I play with your hole." He slid his finger down Daniel's crease and circled his pucker. Daniel moaned and tilted his ass up, silently asking for more. "I've never known a man who liked ass play as much as you," Asher whispered. He bent down and took Daniel's balls into his mouth, sucking on them. "So then I started wondering. What would happen if I combined those two things?"

Before Daniel could process what that meant, Asher

took a cheek in each of his big hands and spread them, then he dipped his face and started licking his way up and down Daniel's cleft.

"Asher!" Daniel cried out, his hands grasping for purchase, his hips rolling up.

"Thought so." Asher chuckled. "Flip over," he commanded. Daniel scrambled to comply, rolling to his stomach and laying his arms flat by his sides. He spread his legs and Asher settled between them, pulled him open, and dove back in, flicking his tongue over Daniel's hole, then flattening it and licking across the puckered skin. "Fuckin' delicious," Asher said. "Gonna get you off this way."

Daniel keened, bending his knees, feet in the air. Asher wrapped his arms around Daniel's lower back and buried his face in his trench, sucking on his opening before pointing his tongue and pushing it inside, fucking him with it. Daniel fisted the edge of the couch cushion, bit into the arm, and rocked back against Asher's mouth, humping his cock against the leather.

He loved being rimmed, it was true, but he'd never had anyone eat his ass like this. He couldn't talk, couldn't think, hell, he couldn't even breathe. All his feelings centered on the pleasure in his ass. His gasps and moans turned into shouts until he was shaking and begging and damn near crying with need and then, suddenly, he was there. He arched, stretched his neck, squeezed his eyes shut and cried out Asher's name as he started coming all over the couch.

Before he was finished, Asher scrambled up, covering his body like a blanket and pushing his erection between Daniel's cheeks, rubbing off on him. His hot breath huffed against the side of Daniel's face as Asher whispered roughly into his ear. "Bet nobody ever did that for you before, right?" he asked while he slid his dick through Daniel's trench.

Daniel just shook his head—words were impossible when he couldn't yet take in enough air.

"That's right," Asher continued. "Only I can make you feel that way. You know why?"

Daniel shook his head again.

"Because I take care of what's mine. And you're mine, aren't you, sugar?"

Daniel nodded and blinked tears away, the intensity of the moment shattering him.

"Say it," Asher demanded. "Say you're mine."

Daniel swallowed hard. "I'm yours," he whispered hoarsely.

Asher stilled, called out his name, and came.

CHAPTER 16

Asher walked into the apartment and all the tension drained from his body. The overhead lights were off and the room was bathed in a warm glow from candlelight. Daniel had a thing for candles, something Asher figured out after he started noticing them popping up on various surfaces: the bathroom counter next to a ceramic bowl Daniel bought that was just the right size to hold Asher's watch and wallet; the dresser and nightstands in the bedroom; on top of mismatched antique candlesticks in various heights; in the kitchen, between the stove and a stoneware vase Daniel used to hold an assortment of wooden spoons and spatulas he used for cooking; on a round teak table Daniel bought and put next to the sofa.

The candles were different sizes, shapes, and colors, but somehow their scents all worked together without being overpowering so when Daniel lit them, their apartment smelled like cinnamon and lavender and vanilla. Not something he would have thought he'd enjoy, but it had grown on him and now he looked forward to the welcoming scent at the end of the day.

He was about to call out to Daniel when he heard him crooning in the kitchen. Asher froze. He had heard the other man sing several times, but never when Daniel realized he was listening. Whenever Asher heard Daniel's warm, soothing voice, he'd walk into the room quietly and watch his fill. The singing always went with dancing and Daniel was sexy as hell when he moved to music. It didn't hurt that he usually sang in the shower. Naked, wet, and gyrating Daniel—nothing better.

This time, Daniel was in the kitchen, slicing bread, shaking his ass in his always baggy jeans, and humming a tune Asher didn't recognize, sprinkling in words every so often. Asher leaned his forearm against the doorframe and crossed his left ankle over his right. When Daniel swayed over to the refrigerator, he noticed Asher and jumped.

"Ash!" he shouted. "You startled me. When did you get home? And why are you lurking like that?"

"I wasn't lurking," Asher said with a leer. "I was enjoying the view."

"Well, announce yourself or something next time. You almost gave me a heart attack." Daniel wiped his hands on his jeans and walked toward Asher. They met in the middle of the kitchen and Daniel slipped into Asher's arms. "Hey, you," he whispered as he tilted his face up expectantly.

What had once been uncomfortable now came naturally to Asher. He dipped down and pressed his lips to Daniel's, kissing him tenderly, tugging that full bottom lip between both of his, and then kissing him again. Eventually, he straightened and looked around the kitchen.

There were bowls everywhere, the sink was full, and he counted three spoons dripping who knew what on their counter. He took a deep breath, counted to ten in his head, and then spoke. "So, what's for dinner?"

"Umm, let's see—" Daniel darted his eyes around. He looked nervous. "Braised chicken with a mole sauce, a butter lettuce, jicama, black bean, and corn salad, and corn tortillas."

"All this mess for chicken and salad?" Asher asked, raising one eyebrow in surprise.

"Chicken and salad?" The pitch of Daniel's voice got higher and his eyes burned, though not with arousal. "Do you know how long it takes to make mole?"

"Uh, I don't—"

"Two days. There are, like, two dozen ingredients in it. Plus there was the chicken itself. Cutting up the vegetables for the salad. Making this dressing, which has lime and cilantro and cumin." He stopped and shook his head. "Gave Marc a nice laugh when I mispronounced that one. And he was working today, so other than getting recipe tips earlier this week and calling him a couple of times today, I was pretty much on my own and I'm still getting the hang of this." Daniel waved his hands around as he spoke, his voice getting louder. "And, just so you know, when someone makes you dinner, you're supposed to thank them, not chastise them."

"Chastise?" Asher repeated.

"Yeah, you know, like I'm a kid who just got caught doing something wrong and you're my dad. When you look at me like that, I feel like I'm about to get grounded or get a spanking or something."

Asher didn't respond to the accusation. He couldn't. Every ounce of mental power he had was stuck on the word spanking.

In reaction to Asher's silence, Daniel hunched his shoulders together and sighed. "You go get changed and I'll clean up. Okay?"

The disappointment pouring off Daniel snapped Asher out of his trance. "Hey." He tilted Daniel's chin up so their gazes met. "I didn't mean anything by that comment. I like that you're learning how to cook and I know you always clean up after. Hell, you keep everything in the place looking nice. But..." Asher paused and grasped Daniel's ass, squeezing and massaging it. "I'd love to spank you, sugar. Fuckin' love it." His voice sounded rough and husky to his own ears.

Daniel stilled and blinked rapidly. He seemed to be taken off guard by Asher's proclamation.

"You've said that before," he said slowly. "In Vegas. I think you were drunk."

"I might have been," Asher confessed, and then he chuckled. "That trip was hell on my liver. But being drunk had nothing to do with me wanting to warm your ass, sugar. I meant it then and I mean it now."

"Why? Why would you want to hurt me?" Daniel asked,

his tone earnest.

It was a fair question. With some guys, pain was the goal. But that was because it was *their* goal. They got off on it. Daniel didn't, Asher realized. But that didn't mean he wouldn't enjoy being put over Asher's knee. The man wasn't into pain, but he got off on being held down, being controlled. Nothing unraveled Daniel as quickly as the times when Asher pinned his wrists to the bed and thrust deep inside him.

"Not hurt," Asher clarified. "Spank. It isn't the same thing." He nibbled his way across Daniel's jaw to his ear and grasped his ass with both hands, squeezing hard. "We both know how much you enjoy ass play. You go wild when I go near your backside. You'll love this."

Daniel gulped. "And if I don't?" he choked out.

"Then we'll stop. But that won't be an issue. Trust me." He massaged Daniel's cheeks as he spoke.

"I do, you know? Trust you, I mean."

Those big brown eyes were wide and adoring as Daniel gazed at him. Asher swallowed down the lump in his throat and nodded. Being turned on in reaction to the plans they'd just made was to be expected, but he found himself feeling something different. His heart ached, like it was too big for his chest, and his breath hitched.

"I know," he said. He twined his fingers with Daniel's. "And I won't let you down."

Daniel blushed. "So, uh, what do we do? I mean, do you want to...now? Or, uh..."

Once again, Daniel had found a way to bring a smile to Asher's face. He was so adorably nervous about a simple spanking, something most subs just took as their due. Whether with a hand or a tool, whether on their asses, their legs, or their backs, they always expected the sensation. It was one of the main reasons they wanted to have a scene with a Dom, with Asher.

"Right now I'm going to get out of my work clothes. Then we're going to eat dinner. I'll know when the time is right to warm your sweet ass. That's not something you need to think about." He rubbed his hand over that pert ass. "Don't I always take care of you, sugar?"

He asked the question, but he already knew the answer. He'd given Daniel everything he needed—he paid for their home, he kept Daniel safe, he made sure the man ate, and the way Daniel cried out his name every night, and lots of mornings, as he spilled his seed left no question about the fact that Asher did it for him in bed. So, yeah, Asher knew he was taking care of Daniel.

"That was actually good," Asher said as he pushed his empty plate forward and leaned back in his chair, stretching his long legs underneath the table.

Daniel shook his head and grinned. "Gee, thanks. You

really know how to flatter a guy."

That was a compliment, wasn't it? He hadn't said the food was bad. Plus, he'd eaten his entire portion, which was more than Daniel could say. Hell, Asher had gone for seconds. All right, so maybe he could have been more appreciative of the meal.

"I meant it, sugar. It was probably the best mole I've had, and I grew up with a Mexican grandmother who used to make it on special occasions."

"I know." Daniel moved the food around on his plate. "You told me how much you liked going to her house for Sunday dinners, so I thought I'd learn how to make mole and some other Mexican dishes. Marc has recipes, and I found a couple of websites and a farmer's market where they sell fresh tomatillos and..." Daniel huffed out a breath and raised his gaze to meet Asher's. "You really liked it?"

He didn't remember telling Daniel about his grandmother's mole, but clearly the story was meaningful to Daniel. Damn, but it warmed him to know that Daniel was trying to please him. He reached for the man's hand and looked at his plate.

"Why aren't you eating?" he asked.

"I'm eating," Daniel refuted.

"You've eaten six pieces of jicama, four pieces of lettuce, and one bite of chicken." He crossed his arms over his chest and raised an eyebrow, quietly challenging Daniel to dispute his statement.

Daniel's jaw dropped open. "You counted my food intake?"

"I did. It's the only way for me to make sure you eat enough to function. Your trick of cutting everything up and moving it around on your plate isn't going to work anymore."

"I don't do that!" Daniel said incredulously.

"Oh, yeah, you do, sugar." Asher chuckled. "I've been watching you."

"It's not on purpose. You're gone all day and I'm excited to see you when you get home, and then we start talking and I like looking at you and..." He sighed and his skin flushed. "I get distracted, I guess."

Not that he didn't like being distracting to Daniel, but the man needed to eat. He was still way too thin. And the protein shakes Asher made for him every morning weren't enough to cut it as an entire day's caloric intake.

Asher pushed his chair back and patted his thick, muscular thighs. "C'mere," he said.

Daniel darted his gaze from Asher's lap to his face, his question clear from his expression.

"You want me to..." He furrowed his brow.

Asher reached a long arm out, curled his fingers around Daniel's bicep, and tugged him over. Daniel followed the motion easily, standing up from his chair and stepping up to Asher's. With a hand on each of Daniel's hips, Asher urged him down until he was sitting on Asher's lap. Then he pulled Daniel's plate over, forked a piece of chicken, and held it up to Daniel's mouth.

Daniel blushed and squirmed, but he opened his mouth and closed his lips over the food once Asher put it on his tongue.

"Good," Asher said encouragingly.

He put more food on the fork and repeated his steps, not stopping until Daniel's plate was empty. Neither of them spoke, and Asher found the moment unexpectedly intimate. He was holding Daniel, feeding him, meeting his needs on a fundamental level. There was something undeniably erotic about it. A quick glance down to where Daniel's jeans pulled across his groin let Asher know he wasn't the only one aroused by the interaction.

"See?" Asher's deep voice was husky. "You were hungry."

Daniel swallowed thickly. His eyes were wide, pupils dilated. The man looked like sex incarnate. Asher kept his gaze locked with Daniel's and reached for the button on his jeans, easily unfastening them.

"Up," he whispered.

It took a few moments, but eventually a dazed-looking Daniel rose to his feet. Asher pushed his jeans and boxers down until they dropped to his ankles. Then he spread his thighs and tugged at Daniel's hip, urging him forward. Daniel's clothes dropped to the floor as he lay facedown across Asher's lap.

He reverently caressed Daniel's firm, pale ass, appreciating the display. The soft sweats Asher wore were thin enough to allow him to feel Daniel's body heat, and he could hear Daniel's breath huff out in quick bursts, whether from arousal or nerves, he wasn't sure. He suspected it was a bit of both.

It had been some time since he'd held a man during a spanking. Usually, Asher forced them to bend over a bench or he'd cuff them to chains hanging from the ceiling in one of the rooms in the club. That allowed him to have more room to extend his arm. Plus, he rarely used his hand, preferring a paddle because it allowed him to strike for longer. So, in some ways, he was as unfamiliar with the current scene as Daniel.

Unfamiliar or not, Asher wanted this, had thought of it almost every time he watched Daniel's ass sway as he walked over the past five months. And with that thought in mind, he raised his hand and brought it down onto Daniel's skin with a loud clap. Though Daniel didn't pull away, he whimpered. Asher paused. That wasn't an aroused sound, he decided, so he reduced the power of his smacks, moving from one side of Daniel's ass to the other, bringing a rosy glow to his fair cheeks but not hitting hard enough to hurt.

"Feel good?" he asked when Daniel moaned.

Though the man didn't answer with words, his body's reaction made the answer clear. Daniel tilted his ass and moved toward Asher's hand as Asher continued to rain swats over his skin. It wasn't long before Daniel's backside was red and hot to the touch. Though the slaps had been light, they'd been at it for some time, and Asher knew Daniel would be feeling sore later. It was time to stop.

"You did so well, sugar," Asher crooned as he gently rubbed circles over that smooth, fiery skin. "So hot like this." The skinny body in his lap went limp in response to the praise.

This was usually the part of a scene when Asher got off. He'd yank out his dick and slam it into the sub's mouth or his ass and then pull out just in time to coat the willing body with his release. But though he was hard, Asher didn't want to fuck Daniel in that moment. He just wanted to hold him.

"Come up here," he said encouragingly.

When Daniel sighed, but didn't move, Asher bent down, rolled him onto his back, and cradled him in his arms.

Daniel lolled his head to the side and blinked up at Asher. "What're you doing?" he asked, his words sounding slow and slurred.

"Taking you to the bedroom." He smiled fondly at the man in his arms, naked from the waist down, dick hard, skin flushed, eyes heavy-lidded. Daniel was an enticing combination of adorable as hell and sexy as sin.

"Mmm 'kay," Daniel sighed. He turned his face into Asher's chest, burrowing close. Then he pushed his hand under Asher's shirt and moved his fingers over Asher's chest hair.

When they got to the bedroom, Asher climbed onto the bed and lay down on his back. Daniel stayed curled on top of him, his breathing heavy, but slow. Asher combed his fingers through Daniel's hair, smoothed his hand down the man's back, and enjoyed the quiet as they lay together.

"I... I didn't know it'd be like that," Daniel said eventually.

Neither did Asher. That wasn't a scene, at least not like any Asher had experienced. He supposed it was a spanking, technically speaking, but it had nothing other than a base similarity to the act as Asher had known it before that day.

"It's not always like that," Asher answered honestly, not wanting to lie to Daniel about something he hoped they'd continue to do.

Daniel folded his arms across Asher's chest and raised his head, propping his chin on his forearms. "What's it usually like?" he asked as he wiggled a little, seemingly trying to find a comfortable spot. "Is it more, uh, intense? Like how it was at the beginning?"

The beginning was when Asher had slapped with strength, which had ended after he'd heard one pained whimper. Some badass Dom he was turning out to be.

"Harder, yeah," he said. "But..." He thought about what they'd just shared, looked at the man in his arms, and felt his chest tighten and his breath stutter. "Not more intense."

If anything, having Daniel lie across his lap and trust him with a light spanking had been more passionate, more intimate, more emotional than any whipping or caning he'd dished out. It didn't make sense, like so many things having to do with Daniel. But it felt good. Asher always felt good when he was with Daniel.

He squeezed the man in his arms tightly, then cupped his nape and tugged his face down for a kiss. It was loving, tender, and so perfect that Asher didn't want to stop, even though it meant waiting a little longer to take care of his hard-on.

A spanking. He'd lain across Asher's lap and let the man spank him. And he'd liked it. Daniel closed his eyes and shuddered with the remembered feelings. It hurt at first, but then Asher changed something and the pain became something good, like the feeling he got when Asher twisted his nipples. So it hurt, yeah, but it felt fucking fine too. Made his dick hard, made his balls ache. Almost enough to make him come if it'd gone on a little longer.

"Ash," he whimpered, pushing Asher's shirt up, trying to get to skin.

Asher looked at him and seemingly saw his need because his gaze suddenly burned. He yanked Daniel's shirt off, then his own. Daniel propped himself up on one elbow and leaned over Asher, who was on his back. He moved his hand from Asher's knee across his thigh, then over his hard dick to his stomach. Asher was just as busy, tweaking Daniel's nipples, skimming over his ribs, massaging his hip. Their mouths moved together, lips tugging, tongues licking. Then Asher lapped at Daniel's lower lip and Daniel started sucking on his tongue, moving his mouth up and down like he was sucking on a dick.

Somewhere along the way, Asher dropped his pants and spread his legs, leaving room for Daniel between them. He knelt between Asher's knees and planted his elbows beside Asher's head, caressing the sides of his face as he dipped down for more kisses. They rocked together, cocks sliding, tongues twisting, Daniel holding onto Asher's face, Asher gripping Daniel's sore ass and squeezing it hard enough to make Daniel gasp.

"Want you," Daniel panted.

Asher put one hand on his back and the other on his ass and flipped them over so Daniel was flat on his stomach with Asher draped across his back. He reached for the lube and slicked his cock, then massaged Daniel's pucker. "Ready?" he whispered into Daniel's ear.

"God, yes," Daniel responded. He lay flat on his stomach and spread his thighs. Asher straddled him, one hand parting Daniel's ass cheeks, the other holding onto his own cock as he pressed it against Daniel's opening and pushed inside. "Asher!" Daniel shouted, reveling in the feeling of skin against skin. They'd gotten tested a month earlier, and he swore he'd been walking around with Asher's cum inside him since that day. The man couldn't seem to get enough, which Daniel loved.

"Good?" Asher asked as he pushed his dick in until his balls cradled Daniel's ass before dragging it out and shoving back inside again.

Daniel couldn't answer. He was biting on the sheet, scraping his hands over it while Asher hovered above him, knees on the outside of Daniel's thighs, hands next to Daniel's chest. He rocked back and forth, using all his strength to pummel Daniel's channel.

"Uh, uh, uh," Daniel grunted.

"Fuck, yeah," Asher responded. He dropped his chest down onto Daniel's back, gripped his arms, and licked his nape as he quickened the pace of his thrusts. "You're so tight. Love this. Gonna fuckin' breed you, sugar."

Hot breath panted over Daniel's neck, the motion of Asher's thrusts had him rocking on the bed, humping the sheets almost hard enough to hurt, and Asher kept him completely immobile, pinned beneath that big body.

"Close," Daniel gasped. "Close."

Asher shoved his arm under Daniel's waist. He got to his knees and pulled Daniel up with him, never severing the connection of their bodies. When they were both kneeling, he wrapped one arm around Daniel's chest and grabbed his dick with the other, stroking in time with his animalistic thrusts, pushing his hard dick into Daniel's tight channel and pegging his gland over and over again.

"Can't... Gonna... Ash..." Daniel mumbled incoherently.

"Do it." Asher grunted. "Fucking come on and do it." He

slammed into Daniel's ass hard enough to make his teeth clack. "Shoot!"

With a desperate cry, Daniel did just that, spraying seed across the bed, shaking, tears running down his face. Asher joined him seconds later, rubbing his groin against Daniel's ass and pulsing deep inside him.

"Damn," Asher said. "Just damn." He kissed Daniel's shoulder and held onto him as he collapsed on his side.

Daniel sighed and pushed back into the curve of Asher's body, enjoying the feeling of hot, sweaty skin. He tightened his ass muscles and squeezed Asher's softening cock.

Asher chuckled. "Having fun?" he asked.

Daniel looked back over his shoulder and Asher met him for a kiss.

"Just playing with my favorite toy."

"Well, your favorite toy needs to recharge for a bit. How about a bath? I think we could both use a little soap right now."

"Not sure I can stand," Daniel said. "You melted me."

Asher chuckled. "Well, since it's my fault, I guess I'll have to carry you."

He scooted off the bed and dragged Daniel with him, then put one hand under Daniel's knees and the other under his neck and picked him up, carrying him into the bathroom. Daniel played with his chest hair.

"Love how strong you are," he said. He really did. It was a major turn-on. All those muscles, the big body, strong enough to overpower him, hold him down, make him stay.

Asher sat him on the closed toilet, turned on the water, and poured shampoo under the tap. He looked back over his shoulder and waggled his eyebrows at Daniel. "Bubbles," he said. Then he slid into the tub and held his arms open for Daniel.

Daniel lit the candles he had scattered on the counter, turned off the lights, and settled between Asher's spread legs, resting his head on Asher's chest. He moved his hands over Asher's knees while Asher caressed his chest and stomach.

"So," Daniel eventually said.

"So," Asher responded.

"That was a spanking?"

Asher chuckled. "Yup."

"I liked it," Daniel whispered.

"I'm glad," Asher said. He took a deep breath and squeezed Daniel tightly. "I like you, sugar. A lot."

CHAPTER 17

"What're you doing tonight? Wanna go get a beer?" Oliver asked Asher.

"You've been working late nights all week and now you want to go out? Don't you want to go spend some time with Shirley? I'd think there would be a million things you need to do for the wedding this weekend."

"Nah, Shirley has all the wedding shit under control. Unless we end up postponing it again." Oliver gave one of his should-be-patented-with-as-often-as-he-used-them shrugs. "So what do you say?"

"Yeah, okay," Asher agreed. Oliver had seemed off lately, a little down, and the mention of yet another delay of the ceremony didn't sound good, so Asher figured he could spare an hour to keep him company.

"Cool. Hey, I'll call Danny and have him meet us at Rusty's Grill. They make a good burger."

And just like that, a beer had morphed into dinner. Oliver already had his phone out, so Asher didn't bother trying to argue. He nodded. "All right. I just need"—he looked at the report he'd been working on—"fifteen and then I can take off, okay?"

"Perfect," Oliver said. "I'll go shut down and get my jacket." Then Daniel must have answered the phone because Oliver started talking to him as he walked out of the office.

Rusty's was right around the corner from the precinct, so Asher and Oliver got there before Daniel. They ordered their beers and settled into a booth.

"Things still good with you and Danny?" Oliver asked. For the hundredth time.

Asher thought about waking up that morning with Daniel tucked into his side, an arm wrapped around his chest, a leg flopped over Asher's hip. Asher had a king-size bed, but Daniel always slept right up against him, partially on top of him, like he couldn't get close enough.

When Asher started sliding out of bed, Daniel had taken hold of his dick, scooted down the bed, and in his half-asleep state still managed to blow Asher's mind by blowing his dick. It was a very satisfying wake-up call, and not at all unusual now that he had Daniel living with him. The man seemed to wake up horny, so Asher had the pleasure of starting his day with a Daniel-induced orgasm most mornings. Morning sex was great. He hadn't ever realized how much he was missing by fucking guys at clubs and going home alone.

"Yeah," he answered Oliver. "Things are good."

"Hey, that's sick, man," Oliver scowled at him. "He's my kid brother."

"He's the farthest thing possible from a kid. And I just

said things are good. How's that sick?"

"It's the *way* you said it." Oliver shuddered. "I can only imagine what you were thinking."

"Well, quit fuckin' imagining my sex life, then. That's a surefire way to make both of us uncomfortable."

"Agreed." Oliver picked up his beer and clinked his glass against Asher's as confirmation of their promise.

Out of the corner of his eye, Asher noticed Daniel walking up. He put his drink down and smiled.

"Hey!" Daniel said happily as he approached their table. He leaned over Oliver and gave him a hug and then sat next to Asher, completely ignoring any social norms about personal space, and tucked himself into Asher's side. And, as if that wasn't enough contact, he squeezed Asher's knee and then rubbed his hand up and down his thigh.

"Hi," Asher said, pushing Daniel's unruly hair out of his face. When Daniel tilted his chin up, Asher bent down and kissed him. "How was your day? Did you..." He decided not to ask about Daniel's job search, because so far it seemed nonexistent. Not that Asher minded. It meant Daniel was always around when he called and when he wasn't working. Plus, there was always food waiting for him when he got home and he looked forward to seeing whatever new change Daniel had made in the apartment.

Asher figured that as long as he could afford it, he enjoyed taking care of Daniel. Though, surprisingly, having the man live with him hadn't impacted his wallet. Probably because Daniel never asked him for money. He still refused to let Asher buy him any clothes, but the groceries and the accessories he bought for the apartment had to be adding up. He needed to talk with Daniel about letting him pay for things rather than buying them on credit or using up all of his savings. But he didn't want to embarrass him, so he wouldn't do it in front of Oliver.

"What'd you do today?" he asked instead.

"I went to that farmer's market," Daniel answered. "And spent some time at that coffee shop on the corner, playing around on my computer." He looked at his brother. "Is Shirley joining us, Ollie?"

"Nah." Oliver shook his head. Asher expected him to leave it at that, like he usually did when the topic of his fiancée came up. But apparently the rules of engagement were different where his brother was involved, because Oliver kept talking to Daniel. "She's all pissed at me."

"What happened?" Daniel folded his arms on the table and leaned forward. Asher immediately missed the warmth of Daniel's hand touching him.

"Apparently the gift I got her for her birthday wasn't good enough," Oliver said drolly.

"Hey, at least you remembered her birthday," Asher said in support. "That's better than you did with your ex."

True story. Oliver had been married to one ex-wife for five years, and if Asher remembered correctly, he had missed every single birthday during that time.

"I said the same thing!" Oliver answered excitedly. "But it just pissed her off even more." He sighed loudly. "Whatever."

"What'd you get her?" Daniel asked.

"A gift certificate to a little clothing store she likes."

"Oh." Daniel frowned. "Why is she mad? That sounds nice."

"Yeah, I thought so too. But Burning Wrath and Indignation is going to be in town on Thursday, and that's her favorite band. I guess I was supposed to get tickets for us. The thing is, we've been busy planning the wedding, and she told me about the show so long ago that by the time they went on sale, I forgot. Now they're all sold out and even shitty tickets are over five hundred a piece from scalpers." Oliver shook his head. "That's just not going to happen."

Asher didn't mention the fact that, to his knowledge, Oliver had had zero involvement in the wedding planning. Nor did he bring up the calendar feature on Oliver's Blackberry... the same calendar Oliver dutifully used to remember every single work meeting.

"Oh," Daniel said, his voice sounding strained for no apparent reason. He looked down at the table and started picking at his napkin, tearing small pieces off, twisting it and then straightening it, and never raising his eyes. "But, well, uh," he stammered. "At least she can go shopping, right? Maybe if you take her to that store where you got the gift card she'll forget about the concert."

Asher straightened in his seat and stopped going over

the list of reasons why Oliver's excuses made no sense. He furrowed his brow and looked at Daniel. The man was acting strange—agitated, shaky, nervous. Like a perp who was hiding something. But he had seemed fine just minutes earlier.

"I tried that, but she refused to step foot in the store. I've never seen her so pissed," Oliver said.

Daniel blanched in reaction to Oliver's words.

What the hell? Asher wrapped his hand around Daniel's neck and gave him a little squeeze. He was about to ask him what was going on when Oliver threw down the gauntlet.

"Hey, maybe I can stay with you guys tonight."

Asher jerked his head away from Daniel and glared at Oliver. "We have a one-bedroom," he reminded the man who'd been to their apartment dozens of times.

"I know. I know. The couch is fine. And it won't be for long. I'm sure she'll calm down in a few days."

"A few days!" Asher shouted more than asked.

"You won't even know I'm there," Oliver wheedled. "I'm at work all the time anyway."

"Shouldn't you go home and apologize and, I don't know," Asher said sarcastically, "work this out?"

"She'll calm down," Oliver assured him. "Six days, tops. I mean, we have the wedding on Sunday so she has to talk to me by then."

"Six days!" Asher was definitely shouting this time.

"Max," Oliver said. "Unless she postpones the wedding

again, and then it might be a little longer."

"If she's that upset, I, uh," Daniel said quietly, the difference in volume between his voice and the previous decibel level at the table startling. "I think I can probably get you tickets."

Oliver's jaw dropped. "Seriously? How? Because, oh, man, Danny, that would be great."

"Where're you going to get tickets?" Asher asked.

"I, uh, know some guys," Daniel answered cryptically. "Let me just send them a text, okay?"

He got his phone out and typed. When he was done, he dropped it back into his pocket.

"What'd they say?" Oliver asked, seemingly having no idea how texts worked.

"Daniel just wrote them, man. They haven't had a chance to respond yet," Asher said, explaining the obvious.

"When are they going to tell us if we can have the tickets?" Oliver asked, channeling a five-year-old. Who thought people could predict the future.

Asher rolled his eyes, refusing to continue engaging in the conversation. Daniel reached his hand out and patted Oliver's.

"One of them'll text back soon. I'm sure it'll be fine. Don't worry."

Sure enough, Daniel's phone buzzed. He took it out, looked at the screen, grimaced, and then seemed resigned as he typed a few words before putting it back in his pocket.

"What'd they say?" Oliver prodded. "They said no, right? I mean, you don't look happy so...it's okay, thanks for trying." He slumped in his seat dejectedly.

"We've got the tickets," Daniel said, which surprised both Oliver and Asher given Daniel's expression when he received the text from his friend. Daniel turned to Asher. "Hey, uh, how do you feel about Burning Wrath and Indignation? Because to get the tickets for Ollie and Shirley, I need to go and I have a ticket for you too, if you don't mind joining us."

"Mind going to a BWI concert?" Asher asked incredulously. "Uh, I think I'll find a way to power through for you, sugar," he said sarcastically. Then he chuckled and tugged Daniel into his arms for a hug. "Why are you all pouty? I know how much you love music, and BWI's a great band. You can't hate them that much."

"No, it's not that. I really like BWI. It's just"—Daniel darted his gaze over to Oliver, who was looking at them— "uh, it's nothing," he concluded quietly.

It wasn't nothing. That much was obvious to Asher. But it looked like Daniel didn't want to talk about whatever was bothering him in front of his brother. Speaking of Daniel's brother...

"Hey, Ollie," Asher said gruffly. "Don't you want to call Shirley to let her know the good news?"

"Oh, right!" Oliver said, as if this was a novel idea. "She'll be so happy." He got out his phone and started tapping at the keys.

"You're texting this information to her?" Asher asked incredulously. "Why don't you call?"

Oliver shrugged and put his phone down on the table. It rang immediately, Shirley's name lighting up the screen.

"Hey," Oliver said in greeting. "Did you get my text?" He smiled and nodded. "I don't know. Danny knows someone or something so all four of us are going. Pretty great, right?" He paused, presumably to listen to Shirley's response. "We're just about to order our food, so I'll still be a while." To hear Oliver tell it, Shirley had been furious with him for days, and now that he'd finally redeemed himself he was going to put off seeing her to have a burger? "Oh, yeah, sure. We're at Rusty's Grill. It's right around the corner from the precinct."

He hung up his phone and smiled at Daniel. "Thanks again, Danny. You're a lifesaver." He picked up his menu and glanced down at it. "What're you guys getting?"

Just then the waitress walked up. "Are you boys ready to order?" she asked.

Oliver set the menu down. "I think I'll have the bacon cheeseburger with fries."

"Ollie?" Daniel said.

"Yeah?"

"It sounded like Shirley was planning to come up here." He inclined his head toward the phone in reference to Oliver's conversation with Shirley.

"She is," Oliver confirmed with a nod.

Daniel stared at Oliver, presumably waiting for the

obvious to sink in, but Asher knew that wouldn't happen. The two divorces and five broken engagements weren't an accident. Oliver was hopeless. Asher took a deep breath and shook his head before turning to the waitress. "We'll need a few more minutes. A fourth person is joining us."

It didn't take long for Shirley to arrive. She was smiling as brightly as ever as she rushed toward their table. Perceptive as always, she looked at the empty table and then turned toward Asher and Daniel. "Thanks for waiting for me. I hope you're not starving."

Daniel stood as much as possible between the bench seat and the table. He reached for Shirley and she leaned in and kissed his cheek. Asher wasn't one for hugging, which, again, Shirley knew, so she just nodded and smiled at him. "Hi, Asher," she said.

Then she slid in next to Oliver and rubbed her hand up and down his bicep. "How was work?"

He shrugged. "Fine. Same as always."

The woman didn't seem as irate as Oliver had described. She didn't even seem upset. Daniel looked at Asher and raised one eyebrow in question, no doubt noticing the same thing. Although Asher wasn't close friends with Shirley, he'd gone to the academy with her ex, so he had known her for years. She had always been easygoing and laid-back, and while he didn't discount the possibility that Oliver could test even her even-keeled temper, it was just as likely that the man had been overreacting.

Whatever. Oliver wasn't bunking at their place. They were going to see Burning Wrath and Indignation. All's well that ends well.

"Danny, thanks so much for getting the BWI tickets." Shirley was practically bouncing in her seat. "I'm such a huge fan. I'm sure Ollie told you." She patted Oliver's shoulder. "Their songs are like poetry." She sighed and closed her eyes, swaying slightly, like she was hearing music in her mind.

Daniel smiled tightly and nodded, but he didn't say anything in response.

"Plus," Shirley continued, "it's so great that we're all going together. I had reservations at Salvador's for before the show. I called on the way here and they said that they can fit all four of us in. What do you think? Should we make a whole night of it? It'll be a blast."

Out of the corner of his eye, Asher noticed Daniel looking at him for a decision. His belly warmed in response to Daniel's deference. "Sounds great, Shirl," he said to Shirley. Then he smiled at Daniel and cupped his cheek, showing him without words that he was pleased. "Salvador's is an Italian restaurant in the Mission," he explained. "It's supposed to be really good."

"That's where Marc works," Daniel said. "So I'm sure it's amazing."

"Marc?" Asher asked, wondering who this man was and how Daniel knew him.

Daniel smiled fondly and squeezed his knee. "Yes. Marc. Your neighbor. The one who's been helping me learn how to cook."

"Oh, right." Asher realized he was frowning and he had no idea why. "Right," he said again, forcing himself to relax. "Marc." Whom he had yet to meet.

The waitress walked up and took their orders.

"I think I need to go shopping tomorrow," Shirley said. "I have the day off work anyway and I don't have anything dressy enough for Salvador's but casual enough to wear to BWI."

"How is that possible? You have a closet full of clothes," Oliver argued.

She rolled her eyes at him.

"Well, at least now you can use the gift card I gave you," he added, seemingly determined to dig himself as far down a hole as possible at any cost.

The smile dropped from Shirley's face and she glared at Oliver.

Asher had a moment of panic, fearing that the fight was going to resurface, which would mean Oliver asking to stay at his apartment. He desperately tried to think of a way to help Oliver out of the impending mess. Shopping made him think of Daniel and how he hadn't been able to talk the man into buying clothes despite multiple efforts. The holes on the bottom of the sweatshirt he was currently wearing were proof. Daniel seemed to have endless patience where his brother was concerned, and he obviously wanted Shirley to be happy.

Asher had just stumbled onto the perfect way to kill two

birds with one stone. Go him. "Daniel, you should go shopping with Shirley tomorrow," he suggested and tried to hold back a smirk.

"Sure thing," Daniel said with a smile. "I have time to hang out tomorrow. Do you mind having company, Shirley?" he asked.

"I'd love it!"

"That's perfect. Because you could use some new clothes too," Asher said evenly.

"I'm good on clothes," Daniel responded.

Asher scoffed. "Sugar, you have two pairs of blue jeans and both are faded and riddled with holes. And your T-shirts aren't in better shape. Those things might be okay for the concert, but you're not going to get into Salvador's wearing anything you own."

"That's true," Shirley agreed. "You actually need to wear a collared shirt. I think jeans might be fine, but they'd have to be the dressy ones, you know?" Daniel's eyes widened comically, as if they'd just suggested he cover his body in honey and roll around in a pile of fire ants. "Don't worry, Danny," she assured him. "I'll help you pick something perfect. I'm really good at this. Ask your brother."

All eyes turned to Oliver. He was stuffing fries into his mouth. When he noticed everyone looking at him, he paused. "What?" he asked around a mouthful of food.

"Okay. Shopping it is," Daniel said, rescuing his brother from himself. Again.

"While you're out, you should pick up some new shoes." Asher figured he might as well go for broke. "Flip-flops won't work, and the soles of your sneakers are peeling off."

Daniel didn't say anything, just nodded.

"This'll be so much fun!" Shirley said. "We can hit the stores and have lunch."

"Hey, Shirl, just make sure my boy here buys something that fits. He seems a little confused about his size." Asher winked at Daniel.

"Never heard any complaints from you before," Daniel grumbled under his breath.

"That's because I'm usually getting you out of your clothes, sugar." He cupped Daniel's cheek with one hand, threaded the other through his hair, and nibbled on his earlobe. "Doesn't much matter what they look like when they're crumpled in the corner. But I've been telling you that you need some new things. And since we're going out to a fancy restaurant, you should probably buy something that fits, okay?"

Daniel shivered and gulped. His pupils were dilated and his skin flushed. "Okay," he squeaked.

Asher smirked at how easily he could unravel the smaller man.

"I'm still here," Oliver said in annoyance. "Along with a restaurant full of people."

Asher raised his hand and flipped Oliver off without taking his eyes off Daniel. He swiped his thumb over Daniel's plump lip. "Thanks, sugar."

CHAPTER 18

"I'll have a large decaf vanilla latte with skim milk. Cold," Shirley said.

"A venti iced latte decaf non-fat add vanilla," the barista repeated.

"I refuse to speak their made-up language," Shirley whispered to Daniel as she handed over her money. "Plus, it's fun making 'em squirm when I say skim instead of nonfat."

He started laughing. "You're funny!"

She wrapped one arm around her belly and held the other out to the side as she took a bow. "Why, thank you, *monsieur*."

"*De rien, madame*," Daniel responded with a curtsy.

Shirley cracked up. "You're all right, Danny." She picked up her drink and took a sip. "I didn't know you spoke French."

"I don't, really. Just a few phrases here and there that I picked up when I worked on a cruise ship. We had a lot of European passengers."

"Mmmm, sounds sexy," she said dreamily. "I bet the French men were romantic and debonair." She sipped her drink and sighed wistfully. "Okay." She breathed out and squared her shoulders. "Are you ready to hit the shops?"

"Ready as I'll ever be. Where do you want to go first?"

"Let's go to Union Square. With all those stores, we're bound to find something."

Two hours later, they still hadn't found anything, and Shirley was coming out of another dressing room, chewing on her bottom lip and frowning. "What do you think of this?"

"I love that sweater. The cowl neck is really flattering and the purple works with your hair and skin tone."

"Yeah?" Shirley asked, sounding relieved.

"Totally. Now we just need to find you some pants. I saw a pair of gray wide-leg pants near the front. They'll be perfect with that sweater. Tell me your size and I'll grab 'em for you."

"Thanks, Danny. I'm a—" Shirley stopped and tilted her head to the side. She narrowed her eyes appraisingly. "What size do you think I am?"

No way was Daniel walking into that trap. "Uh, why do I feel like a giant horse just knocked on my gate?"

"Sorry." Shirley slumped down into an empty chair next to the fitting room. "I wasn't trying to trick you. It's just—" She sighed. "Did your brother tell you what he got me for my birthday?"

"He said he got you a gift certificate," Daniel said.

"Yup." Shirley nodded. "He got me a gift certificate to a boutique called Petite Chateau. Care to guess what they specialize in? Spoiler alert—it isn't castles."

Daniel froze. Shirley was really pretty. Long, wavy red

hair, alabaster skin, sparkling blue eyes, and a curvy body he was sure straight men appreciated. What she wasn't was petite. Though he refused to engage her in the guess-my-size game, Daniel would have put her at around a size sixteen. Plus, she was about an inch or so taller than his five feet eight inches. Nope, not petite.

"All right, so the confused look tells me you get the picture. Needless to say," Shirley said, "I can't even get one boob into their shirts. I don't mean to be ungrateful or bitchy, but don't you think the man who plans to marry me should have some idea of what I look like?"

Daniel sat next to her. "I'm sorry, Shirl. I know Ollie's not the most sensitive guy around."

"No, he isn't. But—" She took in a deep breath. "Do you think he actually wants to be with me? I know some guys have a low sex drive, but..." Daniel must have looked like a deer caught in the headlights—it was sure as hell how he felt—because Shirley stopped talking, squeezed his arm, and smiled weakly. "Never mind. It wasn't fair of me to ask you that. He's your brother."

"I once dated a guy who called me into the bathroom to look at his turd because he swore it was shaped like a dick," Daniel volunteered.

Shirley's eyes widened and she was silent for several beats before she started laughing. "I had a blind date with a guy who called me 'babe' within ten minutes of meeting me. Plus, he was in his forties, lived with his mother, and he wore

Iron Man underwear."

"Oooh, totally dodged a bullet with that one. Umm, okay, I'll raise you babe and cartoon briefs and throw in emotionally unavailable and herpes."

"Seriously?" Shirley asked.

"Swear. The worst part was that he'd use the herpes as an excuse to never have sex. To hear him tell it, he was in a constant outbreak."

"Ugh. Sucks."

"Not well," Daniel said. "But, you know, aside from all that, he was a great catch."

"Right," Shirley said drolly. "I went to bed with a guy who fell asleep with chewing gum in his mouth. I woke up and it was all over the sheets and my hair. Have you ever tried to get gum out of hair?"

"Gum?" Daniel said. "Nope. Got lots of experience getting cum out of hair, though." He winked.

"Nice," Shirley said. "Hair's not bad. Once had a guy shoot in my eye, though. Burned like a bitch."

"Yeah." Daniel chuckled. "Up the nose is no bueno either."

"Totally," Shirley agreed. Then she sighed deeply. "Dating sucks. I swear, guys in their thirties and forties are like parking spots. All the good ones are taken and the only ones left are emotionally handicapped. I finally got to the point where I stopped trying to find the forever guy and, after a date, I'd just ask myself, is this someone who I'll want spending Wednesdays and every other weekend with my kids?"

Daniel froze and stared at the woman who was about to marry his brother. It took a moment, but then she shot up in her chair and gasped, apparently realizing what she'd said and to whom she'd said it. "Danny, listen, I..." She froze, her mouth hanging open but no words coming out. "I have no idea how to finish this sentence. Shit."

They sat together quietly and Daniel thought about what she'd said, about what she'd asked him. Did he think Oliver wanted to be with Shirley? He put his arm around her shoulder and drew her closer. She rested her head on his shoulder.

"Here's the thing. I don't know my brother. Not really. I've lived here for, what? Six months. And I've probably spent ten times as much time with Ollie during that time as I have in the rest of my life combined, phone calls included. So I guess what I'm saying is, you know him better than me. And it sounds like you have some things to work out before you walk down the aisle."

Shirley swung her leg and nudged Daniel's shoe with her foot. "We weren't planning on having an aisle." Her voice sounded a little congested, like she was holding back tears.

"Oh, in that case, fuck it. Bring on the wedding."

Shirley laughed and sniffled. "Thanks, Danny."

"Welcome."

She wiped at the corners of her eyes and cleared her throat. "Okay, pity party's done. Let's go get those pants you saw up front and hope they fit."

"I'm on it," he said as he got up from his seat.

"And then it's your turn," Shirley added.

Daniel groaned.

"Okay, I'm not making fun of you or anything, but—" Shirley took a deep breath. "Do you have body dysmorphia or something?"

"What? No!"

"Then why do you keep choosing things that are four sizes too big? I mean, I know sometimes people are heavy when they're younger and then they lose weight and they don't realize that their body isn't the same anymore and—"

"I know what my body looks like," Daniel assured her.

"Really? Well, those size thirty-two jeans say otherwise. Look, your man asked me to make sure you got clothes that fit and I know you don't want to disappoint him, so you get your tiny butt into the fitting room and I'm going to bring you things to try on."

Daniel wanted to argue, but Asher had been trying to get him to buy new clothes almost from the moment they met. And he frequently commented on the size of Daniel's jeans. And shirts. And boxers.

"Fine," Daniel said, his resignation clear in his tone. "No

flashy colors or fabrics, though. I, uh, don't like to stand out."

"Sure thing." Shirley nodded. "What do you consider flashy?"

Daniel thought about it. "Let's go with black. Easier to blend in that way. I'll be waiting in the fitting room."

Daniel woke in the middle of the night and felt a warm, hairy arm wrapped around his chest and a hard, hairy body pressed against his back. He sighed happily. He had always been a light sleeper, but six months sharing a bed with Asher had him content, settled. Both at night and during the day. So much so that he hadn't woken when Asher finally got home.

Something happened at work that had kept Asher there all night on Tuesday, and so late the previous day that Daniel had stopped waiting up for him and just gone to bed. He blinked his eyes open and saw the beginnings of light coming in from the perimeter of the window. Still too early to wake up, but with Asher being so busy, they hadn't had a chance to talk since before they'd met Oliver and Shirley for dinner on Monday. Before they decided to go to the Burning Wrath and Indignation concert.

He rolled over and kissed Asher's neck. "Ash?" he whispered. Asher grunted and moved his hand down to Daniel's ass, caressing and squeezing even while he slept.

"Asher?" Daniel repeated. Asher needed his sleep and he hated waking him, but if he didn't do it now, he'd fall back asleep and Asher would be at work by the time he woke up.

Thinking a little more stimulation would help, Daniel started kissing Asher at the base of his throat and then up his neck. "Ash?" he said again once he felt Asher stir.

"Mmmm," Asher mumbled. He cupped the back of Daniel's head, tangled fingers in his hair, and pulled him forward until their lips met. Even mostly asleep the man could deliver a kiss that had Daniel hard in seconds. Powerful, all-consuming, like a declaration of ownership with lips and tongue and teeth. Daniel never wanted it to stop. "What time is it?" Asher asked groggily.

"Uh." Daniel blinked and tried to focus on the alarm clock. "Just a little after six, I think."

Asher kissed him one more time and then rolled onto his back. "Fuck," he said with a sigh. "Gotta get up and go in."

"Now? It's still early. And you got home in the middle of the night."

But Asher was already climbing out of bed and walking into the bathroom. "I know. Fucking sucks, but if I don't go now, I might have to miss dinner tonight. Go back to sleep, sugar. I'll call you later."

With those words, Asher closed the bathroom door and Daniel lost yet another opportunity to talk to him about Burning Wrath and Indignation.

"Damn it."

CHAPTER 19

Three cases had blown up at work Monday night, so Asher had practically lived at the office for the rest of the week. When he was able to get home at night, Daniel was already in bed and Asher was too tired to wake him up to fuck. He slept for a few hours, then got up and started the cycle over again. Between the stress, the sleep deprivation, and the lack of sex, Asher was irritable as hell.

He went in early on Thursday because they had the BWI concert that night and he was taking Friday off. But despite his best efforts, he was stuck at work longer than expected.

"Hey, Ash. Are you on your way?" Daniel asked hopefully as soon as he answered the phone. "Because I was hoping we'd get a chance to talk before the concert tonight."

"Afraid not," Asher said. "There're a few things I have to get done before I leave for the night. I'll meet you at the restaurant and we can talk there."

"Oh." Daniel sounded disappointed. "Okay."

It wasn't as if he was happy about working so many hours either, but when shit hit the fan, he was the one responsible for cleaning it up. Getting a guilt trip about that from a man who didn't work for a living just pissed Asher off even further. By the time he was finally done with the most urgent things on his desk, he didn't have time to go home and change. So he took off his tie, unbuttoned the top two buttons on his dress shirt, and headed out to Salvador's, where he was meeting Daniel, Oliver, and Shirley.

The host walked him through the dimly lit restaurant to a table in the back. When Daniel spotted him, he stood up and smiled. Asher's jaw dropped and he forgot to breathe. *Holy shit*. Daniel looked gorgeous.

He was wearing a black button-down shirt made out of a material that clung and shimmered, dark black jeans that hugged his lithe body like a second skin, and black leather boots. His always unruly hair was neatly combed back, the blond streaks gleaming. Without the usual shield of hair, Daniel's angular face was clear of any obstructions, making his brown eyes look even bigger than usual. Asher was certain that he had never seen a more beautiful man. In real life or otherwise.

"Hi!" Daniel said as he reached out toward Asher. When Asher was close enough, Daniel tilted his face up for a kiss.

Asher heard a whimper followed by a clanking sound. Glancing toward the noise, he saw the host raking his gaze up and down Daniel's body and licking his lips, his eyes burning with lust. The menu he had been holding lay on the floor by his feet.

Kiss forgotten, Asher grasped Daniel's arm and pushed

him toward the seat farthest from the aisle, where he'd be obstructed from other people's views by the table and by Asher's larger frame. "I'm all set," Asher growled at the host, hoping the man would take the hint to go back to work.

Unfortunately, even in the low lighting, with just his upper body and face showing, Daniel couldn't be missed. Not with that shirt accentuating his hard chest and exposing a long expanse of glowing skin. And with his hair combed off of his face, Daniel's cheekbones seemed higher, his eyes brighter, his lips more plump. Apparently, the host was well aware of the enticing picture Daniel presented because he hadn't moved an inch and his mouth was practically hanging open as he leered. Thirty more seconds and he'd be drooling.

"I'll have a beer," Asher snapped, sure that a task would get him on his way. But the man didn't seem to hear him. He was too damn busy ogling Daniel. Asher's temper rose.

"Uh." Daniel darted his gaze from Asher to the host. "Can we please have a beer?" he asked.

"Sure!" the host replied enthusiastically, his ears making a remarkable recovery. He stepped as close as he could to the table and completely ignored Asher's presence as he leaned in toward Daniel. "What kind? I'm happy to get you anything you want." His husky tone left no doubt that the last sentence wasn't referring to drinks. Asher wanted to snap his hand out, grab his throat in a chokehold, tear his head off, and spit into the bloody stump left behind.

"It's for my boyfriend," Daniel clarified. "Ash, what kind

of beer do you want?"

Asher was momentarily distracted by Daniel's words. It was the first time he'd been referred to as someone's boyfriend, and while he didn't mind putting a title on what he was to Daniel, that word didn't feel like the right fit.

"But what do *you* want to drink?" the host asked Daniel.

"Oh, for fuck's sake!" Asher shouted, startling the host. "His water glass is full and there's a soda in front of him. He's fine and I'll take an amber. Thanks for asking." He was pretty sure the sarcasm behind that last comment was clear.

"Oh, uh, right." The irritating man finally managed to pry his gaze from Daniel. "Enjoy your meal." He scurried off and Asher rolled his shoulders, trying to relax.

Daniel turned sideways in his chair, put his hands on Asher's shoulders, and started massaging him. "Bad day?" he asked quietly.

Asher didn't have a chance to answer before Oliver jumped in. "Damn, Asher," he chided. "No need to scare the guy. He was just being polite. Now somebody's going to spit in our food."

Shirley laughed. "Polite? Ollie, that man clearly wanted to get into Danny's pants." She looked at Daniel and grinned. "Am I good or what? I told you that outfit was hot!"

Daniel blushed and squirmed awkwardly in his chair. There was no doubt that he looked sexy as all get-out in his new clothes. Any reflective surface would have made that obvious. So why did he seem surprised—or was it uncomfortable?—

hearing it? Was it that he had some ulterior motive with this new look and didn't want Asher to know about it?

A waitress came to the table with Asher's beer in one hand and a tasty-looking antipasto plate in the other. "Courtesy of the chef," she said, setting the plate down.

"Oh, that's so nice." Daniel smiled widely and the waitress gasped, flushed, and widened her eyes. Daniel dipped his head and looked down at the table. "Please thank Marc for us," he said quietly.

Right. Marc the mystery neighbor was a chef at this restaurant. Maybe that was the issue. Daniel was trying to impress Marc. He did spend quite a bit of time with the man. Asher's mood soured further. Not that anybody seemed to notice.

The waitress left, after staring at Daniel and honest-to-goodness giggling. Oliver ate his food like it was his last meal, commenting about how delicious each and every item on his plate tasted. Shirley chatted with Daniel, laughing about various anecdotes from their shopping excursion, and because Asher hadn't been with them, he couldn't participate in the discussion. Not that they cared.

And as if all those things didn't add up to the most irritating dinner of all time, Asher was sure every member of the restaurant's wait staff was making a point to stop by their table to flirt with Daniel. Their bread plate was overflowing. Not a single water glass had managed to remain empty for any longer than the time it took to travel from mouth to table.

And if one more person offered Daniel ground pepper, Asher was going to take the peppermill and shove it up that person's ass. Good service was one thing, but this was ridiculous.

"Ash," Daniel said, the pitch of his tone letting Asher know it wasn't the first time he'd spoken.

"What?" Asher snapped. He closed his eyes and took in a deep breath. Why was he angry at Daniel? He opened his eyes and looked at Daniel. Because he was dressed like a walking billboard for porn, that was why.

"I need to use the bathroom and I'm kind of, uh"— he looked between Asher's chair and his and raised an eyebrow—"pinned in here."

Sure enough, Asher had moved his seat so close to Daniel's that he was only a couple of inches away. And with the wall on the other side, there was no way for him to get up unless Asher moved.

"Oh, sure," Asher said as he slid back, leaving room for Daniel to get up.

He shimmied between Asher and the table, giving Asher a view of his ass in his new jeans. Usually, Daniel wore his pants so loose that they barely stayed on, let alone gave an indication of what he was packing beneath. But in those tight jeans… Asher groaned.

Jesus fuckin' Christ. How could a man with no body fat have a bubble butt?

Asher kept his gaze glued to Daniel's backside as he walked away. He noticed that he wasn't alone. It seemed like all the people at the tables Daniel passed turned their heads and stared at him.

"What's your damage, Asher?" Oliver asked. Apparently there was nothing left to eat within reach because Asher was certain that Oliver hadn't taken a second to talk, let alone breathe, since food had been placed in front of him.

"My damage?" Asher growled and glared at his friend.

Oliver propped his forearms on the table and leaned in. He squinted and lowered his voice menacingly. "Yeah, you've been acting like an asshole all night."

"How would you know? You haven't looked away from your plate long enough to notice anything except the location of the salt shaker."

"Funny," Oliver said drolly. "Quit bein' a dick, Penaz. My brother doesn't deserve it."

"Ollie." Shirley grasped Oliver's shoulder in warning. He rolled his shoulder and shook her off.

"Seriously, you're being a bigger asshole than usual, and that's really saying something. Danny's a good-looking guy; people are going to notice. You should be grateful that he's willing to be with you and kiss his ass instead of punishing him because you think someone's coming on to him."

Asher couldn't hold back his wince at how close to home Oliver's words struck. He knew that he was an attractive man, a little rough-looking, maybe, but not bad. But Daniel, he was more than good-looking. He was stunning, truly. And in that outfit... Asher shuddered and adjusted his erection. Fucking edible, that was what he was. Still, getting relationship advice from Oliver was unwelcome. And absurd.

"Don't psychoanalyze me, Ollie."

"I'll stop doing it when you quit acting like a psycho, Asher."

He told himself not to respond. He needed to calm down and enjoy the evening. It had been a tough, long week, but he wasn't at work, he'd eaten a great dinner, and they were going to see one of the best bands of their generation. No reason to be on edge. The efficacy of the internal pep talk lasted about as long as Daniel's trip to the restroom, because that was when Asher saw him throw himself at another man.

Daniel was walking back to the table, his throng of admirers once again stopping mid-conversation to turn their heads and gape at him. Asher clenched his jaw so tight he could almost hear his teeth grinding. Goddamn, did these people have nothing better to do? Then, seemingly out of nowhere, a tall man with midnight-black hair walked up to Daniel. It looked like he said something, but they were too far away for Asher to hear the words. Whatever it was must have made Daniel happy, because he smiled at the man and hugged him tightly.

Without thought, Asher shoved his chair back and stood, his arms rigid at his sides, fists clenched.

"Where're you going?" Oliver asked him.

He looked down to answer and then Daniel was there.

"Hey, look who I found." The stranger was right behind

him, close enough to touch. "Marc, this is my brother Oliver, his fiancée Shirley, and you know Asher Penaz."

This was his neighbor? Asher peered at the infamous Chef Marc. He did look sort of familiar.

"Nice to meet you," Marc said to Shirley and Oliver before turning to Asher and extending his hand. "We've seen each other around the building, but I don't think we've ever met. I'm Marc Dorey."

His smile was warm, his eyes kind, so Asher took his hand and shook it.

"Good to meet you, Marc," Asher said as he curled his free hand around Daniel's bicep and gently tugged him over to the table, subtly pointing him toward his seat.

"How was dinner?" Marc asked them. "I hope you enjoyed everything."

Oliver nodded, Shirley gushed and asked for the ingredients in the pasta sauce, and Asher smiled politely. Neighbor Marc seemed like a decent sort, even if he did look at Daniel for a little longer than seemed necessary.

"Well, it was great meeting you guys. I'd better get back in the kitchen, but I hope you'll come see us again soon." He turned to Daniel. "Are we on for Italian wedding soup on Monday?"

"You bet," Daniel replied.

"Cool. I want to get your thoughts on whether the dill adds or takes away from the overall flavor."

"Hey, you're the master," Daniel said.

Marc scoffed. "Don't kid yourself, Daniel. You're almost as good as my sous chef and he's been at this for years. Plus, you've got impeccable taste buds. I followed your suggestion and substituted flat leaf parsley for the curled in the lasagna last week and people went wild."

Daniel blushed. "Thanks."

Marc dipped his chin in acknowledgement. "You're a lucky man, Asher," he said. Then he waved and walked away.

Instead of being flattered by Marc's compliment, the words made Asher's skin itch. Was Marc implying that Daniel was too good for him? Did Daniel think that? Was that why he was dressed like a man on the prowl?

"All right, guys, are we ready to head out?" Oliver asked as he got up. "BWI awaits!"

Shirley nodded and followed him away from the table and toward the door. Asher shoved his chair back and stomped after them.

"Ash," Daniel said quietly from behind him. He put his hand on Asher's shoulder and tried to slow his pace. "I've been trying to tell you about—"

"Hey, Asher," Oliver said. "You drove here, right?"

"Yeah."

"Perfect. We took a cab over, so we'll catch a ride with you and Danny to the show."

"Okay," Asher said. Daniel sighed and chewed on his bottom lip. "What were you saying?" Asher asked him.

"Nothing." Daniel shook his head. "I'll, uh, tell you later."

CHAPTER 20

"You got the tickets, Danny?" Oliver asked as they walked up
to the Fillmore.

"They're at will call," he answered. They darted across
the street and walked up to the venue, with Oliver and Shirley
in front. Daniel grasped Asher's bicep and tried to keep him
back. "Hey, listen, before we go in there, I just want you to
know that—"

"Danny, Asher, let's go!" Shirley shouted.

Daniel slumped his shoulders, and they jogged to catch
up with Shirley and Oliver.

"Be right back," Daniel said and walked over to the will-
call window.

"I can't tell you how excited I am about this!" Shirley was
all smiles, bouncing on her toes. "I've wanted to see BWI for
years! My friend Nat saw them last time they were in town
and said they're incredible live. Have you ever seen them,
Asher?"

"No." He shook his head. "But I've heard the same thing."

Though he wasn't into music in the same way as Daniel,
Asher appreciated a live show, and Burning Wrath and

Indignation was rumored to be the best in the industry. It was sure to be a great night. He felt his funk lifting.

Daniel walked back over to them, and Asher put his arm around him, holding him close. "Got the tickets?" he asked.

"Yup." Daniel handed two tickets to Shirley and the other two to Asher.

"Front row?" Oliver shouted. "Goddamn, man! Who'd you have to blow to get these?" He turned to Shirley and showed her the tickets. "Did you see these? We're in the center front. Can you believe it?"

"Oh my God, oh my God, oh my God!" Shirley chanted. She bounced over and pulled Daniel into a hug. "You are officially my favorite almost in-law, Danny!"

"You told me I earned that title Tuesday after four hours of shopping." Daniel scowled, but his eyes twinkled and his lips turned up at the sides, leaving no doubt that he was joking.

"That's true, but now you've earned the title for life!"

He chuckled and kissed her cheek. "Happy birthday, Shirley."

"Best one ever!" she said.

Oliver took her hand and pulled her toward the entrance. "Let's go!" he said.

Shirley hooted, clutched Daniel's hand, and tugged him behind her.

Asher looked down at the tickets. Front row center. He furrowed his brow. How had Daniel gotten those seats?

The Fillmore was loud and packed. They wedged their way through the crowd, looked at the concert posters lining the walls and the chandeliers hanging from the ceiling, stopped at the bar for drinks, and eventually made it to the front.

Asher bent down and spoke into Daniel's ear. "Who did you say you knew that got us these tickets?"

"That's what I've been trying to tell you." Daniel had to raise his voice to be heard above the noise. "When BWI got started, I—"

The lights went dark and the roar of the crowd drowned out the rest of his sentence. Then a guitar started playing, followed by the bass, and finally the drums.

Spotlights lit each of the band members as they launched into one of their most popular songs. There were no fireworks, no complicated stage show; just three guys standing on stage, playing music. They were just as good live as Asher had heard. And just as loud. Trying to have a conversation while BWI was on stage was pointless. He'd talk to Daniel at home later.

"Hey, there," Rob Yearling, BWI's lead singer and guitarist drawled after finishing the second song of the set. "How're y'all doin' this fine evenin'?"

He held the microphone out toward the screaming fans.

Everyone went wild, hooting and hollering, pumping their fists in the air, and Asher found himself being dragged along with the excitement. He put his arm around Daniel's shoulder and squeezed him.

"Soundin' ready for a good time," Rob continued. "Well, I can promise that y'all won't be disappointed. Because not only are you gonna hear the best band in the motherfuckin' world." He shouted the last part of the sentence and then paused to let the crowd roar out their agreement. "But tonight only, you're gettin' the extra special privilege of hearin' the man behind most of our songs." Rob looked at the audience meaningfully and raised an eyebrow. They were close enough to the stage that Asher could see every detail of his expression. "Since I'm the front man, y'all thought that was me, right?"

As loud as it had been moments before, an odd silence descended, and then everyone started murmuring, trying to understand what was going on.

"Well, now, see, y'all probably know BWI as a three-man group, but we actually started out with a fourth member. He cut us loose right when we signed our first major label album. Are there any die-hards in the audience tonight who know what instrument our fourth guy played?"

The room was silent for a couple of beats, and then "Piano!" was shouted out by a few people.

Rob Yearling chuckled. "That's right." A spotlight went up over the right side of the stage, illuminating an electric piano. "Dot plays that baby so fine, he'll either make ya cry or he'll make ya come in your pants. And if any of y'all are still buying CDs, you know his name is next to almost every damn song we put out."

Rob peered into the crowd, putting his hand over his forehead to block the lights. Everyone looked around, trying to follow his gaze, which landed right in the middle of the front row. He grinned wickedly and raised an eyebrow. Time seemed to slow as Asher realized all eyes were fixed on Daniel.

What. The. Fuck.

"Dot, get on up here and help us give these here nice folks a fanfuckintastic show."

Daniel looked at Asher and smiled weakly. He squeezed Asher's hand, dipped his chin and closed his eyes, and then took in a deep breath, seemingly gathering his nerves. When he looked back up, a smile was plastered to his face. It wasn't his usual warm grin or his jovial laugh, and it didn't reach his eyes. Then he put one hand on the stage and propelled himself up, landing in a crouch before straightening.

Rob Yearling walked up and wrapped Daniel in a big hug, lifting him off his feet. The two men hunched together, talking into each other's ears. John Oaks, the bass player, trotted over, flung an arm around Daniel's shoulder, and pulled him into a one-armed hug, giving Daniel's ass a squeeze with his free hand.

In the blink of an eye, or, in this case, the squeeze of an

ass, Asher went from shocked about what was going on to pissed about another man groping Daniel.

John leaned over Daniel's shoulder and spoke into the microphone. "And Rob forgot to mention that Dot's not only mad skilled, but fine as fuck."

Rob chuckled, his deep timbre sounding out over the incredible acoustic system. "No argument from me, guy. Dot's the only man I've ever met who's made me wonder if I could swing the other way." He waggled his eyebrows and the audience erupted in laughter. "I mean it, y'all! Check out his ass."

As if on cue, Daniel turned his back to the crowd and wiggled his tight butt. Asher found himself wishing for the first time that Daniel was wearing his usual baggy, shapeless, worn-out clothes. Well, it wasn't actually the first time; he'd had the same thought in the restaurant. Was this the reason Daniel chose to wear flashy clothes? To impress the band?

"All right," Eric Sear, BWI's drummer drawled. "I know we're in San Francisco, but you boys need to stop molesting Dot. It's time to play." He raised his stick to his forehead and moved it out in a salute to Daniel, who nodded toward him and then strutted over to the piano, taking his seat on the bench.

What was with this "Dot" business? If they'd known Daniel for as long as they said, shouldn't they know his name? Not that Asher knew a thing about *them* and he'd been living with Daniel for half a year.

Daniel moved his fingers over the piano keys, and his button-down shirt pulled tight across his back. He shifted uncomfortably and grunted.

"Got a problem there, Dot?" Rob asked.

"First time in years I'm dressed up and don't it figure you've got to call me up here to play," Daniel grumbled into the microphone attached to the back of the piano.

"Figure it out, baby," John said. "'Cause we've got a show to put on and you're not getting off this stage. Even if that means we have to tackle you and pin you down."

"Sounds like a bonus to me," Rob added cheekily.

"Well, all righty, then," Eric said. "I could use a little extra maneuvering room too, Dot." He stood, grasped the hem of his shirt, and peeled it over his head, exposing a body Asher would've expected to find on a professional athlete, not a scruffy musician.

"Two minutes into this thing and you guys are already getting me out of my clothes," Daniel responded as he got up and started unbuttoning his shirt. "That's officially a record."

"Take it off, baby." John whistled and then yanked off his own top.

If Asher thought Daniel's new black jeans were attention-grabbing before, which he did, once the shirt came off, they were positively orgasm-inducing. The damn things were slung so low on his hips that his chest, stomach, and hip bones showed. Asher was sure that if Daniel stretched the right way, the top of his pubic bush would be exposed.

Daniel reached his arms over his head and clasped his right wrist with his left hand, pulling himself into a stretch. The spotlight highlighted his smooth skin and every muscle showed as he moved. Asher moaned with need. Then he heard people around him gasping and murmuring about the hot guy on stage, and he wanted to growl. Was this a rock concert or a strip show?

"Are all y'all gettin' nekkid?" Rob Yearling shouted to his bandmates as he looked around the stage. He stripped out of his T-shirt and threw it into the crowd. "This here show just got hella good, folks."

Eric tapped his drum sticks together three times. "Here we go, boys. Let's see if we can remember how to keep up with Dot. One, two, one two three four!"

And with that lead-in, Burning Wrath and Indignation— plus Daniel—started playing.

It was, unquestionably, the most incredible performance Asher had ever seen. And from the chattering in the crowd, he wasn't alone in that opinion. BWI was on top of their game, their energy level high enough to carry into the crowd so everyone was dancing and singing along with every tune. And there was no doubt that Daniel's addition to the ensemble was part of the reason.

He'd started out sitting on the piano bench, but that didn't mean he was still. This was no sedate piano recital. His hands flew over the keys, his body rolling in time with the music, all fluid grace and sexy heat. His smooth, warm voice joined with Rob's raspy mumbles in a way that should have been awkward but was, instead, a perfect union of soft and rough. By the end of the set, Daniel had kicked back the bench and was on his feet, slamming his fingers on the keyboard, sweat dripping down his back and body swaying as he belted out song after song.

When the lights finally flickered off, signaling the end of the show, the audience had shouted themselves raw. The spotlight came back on, and the four men stood together at the front of the stage, arms wrapped around each other, saluting the crowd and taking bows. It was an epic night and it was clear they knew it. Rob Yearling spoke to the fans, but Asher couldn't hear his words. He was too focused on Daniel hugging the other men, listening to whatever they were saying into his ear as they rubbed his arms or back. He looked so natural on stage, like a real rock 'n roll star. Hell, he *was* a real rock 'n roll star.

Daniel looked like he'd been born to entertain, and Asher couldn't help but wonder what in the hell he was doing living in his apartment, searching for jobs. Not that Daniel had been doing all that much searching. Which, now that Asher knew all the facts, made sense.

Didn't Rob Yearling say Daniel was still writing their songs? Every album Burning Wrath and Indignation released went platinum. How much money did the people who wrote the songs on those albums make? Fuck more than a police captain, that was how much.

"Did you know about Danny?" Shirley rasped out as soon as the band, plus Daniel, left the stage. All the singing and cheering had wiped out her voice.

Oliver shook his head. "No. We didn't grow up together, and Danny's never been a talker. My dad would've told me if he knew, so I'm guessing he doesn't have a clue either. Asher, did you know?" Oliver asked.

Asher grunted at him, not wanting to admit that apparently he had no knowledge about the past, hell, even the present, of the only man he'd ever asked to share his bed.

"Asher Penaz?" a man almost as big as Asher, wearing a BWI T-shirt and headphones, called over to them.

"Yeah?"

"Come on out this way." He waved Asher over to him. "Dot's waiting for you backstage."

Shirley found enough vocal power to shriek. "We're going backstage!"

The three of them followed the security guard down a hallway and past a locked door. "He's right in here," the guy said as he marched over to a door off to the left, knocked three times, and then opened it up.

Asher walked in first, followed by Shirley and then Oliver. The room wasn't big, and in addition to the band members, there were several other people in the space. Everybody was huddled in groups, laughing and talking about the show. Asher spotted Daniel in a corner, pinned in by Rob Yearling and John Oaks.

"Come on, Dot," John wheedled. "Don't act like you didn't love it up there tonight." He was touching Daniel's arm, his neck, his chest, hands, basically everywhere.

"You fuckin' light up when you're on stage and you know it. You belong with us." Rob was standing close enough while he was speaking that Daniel surely could feel his breath on his skin.

Asher hated them in equal measure because they were all over his boy and because they were right.

"It's not what I want. It's never been what I wanted," Daniel explained gently.

"That was before. None of us wanted Bobby, Johnny, Ricky, and Danny. It was boy-band bullshit. But it's different now, Dot. It's real," Rob said passionately.

"I know it is," Daniel said, reaching for Rob's cheek. Something in the edge of his vision must have caught his attention, because his gaze darted to the right, where Eric Sear was standing, and he dropped his hand. "Listen, I'm really proud of you guys, okay? And you can count on me in the background, just like we agreed. But I'm done playing live. Nothing's changed. I don't want this."

John and Rob started arguing with Daniel. He white-knuckled his shirt and shook his head. Then John stepped even closer, pressing his bare chest to Daniel's, and Asher saw red.

He marched over to Daniel. "Put the fuckin' shirt on," he barked.

Rob's back was to Asher. He flipped around to see who had spoken. "And you are?" he drawled, one eyebrow raised.

No fucking way was he answering to this man. "Daniel," he warned. "Shirt. On. Now."

John turned and stood in front of Daniel protectively. "Chill out, friend." He looked back over his shoulder at Daniel. "Is he yours, Dot?"

That phrasing snapped Asher's last nerve. So did the fact that these men were standing between him and Daniel. They had no right to keep him from what was his. "It's the other way around, *friend*," Asher said, his tone making clear that he felt anything but friendship. "Now step the fuck back."

Daniel frantically tried to put his shirt on, no easy task when he was squished against the wall, unable to move because of the wall of bodies in front of him. Asher could see that, could see that Daniel was trying to do as he was told. But somehow it wasn't enough.

Why had the man taken off his shirt to begin with? Why had he even bought that damn shirt? And the jeans! Every curve and asset on display. Why? To impress a bunch of pretentious rock stars? And, really, why would Daniel need to impress them? He was more talented than these men. Two hours on stage had made that abundantly clear to anybody with ears and eyes.

Right.

"You know what?" Asher sighed. "Forget it."

He turned on his heel and pushed through the throng

of people, making his way to the door. Once he stepped into the hallway, he twisted around until he saw the glowing red exit sign. He was almost to the door when he heard his name being called.

"Asher!" He kept walking. "Asher, goddammit! Stop." Oliver jogged over to him. "Where're you going?"

"To the Leather Lounge." Until the words had left his mouth, he hadn't planned to go to the Lounge. He didn't have a plan at all, other than to get away from the sight of Daniel, half-naked and surrounded by other men. Wealthy, successful, talented men.

Oliver's expression turned icy. "Why?"

"Because there are other people like me there, Ollie." Guys who needed him to make them feel or fly or scream or cry. "I feel comfortable there."

"You haven't been to that bar in half a year," Oliver reminded him. They both knew when he'd last been to the club: before he'd met Daniel.

"Yeah, well, clearly it's been too long."

And for what? It wasn't like Daniel would stay with Asher. The man had lived in dozens of places and none of them for long. Being a successful dancer in New York didn't hold him, neither did his masseur gig in Santa Fe, or his Taekwondo job in Oregon. And didn't Daniel once tell him that he'd been a jewelry maker? And he met Chase Rhodes working on that cruise ship doing fuck knew what.

Asher dragged his hand over his bare scalp and rubbed

the back of his neck. *Goddammit*. Those were just the jobs and places Asher knew of. Given that he hadn't heard word one about Daniel's past as a member of the hottest motherfucking band in the world or about his present career writing their songs, it was safe to guess he didn't even have a complete list of the pit stops on Daniel's walk through life.

He had changed every part of his life to accommodate Daniel. His apartment looked different. He never went clubbing. He'd gone down on the man, for fuck's sake! First time he'd done that in decades. And for what? Someone who'd leave to go on a tour or record an album or shit knew what the next thing would be, but Asher could be damn sure it wouldn't be crashing in a one-bedroom apartment in a mediocre neighborhood and cooking him dinner. He turned away.

"Don't do this, Asher," Oliver said.

But he was already at the exit door, walking out into the night air.

CHAPTER 21

It was after midnight by the time Asher stepped into the Leather Lounge. Not particularly late, and Thursdays were usually pretty busy, so there were sure to be a decent number of people in the club.

"Asher Penaz." The bouncer shook his hand and clapped his shoulder. "Haven't seen you here in a while."

"I've been busy." He shrugged. "You know how it goes."

The man laughed. "I figured that was it. Some guys were spreading shit about you having settled down, but I was saying it had to be work. You're just not that way."

It wasn't intended as a dig, Asher knew. Hell, it was probably something he would have said about himself. So why did it bother him?

He shook off the awkward feeling, chuckled along with the bouncer, and then went into the club. The lights were dim, but he could see that most of the tables were taken, the corners occupied by shadowed figures moving in a familiar rhythm. Asher stilled and took stock of the room.

It felt strange being there. He wasn't sure what to do next, which was ridiculous. He had walked through those doors hundreds of times, always knowing he'd get what he wanted before he left. So what did he want?

Memories of his erotic experiences at the club flickered through his mind like a pornographic Rolodex: men kneeling, writhing under his cane or whip, sucking his dick, spreading their cheeks and begging for his cock. Without his permission, the pictures morphed, and he saw Daniel leaning up to kiss him. Daniel lying on his back, a happy smile on his face as he welcomed Asher into his body. Daniel over Asher's lap, cheeks hot and red as he moaned in reaction to the most gentle spanking Asher had ever delivered. Daniel, moaning and whimpering as Asher sucked him down and swallowed his seed.

Just like that, Asher was achingly hard and his chest burned. He gulped down the lump in his throat and closed his eyes, trying to catch his breath. What in the hell was wrong with him? He viciously shoved the memories of Daniel away. He was a skilled, demanding Master. He could have subs lined up to experience his whip with a snap of his fingers. And maybe that was exactly what he'd do.

With that decision made, Asher strode up to the bar and settled on a stool where he could scope out the available men and pick the lucky one who would be kneeling before him in a matter of minutes.

The heavily pierced woman tending bar approached him. "Tina," he said and dipped his chin in greeting. "How've you been?"

"Not bad, Asher," she responded. "What can I get for you?"

"Nothing right now. I'll vacate the spot in a minute—just looking for someone."

"Who?" she asked. "I'm sure I've seen every man here at some point tonight."

"I'm not sure yet," Asher said with a shrug. "I haven't picked him yet."

She laughed. "Oh, I see. So it's like that, is it? What'll it be tonight? The whip or the cane?"

"You're doing a whipping, Penaz?" a snide voice said from behind him. "I heard you were done with the scene."

Nicholas Pike. Even the man's voice was grating.

"You heard wrong," Asher said, not bothering to turn his head, the dismissal intentional and obvious.

"What's the matter? Did your boy walk out on you already? When I heard you were living with someone, I figured it wouldn't last. And I was right. Here you are, looking for the next guy to disappoint."

Asher's jaw ticced. He clenched his fists and willed himself to ignore the taunt. Other than bumping into a couple of people on the street, he hadn't talked with anyone from the club since the last time he'd been in. So how did Nicholas know anything about what he'd been doing? And why did Nicholas care?

The man hated Asher, something to do with him caning and fucking Nicholas's sub years earlier. Never mind that

Darwin had asked for it and that Asher had seen Nicholas fuck dozens of men on the side. Somehow he was responsible for not knowing the rules of their screwed-up relationship.

"The regulars know you're nothing more than smoke and mirrors. So you'll need to find someone new to endure your brand of whipping," Nicholas taunted, pretending to survey the crowd. "So what poor guy are you going to take to the back tonight, Asher?"

That was it. Asher planted his hands on the bar, ready to push himself up and deck the gnat, who was now standing next to him.

"It'll be me."

Asher spun around at the sound of Daniel's voice. What was he doing at the Lounge?

"Well, you're a pretty one, aren't you?" Nicholas dragged his gaze over Daniel's body appreciatively. "You don't want him, sweetheart, believe me. But I'd be happy to take care of you."

"Ash?" Daniel sounded unsure and frightened. He darted his gaze between Asher and Nicholas.

"Ash?" Nicholas repeated incredulously. He stared at Asher. "*This* is your new boy?"

"Yes," Daniel responded. "I am." He moved closer to Asher, pressing himself to Asher's side.

"Oh, ho!" Nicholas chuckled. "I am going to enjoy this. His skin looks delicate." He moved his finger toward Daniel's neck. "Wonder if you'll make him bleed."

Asher shot forward and grasped Nicholas's wrist before he could connect with Daniel's body. Daniel folded into him, pressing his face into the side of Asher's neck, wrapping his arms around Asher and clinging to his back with his fingers.

"Interesting," Nicholas said. Then he yanked his hand out of Asher's grasp. "I'll follow you to the back."

He should have told Nicholas to fuck off. He should have asked Daniel what he was doing at the Lounge. But several men were gathered around, looking at Daniel lecherously, and Asher knew that if he walked away, he'd never hear the end of it from Nicholas. Before he realized what he was doing, Asher was standing next to a St. Andrew's cross and gripping Daniel's arm.

"I wonder if pretty boy looks as good out of his clothes as he does in them." Nicholas sneered as he spoke. Darwin, his sub, was kneeling at his feet, head bowed, the perfect picture of submission. It would have been more believable if Asher hadn't seen the man ass-up, begging for a fucking while, as it turned out, his Dom was out of town, oblivious to his sub's proclivity to cheat.

"Ash?" Daniel whispered, the question obvious from his tone and expression. "What...what—"

"Have you trained this boy at all, Asher?" Nicholas interrupted. "Because it seems like he doesn't have a clue what's going on. Or is it that you can't control him?" He scoffed and looked around, trying to catch the eyes of the men standing around him. "Figures. Like I've always said, smoke and mirrors."

Asher refused to acknowledge Nicholas's barrage of digs, but it wasn't easy, not after the week he'd had. He was running on very little sleep, a lot of stress at work, and a night that left him feeling shaken and off-balance. Asher needed to regain his control. He looked at Daniel.

"Strip," he ordered.

Daniel looked dismayed, his eyes wide as saucers, his mouth open, but after several heartbeats, he obeyed, moving his hands over the buttons on his shirt until it hung open. He paused and looked at Asher, then pulled it off and laid it on a nearby table. When Daniel's shaking hands went to the button on his pants, all Asher could see were hungry eyes staring and waiting. Nothing about this scene felt comfortable or normal, but he didn't know how to make it stop. By the time Daniel was standing naked in front of him and a dozen other men, Asher realized he had never felt less in control.

"Arms spread, wrists in the buckles," he said reflexively. He was on autopilot, going through the motions, the words spoken by rote. It wasn't until he was starting to clasp one of the buckles around a skinny arm, and he noticed Daniel trembling, that something in Asher awoke. This was a man who had hated a hard slap from his hand. How would he react to a whipping? Terribly, that was how.

"What're you doing here?" Asher whispered quietly, talking to himself more than Daniel.

"You were here," Daniel answered. "Where else would I

be?"

Asher squeezed his eyes shut. He clenched and released his fists, and then he straightened and spoke in a louder voice. "Change of plans. We're leaving."

There were grumbles of disappointment, but most of the men standing around disbanded. Unfortunately, most did not mean all.

"So that's it, then. You can't even make a man take a simple whipping." Nicholas spoke much louder than was necessary. "Never thought I'd see the day Asher Penaz went soft."

"Not every sub gets off on pain," Asher snapped. "Daniel isn't a pain slut. He'll take the whipping if I order him to do it. Hell, he's my sub, so he'll do whatever I say. And I say we're leaving."

"Oh, please," Nicholas scoffed. "That man isn't your sub—he's your boyfriend. Face it, Asher, you're no Dom. Never have been."

Really, why had Daniel followed him to this club? It wasn't bad enough that he had spent the night flaunting his body in tight clothes, that he had let men who Asher had no idea were a part of his life touch him like he belonged to them, that he had lied to Asher about everything from the first day they'd met? Now he had to come to Asher's club and undermine him in front of dozens of people, including the one man who'd never let him hear the end of it.

"I'm a better Dom than you'll ever be," Asher responded.

"I think Darwin proved that when he came onto me, asked me to cane him, begged me for my cock." He was taunting Nicholas, he knew, just aggravating an already tense situation. But he couldn't stop himself.

The two men glared at each other, and then Nicholas's eyes narrowed in triumph. "Good point. And since you took my sub, I think turnabout is fair play, don't you?"

Asher froze.

"You knew he was mine, Penaz. But we can call it even. Just give me your boy."

Nicholas wasn't alone in thinking Asher had acted out of turn when he'd had a scene with Darwin without his Dom's permission, mostly because Nicholas wouldn't stop talking about it to anybody who would listen. So when he made the suggestion, several men nodded.

"I just told you—he doesn't like pain. I'm not going to let you cane him. Darwin asked for it."

"No problem. I'll take caning off the table. You fucked my boy, I'm going to fuck yours. That's it. No cane, no whip, no pain." Nicholas reached for Daniel, and Daniel stepped back out of his grasp, practically hiding behind Asher. "Tell your boy to come to me, Asher, or can't you control him even that much?"

At that moment, Asher didn't feel like he could control himself, let alone Daniel. But he couldn't bring himself to admit it. "Fine," he heard himself saying. "But, after this, we're even."

It was, Asher knew, a strange compromise. He hadn't enjoyed the feud with Nicholas, but it hadn't ever bothered him much. Being even didn't matter to him, not really. And besides, Nicholas was right—he had no control over Daniel. The concert earlier that night had made that abundantly clear. There was no way Daniel was going to agree to this. No, he would refuse, proving, in a very public way, that Nicholas was right about Asher having no control over his boy.

But Daniel didn't refuse. When Nicholas reached for him again, Daniel let the man grab his wrist and start pulling him out of the room.

"Wait," an unfamiliar voice bellowed. "I want him first."

Every head turned to see the club's owner blocking the hallway. Riley Sands was a huge man, even bigger than Asher. And though he had a warm smile and kind eyes, people tended to steer clear of him because he rarely spoke, just glared and watched everyone and everything in a disconcerting way. And to Asher's knowledge, he'd never hooked up with anyone at the Lounge.

"I—" Nicholas started to protest, only to be interrupted by Riley.

"My club, my rules. Let's go, boy. Grab your clothes and follow me." Riley turned on his heel and started walking away. When nobody said a word, Daniel scooped up his clothes and shoes and followed. He looked at Asher as he passed, his expression full of confusion, betrayal, and so much pain that it almost brought Asher to his knees. But still, Daniel didn't refuse, didn't say a word, just trailed after Riley down the hallway.

It wasn't until the two men were out of sight and Asher heard the door to the office in the back close that he realized what he'd done. But even then, he saw no way out of it. And Daniel had gone willingly. Hell, maybe this was what he'd wanted all along. After all, he had been trying to get other men's attention all night, right?

A few people Asher knew approached, trying to make light conversation and see what he'd been doing during the time he'd been away, but he couldn't focus. He couldn't stop thinking about Daniel alone in a room with Riley Sands. And why? Because he didn't want to appear weak in front of men who he didn't even care enough about to see, let alone talk to, in more than half a year? These weren't his friends. Hell, they were barely acquaintances. Just people who had similar itches to scratch. And Daniel was... Asher gasped as realization set in. He'd made a mistake. A huge mistake.

Asher walked away from whoever was talking to him and marched down the hallway over to the office. He tried the door, expecting to find it locked, but it swung open.

Riley Sands was sitting at his desk, paperwork spread in front of him. He looked up when he heard the door open, his expression fierce, stare unwavering.

Asher glanced around the office and then looked at Riley. A sick feeling washed over him when he realized Daniel wasn't there. How much time had passed? Had Nicholas already collected him?

"Where's Daniel?" he asked.

"Gone," Riley answered.

Asher waited for an explanation, but true to form, Riley didn't say anything else. Just glared at him with those disconcertingly piercing eyes.

"Gone where?" he said. "Where does Nicholas have him?"

Disgust spread over Riley's face. "Do you honestly think I'd hand a sub over to a man he didn't want because of some pissing match?"

The message was clear, and Asher winced as if he'd been struck.

"I made a mistake," he said. "Biggest mistake of my life." Which, Asher knew, he should have recognized much earlier. "Where is he?"

"Yes, you did. And I don't know where he is. I called him a cab, took him out through my private exit." He gestured toward a door in the corner of the office. "And stayed with him until they drove away."

Holy shit, what had he done? If Daniel hadn't been planning to leave him to join BWI, he'd no doubt do it now, even if it wasn't to go on tour. The pain in Asher's gut was so intense his vision went gray around the edges. He leaned against the doorframe to keep himself from collapsing.

"Asher," Riley said, reminding Asher that he wasn't alone. He looked up, but couldn't respond. Hell, it felt like he couldn't breathe. "The way your boy kept looking over his shoulder when we were waiting for that cab told me I wasn't the one whose company he wanted. Better late than never. Isn't that what they say?"

Asher didn't know who *they* were or what *they* said. But he knew he had to go to Daniel, apologize, and come up with a way to get him to stay. Because after living with the sweet, funny, kind, sexy man for the past several months, Asher couldn't go back to being alone, couldn't go back to a life without Daniel at the center of it.

CHAPTER 22

Asher was disappointed when Daniel's phone went straight to voice mail, but he wasn't surprised. He slipped his phone into his jacket pocket, put the key in the ignition, and started driving home. Almost half an hour later, he still hadn't come up with the right words to say. "I'm sorry" wasn't going to cut it.

The apartment was dark when he walked in. "Daniel," he called out, even though he knew there'd be no response.

He rubbed his hand across his head, took in a deep breath, and then shuffled through the great room into the bedroom. Daniel wasn't there, either. Asher sat on the edge of the bed, clasped his hands over his spread knees, and closed his eyes. He was so damn tired. And he ached. Bone deep.

With a sigh, he picked up his phone and called Daniel again. Voice mail.

"It's me. Listen, I... Shit. I fucked up, Daniel. I know that and I'm sorry and I want to tell you that I'll never do it again, but I feel like I..." Long sigh. "Please don't make me do this in a recording. Come home, okay? Just...please, sugar, come home."

He didn't remember falling asleep, but the next thing Asher knew, light filled the room and he was lying on top of his comforter, fully dressed, shoes included. He had a crick in his neck, his back was sore, and his feet were numb. But none of those things compared to the pain in his chest when he realized Daniel hadn't come home.

Asher sat up and scrubbed his palms over his dry, gritty eyes. He looked around the room again, as if Daniel had magically appeared in the last few seconds, which he hadn't, then sighed as he unfolded his tall frame and stood. He walked into the bathroom, shedding shoes and clothes as he went, and stepped into the shower, not bothering to wait for the water to heat.

After absently running the soap over his body, Asher rinsed off and then stepped onto the bath mat. He didn't know how long he'd been standing there when he realized he was cold and dripping. He reached for his towel, his arm feeling unaccountably heavy, and wiped it over his face and body, then let it slip from his hand onto the floor.

A quick check of his phone showed no missed calls, so he walked over to the closet. And that was when he noticed that Daniel's clothes were gone. He choked back the tears that threatened, pulled on a pair of jeans and a long-sleeved shirt, stuffed his wallet, phone, and keys in his pocket, and grabbed his jacket. He was standing on the sidewalk outside of his apartment before he realized he had no idea where he was going. His brain felt murky and he just couldn't seem to think straight.

Where would Daniel go if he wasn't home? Would he go to his brother's place? Not knowing where else to try, Asher headed to Oliver's apartment.

The door swung open seconds after he knocked, and a furious Oliver glared at him. "Fuck you, Asher. Get the hell out of here," Ollie shouted, and then he slammed the door. Lovely. Asher didn't move, just stood there with his hand poised to keep knocking, when Oliver opened the door again. "Fine, you can come in, but only because Danny told me I couldn't be mad at you." He glared at Asher, disgust clear on his face. "Asshole."

"Daniel's here?" Asher asked hopefully, choosing to ignore Oliver's rant.

"Pfft, you think I'd let you in if Danny was here after the way you treated him? Nah, man, he's gone."

"Gone?" Asher felt like he'd been socked in the stomach. "Gone where?"

"I have no idea, and even if I did, I wouldn't tell you. What'd you do to him last night, Asher? I've never seen him so... What'd you do?"

God, he didn't think he could hate himself more, but hearing Oliver confirm what he already knew—that he'd caused Daniel pain—made him feel physically ill. "I need to talk to him, Ollie. I messed up, but I promise you that I'll make it up to him and—"

"You promise? Really? Just like how you swore to me

that you wouldn't hurt my brother? Because we both know how that promise turned out." Oliver glared at Asher. "Your word doesn't hold any currency with me."

"Damn it, Ollie, what do you want me to say? I just want—"

"What you want is to be worshiped. You want someone who'll follow you around and bow at your feet."

Asher opened his mouth to deny that statement, but found that he couldn't. It was true, wasn't it? That was exactly what he'd wanted. And it was exactly what Daniel had given him.

"Why is that so wrong, Ollie?" he said instead. "It works both ways. You've got to know that I lo... I adore your brother."

"How does it work both ways? He moved to your city, lived in your apartment, went wherever you wanted, and I don't even want to know how much of your kinky sex stuff you made him do. You held all the power in your relationship, and what did Danny get in return? Tell me, Asher. Tell me how it worked both ways."

Asher leaned back against the wall and slid down until he was sitting on the floor, looking up at Oliver. "He is my entire world, Ollie."

Asher had no idea how that had happened, but it was true. What had started out as an out-of-character infatuation had bloomed into so much more, until now Asher found himself thinking about Daniel almost constantly. He'd go to a restaurant and scan the menu for items Daniel would like, even if the man wasn't with him. He'd catch himself glancing at the clock every ten minutes at the end of the day because he wanted nothing more than to go home and be with Daniel. He'd walk down the street and see some ridiculously loud accessory or he'd smell a scented candle, and he'd be reminded of Daniel. The man filled his mind, his heart. And now he was gone.

"Do you know what that's like?" Asher choked out, forcing himself to keep his feelings in check. "To be with someone who shines so brightly he's all you can see? That's how I feel when I'm with your brother. To me he's…everything." Asher swallowed down emotion threatening to rage out of control. "If that's not power, I don't know what is."

Oliver didn't speak for several minutes. He just stood and stared at Asher. Eventually, he walked over to the couch and sat down. "Get over here. We're too old to be sitting on the floor. My ass will go numb and my back will hurt all day."

Asher stood up and winced at the pinch in his lower back. Oliver smirked at him.

He flopped on the sofa next to Oliver and leaned back, closing his eyes and trying to clear his mind.

"What happened last night?" Oliver finally asked.

"Daniel didn't tell you?" Asher asked in surprise.

Oliver scoffed. "Are you kidding? He called me specifically to tell me not to be mad at you. He wasn't about to fill me in on whatever you did, but that's not what I'm asking, anyway. What I want to know is, why were you acting like such a—"

"Did you see the way he was dressed last night?" Asher interrupted. "Made me fucking crazy."

"The way he was dressed? Asher, he was wearing black jeans and a black button-down shirt. He wasn't parading around in a loincloth."

It was true. Now that Asher thought about Daniel's clothes without the red veil of fury that had fallen over him in reaction to watching every man and woman in their time zone flirting with his boy, he realized that the clothes weren't over the top. But somehow the simple pants and shirt didn't look so simple on Daniel's stunning body.

"He's so good-looking it hurts."

"And that's a problem?" Oliver asked, making Asher realize he'd spoken the thought out loud. Oliver shook his head and pursed his lips in disapproval. "A fixation on a person's appearance is the hobgoblin of shallow minds."

Was that English?

"Huh?" Asher said.

Oliver rolled his eyes. "I'm saying that if I understood you correctly, you treated my brother, who you claim to care for deeply, like crap because he's good-looking. Does it sound as ridiculous to you when you hear me say it as it did to me when I heard you say it?"

Phrased that way, yeah, it made no sense. But it wasn't just that Daniel was movie-star gorgeous. It was also that he was so skilled at seemingly anything he tried. How many people had successful careers as dancers and musicians and

martial arts trainers and jewelry makers and masseurs and...
Anyway, the list went on and on.

Plus, there was something about Daniel that drew
people to him. Asher had witnessed it when they'd gone to a
coffee shop on a Saturday morning and Daniel seemed to be
best friends with the owners and several customers. Asher
had been going in there for half a decade and nobody knew
his name. Same with Asher's neighbor, Marc. Years living
under the same roof and Asher was just a man he'd seen in
the hallway, but within days, Daniel had Marc giving up his
free time to provide cooking lessons. Asher had seen Shirley
around dozens of people over the years, including a husband
and a fiancé, and he'd never seen her smile and laugh as
freely as she did in Daniel's presence.

So, yeah, it wasn't just Daniel's appearance that troubled
Asher, it was that he was so... God, so perfect. Daniel was so
fucking perfect. Asher heard a pained whimper. When Oliver
looked at him in pity, he realized he'd been the one to make
the pathetic sound.

"Damn it, Asher. Half of me is pissed as hell at how you
treated Danny, half of me feels sorry for you, and half of
me—"

"Is horrifyingly bad at math?" Asher asked. Oliver glared
at him. "Sorry."

Oliver punched him lightly in the shoulder. "'S okay. I
walked right into that one."

Asher smiled weakly and took a deep breath, gathering

his strength. He'd never begged anyone for anything in his life, but for Daniel... "Will you tell me where he is, Ollie? Please."

"I honestly don't know." Sincerity poured off Oliver. "Look, Asher, I don't know what happened between the two of you, but I can tell you that unless Danny wants you to find him, you won't."

Asher scoffed, his usual arrogance reasserting itself. "I'm a cop."

"Great, well, if he gets arrested, maybe you'll have a shot. But otherwise—" He breathed in deeply and then let it out in a sigh. "Danny lives off the grid. How're you going to track him? He doesn't use credit cards, doesn't own a house or a car. And he has enough money to go anywhere. You need to realize that—" Oliver swallowed and sounded genuinely regretful when he continued speaking. "He left you, and that probably means he isn't coming back."

No. Asher refused to believe that. What they had between them wasn't one-sided. Asher had seen the way Daniel looked at him—full of desire, happiness, contentment, and pure, unadulterated need. It was easy to recognize, at least for Asher, because those emotions were a reflection of what he felt for Daniel.

"He'll be back," Asher said, certain that he'd be proven right.

Two weeks later, Asher felt like nothing would ever be right again. Daniel hadn't returned, hadn't taken any of his calls, hadn't so much as sent him an e-mail or a text. And Asher felt like he was crawling out of his skin. He worked all day and all night, only leaving the office when he was about to collapse, and sometimes not even then. There had been more than one morning when he'd woken up slumped over his desk, splashed some water on his face, and gotten right back to it.

"Asher."

Thankfully he had a job with a never-ending pile of tasks to get through, so there was always something to occupy his time.

"Asher."

He rubbed his dry eyes and blinked, trying to focus on his computer screen.

"Asher!"

Asher jerked and looked up.

"Ollie. Hey. Have you heard from your brother?"

"Fuck," Oliver whispered. He closed Asher's office door and walked over to an empty chair, sitting with his feet shoulder-width apart and resting his forearms on his knees, clasping his hands tightly together. The sorrow on his face was a completely foreign expression. And Asher had known him through two broken engagements and a divorce.

"What happened?" Asher asked frantically. "Tell me. Is he—"

"Nothing happened to Danny," Oliver said. "Calm down."

"Oh." Asher started breathing again. "Okay. You scared me there."

"The feeling's mutual."

"Huh?"

"Asher, I'm worried about you."

"I'm fine," Asher said reflexively.

"You are the furthest thing possible from fine. You look like shit."

"Thanks," Asher grinned wryly. "That helps."

"Your shirt looks like it was slept in. There are coffee stains on your pants. And you're wearing one blue sock and one black one."

Asher frowned. "I'm sitting behind my desk, how can you—"

"You haven't changed your pants in three days and the coffee stain has been there since yesterday. And I heard about the socks when I poured myself a cup of sludge in your break room earlier."

"Who was talking about my socks? If one of my officers has so much free time, then I can—"

"What? You can what? Bite his head off? Snap at him for no reason? No worries, you've got it covered. There isn't a person on this floor who hasn't been subjected to your piss-poor mood."

"How would you know? You're in another part of the building. I haven't—"

"I know because five different people have come to me separately to tell me they're worried about you and they're too scared to say anything. Asher, listen to me. This needs to stop."

Asher didn't say anything. He just looked down at his desk and started shuffling papers around.

"I was wrong," Oliver said sadly.

The words took Asher off guard, startling him enough to get him to dart his gaze over to Oliver.

"I was so focused on your kinky sex stuff and your temper that I was sure you'd hurt my brother."

The comment hit so close to the mark, it felt like an arrow to Asher's heart. He'd lashed out at Daniel in more than one jealous rage. And the way he'd treated Daniel at the Leather Lounge... Asher squeezed his eyes shut in horror at the memory.

"But I should have realized that I had it backwards," Oliver continued.

Asher opened his eyes and blinked at Oliver in confusion.

"Do you know that in all the years we've known each other, we've never double-dated?" Oliver asked.

"That's because we're not in junior high school," Asher replied sarcastically.

Oliver ignored him. "You never brought a date to any

parties I've thrown, and I'm including my wedding and my engagement parties."

"Which is a real tragedy, because we all know how well those turned out."

Oliver kept talking, letting the taunt fly past him. "I can't tell you the name of a single guy you've dated. Hell, I'm not even sure if you've ever really dated."

"Are you working up to a point, Ollie, or are you just here to kick me while I'm down?"

"You see? That's what I'm saying. A year ago, you wouldn't have taken offense at any of those qualities. You would've made some off-color joke and gone out to wherever it is you go to find men to beat. But now, it's different. You're different. And I should have realized that when you followed my brother around Las Vegas—"

"I didn't follow—"

"Save it. I was there. You walked into that casino with him like you owned him and you didn't let him out of your sight the whole time we were there. Then you moved him into your place, which was totally out of character. And the way you doted on him—" Oliver shook his head. "I should have realized you really cared about him, that you were falling in deep. I love my brother, you know that, but he isn't somebody to build a life on. His running was inevitable. Danny's a vagabond, has been since he was a kid. The longest he's lived in one place since he left his mother's house was…" Oliver paused and furrowed his brow in thought. "Hell, it was probably the six months he spent here."

And while Daniel had lived with him, he'd been happy. He'd never seemed itchy to leave. Hell, if anything, the man acted like he was putting down roots, decorating their home, making friends in the neighborhood, becoming an integral part of Asher's life. Why Asher couldn't have realized that before flying into a jealous snit and pushing Daniel away, he didn't know. But it wasn't too late to fix what he'd broken. It couldn't be.

"There has to be a way for me to find him."

"How? Asher," Oliver sighed. "We've talked about this. You're not going to be able to track him if he doesn't want to see you."

"What about your father?"

"What about him?" Oliver asked.

"Maybe he knows something."

"He hasn't talked to Daniel in months."

"His mother, then," Asher tried. "You can get her number right? Just give it to me and I'll—"

Oliver stood. "Let's go," he said gently, gesturing to Asher to get up.

"You have an idea?" Asher asked hopefully as he quickly got up from his chair.

"It's eight o'clock on a Friday. My idea is for you to go home, take a shower, and get some sleep. It's time to move on."

He wasn't moving on. And neither was Daniel. Oliver

was wrong on both of those counts. But he was right about Asher needing some sleep. He was so exhausted that every part of him hurt.

It didn't take long to get home. He stumbled groggily up the stairs, down the hallway, and into his apartment. He was standing in his great room, trying to figure out why all the lights were on, when he heard a noise coming from the bedroom. Slower than usual reflexes meant he hadn't quite gotten his gun out of his holster when Daniel walked in from the hallway.

CHAPTER 23

Daniel's gaze met Asher's. He opened his mouth. And then he stumbled, tripped over his own feet, and hit the floor.

Asher dropped his hand from his piece and hurried over to Daniel, squatting down next to him and helping him sit up. "Are you okay?"

Those beloved brown eyes widened from behind a curtain of shaggy blond hair. Then the freckled nose scrunched up. "When was the last time you took a shower," Daniel asked. "Because you smell like...well, kind of like this apartment before I scrubbed everything."

As reunions went, it was unexpectedly low on the romance.

"Uh," Asher said as he looked around the sparkling-clean great room.

Daniel pointed a rubber-gloved finger toward the door. Asher looked over and noticed four full trash bags.

"If you're looking for your Chinese food, empty pizza boxes, and beer cans, they're over there. Seemed like a better place for them than all over my living room."

Asher snapped his head back and looked at Daniel

hopefully. "*Your* living room?"

With his arms crossed over his chest, Daniel glared at Asher mutinously. "Yes, my living room. You told me I could live here and you don't get to take that away." He raised his eyebrows as if he was waiting for Asher to argue with him. When it didn't happen, he kept talking. "And tomorrow we're going to buy some paint and do something about these walls. I'm tired of living in a hospital. We're painting those three a light green." He pointed to the walls. "And the kitchen a bright yellow."

The discussion was surreal in light of the radio silence and loneliness he'd endured the past couple of weeks.

"Okay," Asher agreed eagerly.

"Okay?" Daniel asked.

Asher nodded and wrapped his arms around the smaller man, pulling him close and burying his face in the curve where his neck met his shoulder.

"And the bedroom's going to be a silver gray."

Asher nodded and squeezed tighter.

"With a blue stripe around the top as an accent," Daniel added.

"Anything," Asher choked out, not sure if it was through laughter or tears.

The silence stretched.

"Was it because I didn't tell you about BWI?" Daniel said eventually. "Because I wanted to. I tried. But you were at work almost nonstop from the minute we heard about the concert and every time I tried to bring it up something got in the way and…"

It was hard to answer that question with Daniel in his arms, clinging to him like he was the second coming. How could he say he'd felt like he wasn't needed, like there was no reason for him to be there when Daniel was surrounded by rock stars? Literally. Daniel was babbling, red-cheeked, flustered, desperate, and adorable. And Asher couldn't stop himself from cupping his cheeks with large hands, holding him still, and kissing those plump red lips.

Daniel opened for him right away, whimpering into his mouth and licking at his tongue. Their mouths moved together, getting reacquainted, and Asher thought he'd cry from how perfect it was. Then Daniel pulled away and twitched his nose.

"Seriously, Ash, you stink."

Asher resisted the urge to smell his pits, but it was a near thing.

Daniel climbed to his feet. "Let's get in the shower. I just finished cleaning the bathroom."

They walked through the bedroom, and Asher noticed that the sheets had been changed, the room aired out, and that his dirty laundry was no longer strewn about. "Thanks for cleaning," he said quietly.

"I've been cleaning this apartment for half a year," Daniel said matter-of-factly as he peeled off the yellow rubber gloves. Then he removed the rest of his clothes and put them in the laundry basket.

Asher followed his lead. "I know you have, and I'm grateful for that too," he said as they stepped into the shower. He waited for Daniel to finish adjusting the water temperature, and then he pulled him back so he leaned on Asher's taller frame. He kissed Daniel's shoulder. "I'm sorry if I didn't tell you."

"You did," Daniel whispered. "I've always been kind of messy, but I know you appreciate having our apartment look nice. That's why I did it." He reached for the soap and rubbed it over his golden skin, covering himself in white suds before stepping under the spray and rinsing off.

Then he dropped to a squat and started soaping Asher's legs—thighs, knees, calves, then each foot in turn. He stood and ran soapy hands over Asher's stomach, up his sides to his underarms, and then nudged him to turn around and paid the same attention to his back.

"I got jealous," Asher said after several minutes of silence. "You're so beautiful, Daniel, and—"

"I can't help how I look!" Daniel shouted, stopping his soapy massage. "I'm usually better about—" He took in a deep breath. "You told me to buy new clothes, went on and on about how they needed to fit, and I—" His voice broke. "I did what you said. You don't get to be mad at me because I listened to you."

Asher turned around and dragged Daniel into a tight hug. "You're right. I'm sorry." He kissed Daniel's shoulders and neck and rubbed circles on his back, thinking about what Daniel said. "Is that why you wear your clothes so loose? Are you hiding?"

Daniel shrugged. "Not hiding, just making things easier. You think I liked how people acted around me in that restaurant? Or at the concert?" He paused briefly. "You think it's fun to make everyone nervous, have them come onto me without knowing me, make whatever guy or girl they're with pissed?"

"I didn't think," Asher said. "I didn't know."

"Well, I do. I've had it happen all my life and I hate it. I hate having them look at me, hate having them touch me."

Asher nodded and held Daniel close. "Shhh," he said until Daniel stopped trembling.

Eventually, he pulled back and met Asher's gaze. "It's not what I want," he said. "*They're* not what I want.

"And John Oaks?" Asher asked.

Daniel furrowed his brow. "What about John?"

"Do you want him? The way he was touching you—" Asher frowned at the memory and shook his head. "Rob Yearling too. They had their hands all over you, kept calling you some nickname I'd never heard. Made me nuts."

Daniel's expression softened with understanding. He rubbed his palm over Asher's cheek. "They're my initials. Daniel Owens Tover. I use them with the band stuff instead of my name because it's easier to keep my anonymity that way, so they started calling me Dot. There's nothing intimate about it. And John's straight. He's just a touchy guy. Rob—" Daniel pursed his lips and furrowed his brow. "Rob's... clueless. I don't have any interest in either of them, not that way. Never have. And the feeling's mutual."

"I'm sorry I freaked out," Asher said. "The way they looked at you...and then when I heard them asking you to go on tour with them, I thought you'd do it." He dropped his gaze and lowered his voice. "I thought you were going to leave me."

"I walked away from that life more than ten years ago, Ash." Daniel sounded frustrated. "We started playing together when we were kids, barely out of high school. One of my mother's exes is Eric's dad, and he had a buddy who worked for a record company. We had a good time, but when I realized that it wasn't just fun for the other guys, that they wanted to make it big and tour the world, I told the record company guy to kiss my ass and—"

"Not unless he wants to start walking with a limp," Asher growled.

Daniel scoffed. "Right, because the only way a guy is allowed to touch me is when you give me away. Is that it?"

Asher's whole body jerked.

"I'm sorry," Daniel said right away. "I didn't mean—"

"No," Asher said, shaking his head. "Don't be sorry. I deserved that." He sighed. "The water's getting cold and I haven't had a full night's sleep in long enough that falling over seems like a real possibility. Can we finish this conversation in bed?"

It didn't take long to dry off, brush teeth, and crawl under the crisp, clean sheets. Daniel automatically curled into Asher's side, and Asher sighed in pleasure and held him close, pushing his damp hair out of his face and kissing his forehead.

"I don't have any excuse for what I did at the Lounge that night," Asher finally said. "None. When I've thought back about it, which I've done over and over since you left, it's almost like I can't believe it really happened. I see a guy look at you and I want to punch his teeth out. Making you strip in front of a room full of people and then sending you to..." Asher shook his head, unable to complete the sentence. "No excuse. And I know this isn't the first time we've had a conversation like this, this isn't the first time I've fucked up. I want to tell you that I'll stop being so possessive, that I'll never be jealous like that again, but—"

"You'd better not stop!" Daniel said, his eyes blazing.

"Huh?"

Daniel blushed. He dropped his gaze. "I left because you sent me off with that guy, like it didn't matter to you if someone else fucked me." Daniel swallowed thickly. "Hurt," he finally rasped out.

And Asher understood then, really understood what Daniel needed and how it meshed so well with his own needs. No whips or ropes or props or pain. He wanted to own the man in his arms, and Daniel wanted to belong to him. Yin and yang. When that had been threatened, Asher broke and Daniel ran.

"You told me once that all you ever wanted was to be needed," Asher said. "Well, I need you." He swallowed hard and cleared his throat. "I need to know that you belong to me. And when I felt like that was being challenged, when I thought I was going to lose you, I just... I lost it. Please forgive me."

"I do need you," Daniel said desperately. "Need you so much." He pressed his lips to Asher's and mumbled into his mouth, "Only you."

Asher nodded. "I know." He shuddered. "And fuck, do I ever love that." He ran his hand over Daniel's ribs and belly. "You've lost weight and you didn't have any to spare."

Daniel sniffled, blinked back tears, and smiled. "Nobody was making me protein drinks every morning and hand-feeding me dinner every night."

"'S my job," Asher said.

"Still?" Daniel asked, his voice rough with emotion, his face full of hope and yearning.

"Always," Asher said.

They came together—hands possessing, bodies gliding, and mouths moving over skin and tongues and lips. Asher could never get enough of the man in his arms. He wanted to consume Daniel. He scooted down the bed and licked at Daniel's balls, mouthing them gently before swiping his tongue up Daniel's cock and then sucking him down. Daniel moaned, running his hands over Asher's skin. Then he somehow twisted his body until he was underneath Asher, taking his thick, long cock into his mouth.

Asher thrust down, fucking Daniel's face at the same time that he bobbed his head up and down on Daniel's dick. It was ungraceful and hurried, but it felt so damn good Asher wanted to cry with it. Then he popped his mouth off Daniel's cock and flipped him over.

Daniel was on his belly, his head at the edge of the bed, his shoulder next to Asher's knee. Asher pulled him up until his chest was flat on the bed but his knees were tucked under him, raising his ass. Then he draped his torso across Daniel's back, wrapped his right arm around Daniel, and planted his hand on the bed. He rubbed his left hand up Daniel's thigh to his ass, pulling his cheek to the side before he buried his face in Daniel's trench and plundered his hole with his tongue.

"Oh, holy shit, Asher!" Daniel yelled. He reached back with his left hand and gripped Asher's arm, rolled his neck, and bit down on his bottom lip, grunting in pleasure.

Asher thrust his left hand between Daniel's legs and started pulling on his dick, jacking him hard as he feasted on his ass, licking, sucking, fucking that hole with his tongue. When he couldn't wait another minute, he flipped Daniel onto his back, spread his legs apart, draping his knees over his forearms, and shoved his aching cock into that tight, glistening hole.

"Ah!" Daniel shouted, his face contorting with a pained

pleasure.

"Fuck, yes, take it!" Asher grunted, fucking Daniel hard and deep, pushing into his body so hard his head dropped back off the side of the bed.

Asher wrapped a meaty hand around the back of Daniel's neck and pressed his thumb against the base of Daniel's throat, exerting just enough pressure against the man's windpipe for him to feel it.

Daniel grasped his cock and yanked desperately, his eyes closed, a litany of cries escaping his mouth as Asher shoved mercilessly into his hole. They grunted and groaned, pushed and pulled together, rising higher and higher. And then Daniel's eyes shot open and met Asher's.

"Love you!" he shouted, and he came, long and hard, white cream pouring over his hand and streaking across his stomach.

Asher lost it, shouting and thrusting and sweating and coming until his body shook too hard to hold him. He collapsed on top of Daniel, pushed his sweaty hair off his face and gazed at him in wonder.

"I love you too," he whispered.

Daniel whimpered and then pressed his mouth to Asher's, licking and nibbling before sucking Asher's tongue into his mouth. When the need to breathe became imperative, they separated and Daniel gasped in air. "Love you so much," he said, and then he searched Asher's lips out again. "You gave me a home. First time I ever had that. Only person I want it with. Please don't take it away from me."

"Never," Asher growled. "You're mine."

"Why?" Daniel asked. "Why me?"

"Because my life was cold and empty before you came into it. Because my house was sterile and boring before you made it a home." He looked into Daniel's eyes and let everything he felt for the man shine out. "Because I love you, Daniel. You're my family."

THE END

ABOUT THE AUTHOR

Cardeno C.—CC to friends—is a hopeless romantic who wants to add a lot of happiness and a few *awwws* into a reader's day. Writing is a nice break from real life as a corporate type and volunteer work with gay rights organizations. Cardeno's stories range from sweet to intense, contemporary to paranormal, long to short, but they always include strong relationships and walks into the happily-ever-after sunset.

Email: cardenoc@gmail.com

Website: www.cardenoc.com

Twitter: https://twitter.com/cardenoc

Facebook: http://www.facebook.com/CardenoC

Pinterest: http://www.pinterest.com/cardenoC

Blog: http://caferisque.blogspot.com

OTHER BOOKS BY CARDENO C.

AVAILABLE NOW

More than Everything

Time might not heal all wounds, but with two motivated and strong-willed men on a campaign to win him back, Charlie will get more than he ever thought possible.

As a teenager, Charlie "Chase" Rhodes meets Scott Boone and falls head over heels in love with the popular, athletic boy next door. Charlie thinks he's living the dream when Scott says he feels the same way. But his dreams are dashed when Scott unexpectedly moves away.

Years later, Charlie meets brash and confident Adan Navarro, who claims all he wants is a round between the sheets. After eight months together, Charlie is convinced Adan returns his love. But when the opportunity comes to be open about their relationship, Adan walks away.

Time passes and life moves on, but when Charlie learns the only two men he's ever loved are now in love with each other, his heart breaks all over again. Scott and Adan tell Charlie they want him back, but Charlie doesn't know if he can trust two people who have hurt him so deeply. Time might not heal all wounds, but with two motivated and strong-willed men on a campaign to win him back, Charlie will get more than he ever thought possible.

Strong Enough

When a casual hookup turns into the potential for love, staid Spencer realizes he wants to build a life with vibrant Emilio.

When twenty-two-year-old Emilio Sanchez sees handsome Spencer Derdinger walking by his construction site, Emilio makes it his goal to seduce the shy professor. Getting Spencer into bed isn't difficult, but Emilio soon learns that earning the trust of a man deeply hurt will take time and patience. With a prize like brilliant, sweet Spencer on the line, Emilio decides he is strong enough to face the challenge.

Spencer is surprised when he's approached by the gorgeous construction worker he's admired from the safety of his office window. Acting spontaneously for the first time in his thirty-eight years, Spencer takes Emilio home. When the casual hookup turns into the potential for love, Spencer realizes that if he wants to build a life with Emilio, he'll need to be strong enough to slay his personal demons and learn to trust again.

The Half of Us

If short-tempered Jason can open his heart and life to optimistic Abe, he might finally find the family he craves.

Short-tempered, arrogant heart surgeon Jason Garcia grew up wanting a close-knit family, but believes he ruined those dreams when he broke up his marriage. The benefit of divorce is having as much random sex as he wants, and it's a benefit Jason is exploiting when he meets a sweet, shy man at a bar and convinces him to go home for a no-strings-attached night of fun.

Eight years living in Las Vegas hasn't dimmed Abe Green's optimism, earnestness, or desire to find the one. When a sexy man with lonely eyes propositions him, Abe decides to give himself a birthday present—one night of spontaneous fun with no thoughts of the future. But one night turns into two and then three, and Abe realizes his heart is involved.

For the first time, Abe feels safe enough with someone he respects and adores to let go of his inhibitions in the bedroom. If Jason can get past his own inhibitions and open his heart and his life to Abe, he might finally find the family he craves.

Jumping In

When love's on the line, the brave jump in with both feet...

Small town cop Clint Rivera can't catch a break. His ex of two weeks is suddenly getting married, his dogs tore up his furniture, he's getting evicted, and he's out of beer. When he decides to solve his alcohol shortage by going to his ex's engagement party, Clint winds up too drunk to drive himself home.

Enter gorgeous deputy mayor Hawk Black, the man who constantly shows up unexpectedly and sends Clint's body and mind into a tailspin with nothing but his whiskey voice and blue eyes. After months of patience, Hawk can finally seduce the man he's been craving.

Clint's day might not have started out well, but Hawk's going to make sure it ends with a bang, preferably in bed. He'll show Clint some rewards are worth the risk. With love on the line, Clint will need to decide if he can open his heart, tear down his shields, and jump in with both feet.

Home Again

Two men whose love has never faltered must relive their most treasured moments in order to secure their future.

Imposing, temperamental Noah Forman wakes up in a hospital and can't remember how he got there. He holds it together, taking comfort in the fact that the man he has loved since childhood is on the way. But when his one and only finally arrives, Noah is horrified to discover that he doesn't remember anything from the past three years.

Loyal, serious Clark Lehman built a life around the person who insisted from their first meeting that they were meant to be together. Now, years later, two men whose love has never faltered must relive their most treasured and most painful moments in order to recover lost memories and secure their future.

www.ingramcontent.com/pod-product-compliance
Lightning Source LLC
Chambersburg PA
CBHW070655180626
46817CB00006B/2387